I0586907

Peeping *through my* fingers

SHARYN MUNRO is an author, award-winning short-story writer, essayist, public speaker and 'literary activist'. Her three non-fiction books are *The Woman on the Mountain* (Exisle 2007), *Mountain Tails* (Exisle 2009), and *Rich Land, Wasteland* (Pan Macmillan/Exisle 2012). Her favourite genre is the short story, and hers have won many awards, including first prizes nationally, as in the Alan Marshall Award and the Boroondara.

She lived alone for years in a solar-powered mudbrick cabin on her remote NSW mountain wildlife refuge, where her first two books were set. Now she lives on the NSW mid north coast. She received the 2014 NSW Nature Conservation Council's Dunphy Award for 'The most outstanding environmental effort of an individual'. Her website, www.sharynmunro.com, houses her ongoing nature blog, background information and her earlier books, and she continues to have a large following on Facebook.

Peeping
through my
fingers

Stories by
Sharyn Munro

Glimpses of childhood, old age —
and the dangerous bits in between

K

Knocklofty
Press

First published 2022
Copyright © 2022 Sharyn Munro

Sharyn Munro asserts the right to be identified as the author of this book.
This work is copyright. Apart from any use as permitted under the Copyright
Act of 1968 and its amendments, no part may be reproduced, stored in a
retrieval system or transmitted by any means or process whatsoever without
the prior written permission of the author. All rights reserved.

Published by Knocklofty Press 2022

Printed on demand by IngramSpark using sustainably sourced paper,
reducing supply chain waste and greenhouse emissions and conserving
valuable natural resources.

ISBN: 978-0-6456106-0-4

CONTENTS

For Tony, who showed me how to turn my
observations into stories
— and how to deal with dying.

FOREWORD

If youth knew; if age could.
(Si jeunesse savait; si vieillesse pouvait.)
Henri Estienne, *Les Prémices*, 1594

W E STUMBLE along on our individual paths through life — tripping over rocks, clawing up slopes only to slip down the other
side, occasionally skating along a flat stretch before tipping off at the
next hidden hairpin bend.

No matter that billions have made the trip before us; no two journeys are ever the same. The only common factors are the start and finish points and the lack of any chance to go back.

There is a sort of map, signposting the named ages and stages of life. Some are physical enough to be indisputable — childhood, puberty, parenthood, and very old age. Others — adulthood, maturity, and the middle-to-old ages — are far less clear until we are looking back at them. They are not only highly variable amongst individuals, but highly subjective.

The artificial signposts that society creates do not help: seven is not the age of reason, since I know children who reached it much younger and others who still don't function that way at 47; the 21 key does not open the door to adulthood, which may not begin for another 15 years; and 50 does not mark the middle of most people's lives.

My window into how other people have navigated this chaotic journey has been through reading. I prefer fiction because it's usually better written, in language where I can expect at least an occasional phrase of such crystalline insight and originality that it jolts my heart and mind.

Not that my reading stops me from making mistakes as I stumble on, but perhaps it lessens them. Books give me glimmers of hope for humanity; books keep me going.

I also write to make sense of life, but I do that best with the stages of life which I think I now understand — childhood, adolescence, and old age. In between lies a tangled muddle, the messy ups and downs of relationships, which I still can't quite unravel — so I'm writing towards the middle from both ends, hoping to reach a waiting lightbulb.

In my first two books, *The Woman on the Mountain* and *Mountain Tails* (Exisle 2007 and 2009), set on my remote mountain wildlife refuge, I told true tales of the observed lives and loves of my animal neighbours — and a little bit of mine. The following smattering of short fiction is about human lives and loves — and a little bit of mine.

I didn't always live like a hermit with wild animals as my only companions, and I did sometimes venture down from my mountain into that other world where people dominate, and where I was as equally fascinated an observer. I would often feel like Rip Van Winkle, sitting at city railway stations, cafés or shopping malls, perhaps leaning on one elbow, hand propping my cheek and forehead, the better to discreetly peep through my fingers — and write down what I saw, heard, and thought.

Most of my short stories begin with one such captured image or overheard soundbite from real life. I am never without a small notebook. From the shelf behind me, a row of past companions peek at me through the long curling lashes of their black spiral edges, enticing, seductive, demanding — 'Open me!' 'No, me!' I pick one at random, flip through. If I spot an entry which appeals to my present mood, I type it into my laptop. As I do, my imagination begins to roam around it, characters creep in — and a story takes off. Where to, I never know. Magic.

My very different third book, *Rich Land, Wasteland* (Pan Macmillan/Exisle 2012), was essentially about man's inhumanity to people and places as I shared the stories of those in the path of runaway coal and coal seam gas, and revealed the shameful truth behind government and industry spin. For my grandchildren's sake — and yours — I am still very involved in the battles to stop that fatal fuelling of global warming.

It has become my best known book, and my reputation is now as a literary activist and speaker rather than a nature writer or an award-winning short story writer. It has taken me away from my short stories for too long; now I need to work them back into my life. Revisiting some of them for this collection is my way of starting.

Readers of *The Woman on the Mountain* will recognise factual 'germs' from my own life in some of these stories, while others have no connection at all, but, once having germinated, they are all fiction. 'Truth' is whatever is credible in a story.

For me, a story must be more than its plot, or what happened. It should also carry an underlying elusive note, a hinted 'why', either as question or answer. It should be more than the sum of its parts. If not, it's just a yarn.

Because I love the short story form, I concentrated on it over the years since I 'got serious' about writing — until *Rich Land, Wasteland* captured me. As I wrote in my first book…

'On my 49th birthday I vowed to take action to regain that creative path, so as to be able to greet 50 with pride and pleasure. By then I knew that life did not usually drop gifts into the laps of we poor sods, no matter how talented. Success, happiness — they all have to be worked for. Even then we might miss out, but the trying brings unforeseen benefits.

'Firstly, I would get serious about writing. I did not want writing to be just another 'if only' at the end of my life. I'd been dabbling with short stories for too long. I would start treating them as work, getting them up to scratch and sending them out to competitions. Only when they were acknowledged as top standard would I try to get them published. I had my first major win two years later.

'Secondly, I would stop dyeing my hair, whose Scottish black had begun greying too soon, after the insanity of my marriage break-up. When I did, there were unexpected side effects, like suddenly becoming invisible as a female. No more wolf whistles. I'd have cherished those last two uncouthly shrilled syllables if I'd known; I might even have taken a bow.

'So by 50 I was ready for the perception of my older age by others, which mattered less and less because I was writing often enough to know I was a writer, so I was excited at the years ahead of plunging into that addictive world. The next 50 years, I told myself, re-polishing the thought that Elizabeth Jolley wasn't published until her fifties.'

As I am now in my mid-70s, feeling more mortal, I have realised I'd better get a wriggle on as far as my fiction goes! I hope you enjoy this selective fictional ramble through my take on our human lives.

— *Sharyn Munro*

GROWING UP

*'There is always one moment in childhood when the door opens
and lets the future in.'*
Graham Greene, *The Power and the Glory*, 1940

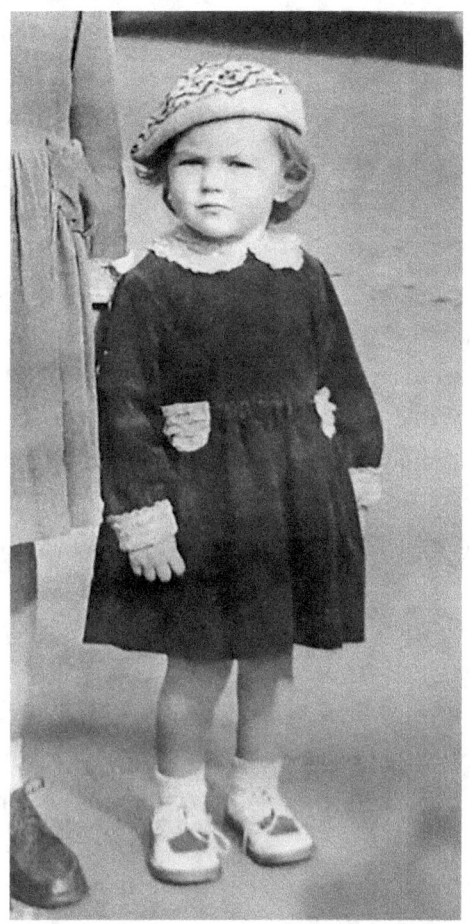

M Y CHILDHOOD was spent in the fibroland of Sydney's west,
then from seven to sixteen on a small farm on the NSW Central Coast, at the time a quiet rural area, before I left home to attend

Newcastle University. I have vivid memories of those times; I can still inhabit that child and that confused girl, whirling in the currents from that open door.

Since my own childhood, one way or another, I've had a fair bit to do with children.

After fleeing from the disciplinary horrors of teaching in a tough public high school, I taught Kindergarten. There I fell in love with several mischievous and quirky little boys — and decided that, after all, I would have children. The threat of The Bomb, of nuclear warfare, had given many of my generation cause to consider the wisdom or fairness of such a move.

I bore one of exactly that kind of boy, and then, 22 months later, a sweet little girl. I loved pregnancy, had no nausea, and would have had more children if my husband had agreed. I found them endlessly engrossing, the whole process of their 'becoming' both fascinating and fearful. While rearing them, I ran playgroups in the old courthouse part of my historic village home, and held craft workshops there in the holidays for older children.

Now those two children are nearing 50, and I have five grandchildren!

Byron reckoned 'the days of our youth are the days of our glory' — but they certainly weren't for me.

The hormonal raging, the impulsiveness, the uncertainty, the agonising struggles between idealism and emerging reality, and the resulting seesawing of positions, beliefs, decisions: who am I and where am I going?

So would I wish to be young again? Oh no, it was too painful — trying to fit in, to win the approval of peers, to seem confident and cool when faced with new situations and dilemmas, when in reality I was always the opposite. My body was in better shape then, but not the more important other half, whatever you like to call it — mind, personality, soul. It hardly even had a shape back then.

Some girls seemed to know who they were and what they wanted. Perhaps they were just better at acting, yet they had at least been capable of choosing which roles to play. No character suited me, no costume fitted the amorphous yet prickly thing that I was, anxiously awaiting my own future and fearing for that of the world. Now only the latter concern remains.

My stories grow more fanciful as the years they deal with creep up towards theoretical adulthood; they shy away from anything too close to the flesh and blood life, when I am as yet unclear as to which bone connects to which and where the heart fits in.

Twenty to thirty is where many of us skid into a life that may prove to be a hole that is hard to climb out of, where we understand least about what we are doing but nevertheless acquire dependents to drag stumbling along beside us.

I blame the witchery of 'love' but have yet to write my way into the essence of how and why that works and how we could deal with it differently.

Wise societies do not allow young people to commit to lifetime attachments until after thirty.

THE VISIT

FRAN was bored. She often was lately. Her mother said so, and that the sooner she started school, the better. Fran was sitting on the back steps in the morning sun, absently stroking the sleepy tabby. She could still taste her breakfast Weetbix, so she knew it would be a long time till the baker came with the soft white bread for lunch.

That was always a high point of her day. If she hadn't annoyed her mother too much she would be allowed to have banana sandwiches. It was the way she made these that most convinced Fran that her mother did love her after all, despite the fairly constant frowns and snaps and slaps bestowed on this youngest daughter.

Other kids' mothers mashed the banana first, making it go all brown and ugly, but her mother sliced it and laid the circles in beautiful overlapping rows so that they exactly covered the buttered bread, then gently pressed them into place with the flat of the knife before giving them a twinkling coating of crunchy sugar. With its lid added, and cut into four dainty triangles, Fran could not imagine anything more wonderful. She always felt like hugging her mother for such a gift, but knew better than to try; sticky fingers were abhorred far more than hugs were valued.

Her daydeaming was broken by a loud burst of song from over the paling fence. *'I'll be loving you-oo, oo-oo-oo, oo-oo-oo!'* It was the fat lady who lived on the other side of the paddock where they had their Cracker Night bonfires. Her kitchen window faced their house, and she often sang over the washing up. Mum said this song was the 'Indian Love Call'. Fran could almost imagine the fat lady in pigtails like an Indian squaw, but no matter how hard she tried, she could never see her very small husband as an Indian brave.

Fran sparked up. Holding on to a happy feeling from the song and the hope of banana sandwiches, she vowed not to whinge or hang around her mum today. As she was nearly five, she was allowed to visit certain neighbours on her own.

'Mu-um, can I go see Mrs Graham, please?' she called down the hall.

Her mother stuck her head out from the kitchen, where she was, as usual, extremely busy. 'May I,' she corrected. 'All right, but don't stay too long and don't ask for anything to eat. And don't talk too much!'

'Talk the leg off a chair, that one would!' Fran heard her mother muttering behind her as she raced out the door. This puzzling concept momentarily held her attention before she had to give it to alternating her feet on the cement drive strips and the stiff buffalo grass in between. Always a challenge to get this right when going fast, today felt extra sunny when she got to the gate without once putting a foot wrong.

She balanced on the gutter, dramatically looking 'first to the right, then to the left, then to the right again' as her mother had drilled her. Not many cars came along their street, as the suburb was very new, and in this year of 1952, what few vehicles belonged to the scattered fibro cottages were of course at work with the men. Women caught buses.

However, checking traffic was a vital part of the adventure of visiting, so she did it twice, then 'walked, not ran' across the road and down two doors to Mrs Graham's. For the hundredth time she paused to inspect the strange plant in the pot by the porch. It was dark green, stiff and glossy, and bore small, fat, pointy berries of red, purple or orange. She didn't know its name, but she knew it was very special and not to be touched.

It was just like Mrs Graham to have such a mysterious plant! Her mother's front garden had dwarf golden cypresses, a few sticklike roses, and sharply spaded beds of pansies or primulas, as did most of their neighbours. Her mother said Mrs Graham had no pride because she had no garden and no front fence, just lawn with one young jacaranda tree smack in the middle. But Mrs Graham was odd — she had no husband either.

Fran turned the little handle on the front doorbell twice and waited anxiously. She hated people not to be home when she had decided to visit; it made her feel sad, as if they were cross with her. Ah, she could hear heels clicking on the polished floors, she was home! The door opened and Mrs Graham smiled down on her.

'Why, Fran, how nice of you to call on me! Come in, we're just about to have morning tea. Would you like some?'

A flicker of guilt, but no, she wasn't asking, she was being asked, so it was all right. She smiled back an eager 'Yes please.' But what had she said? — 'we're just about to'?

In the lounge room, Fran settled herself on the round cushion of coloured leather shapes that Mrs Graham called a 'pouffe'. As always, she looked immediately at the china cabinet, whose glass shelves were full of miniature shoes. Only Mrs Graham would collect something like that!

For Fran this collection had changed the shape and flavour of the word 'shoes' forever. None of the many varieties here were the everyday sort. They ranged from pink porcelain high-heeled slippers from France, with clusters of gilded flowers at their toes, to blue wooden clogs from Holland with tulips painted on their sides. Mrs Graham's grown-up son travelled all over the world, and brought them back for her.

Fran thought that perhaps he bought Mrs Graham's real shoes too, as they were unlike any her mother or her aunts wore, even to go to Parramatta on 'endowment' days. It didn't matter what time Fran called, Mrs Graham would be wearing shiny stockings and high-heeled shoes — once even a red pair. She had never seen her without lipstick — or with her hair in pincurls.

She had stopped telling her mother about the marvels of Mrs Graham; they only made her mother wrinkle up her nose and snap out things that didn't make sense, like 'Humph! Mutton dressed as lamb!' or 'China shoes indeed; dust collectors!' or 'It's all very well for people with nothing better to do!'

Mrs Graham came back with the lacquered tea tray, which she set down on the spindly coffee table that straddled a whole 'nest' of tables that got smaller and smaller till the last one, just big enough for a cup and saucer. Mrs Graham drew this out and placed it by the pouffe. Smiling as she set Fran's glass of milk down on it, she said, 'I've got another visitor today — my niece, Veronica. She's having a little holiday from the Home.'

Fran was till trying to work out why she had said it like that — 'the Home' sounded wrong somehow — when Mrs Graham returned, leading a big girl by the hand. 'This is Veronica, Frances.'

'Frances' looked at the girl, feeling very grown up, and shyly said hello. The girl just smiled and nodded her head a few times, which Fran thought rather rude. Her mother would have given her a poke and made her reply properly. Turning her attention to the Sao biscuits, Fran steered clear of the ones with tomato on them, knowing from past experience that the first bite always left her with half a tomato slice dangling from her lips. Cheese was safer.

This Veronica must be a special visitor, as today there was rainbow cake as well. Fran eyed her as she ate. Veronica looked steadily back and didn't say a word while Mrs Graham chattered on. Then, as if Fran was the big girl, she said, 'Why don't you take Veronica outside to play, Frances?'

This really was an odd visit, thought Fran, but she nodded politely and stood up, knocking over the little table, glass, milk, plate, crumbs and all. The fright and the clatter were made worse by a long croaky shriek from Veronica, who was waving her arm, pointing at Fran and the mess.

'It's all right, Veronica, it's all right,' soothed Mrs Graham, patting her. Fran's apologies tumbled over themselves, but nobody seemed to be listening. 'Come on you two, outside while I clean this up.' More pats to Veronica.

Finding themselves bundled out onto the front porch, they stood staring at each other. Confused, Fran looked about for some way of entertaining this stuck-up, silent person. Her eye fell on the special plant.

'I'll bet you've never seen one of these,' she said, pointing.

Veronica's eyes followed the proudly outstretched arm. She bent closer, reaching out to touch the bright berries.

'No, no,' said Fran, 'we're not allowed. Mrs Graham said!'

The dreadful girl ignored her.

'You mustn't, we'll get into trouble!' hissed Fran more urgently. Veronica still paid no attention. Fran felt panic and jealousy all mixed up as bold Veronica gave a little tug and turned to her, smiling, with a red berry in her hand. Before Fran could say another word, she had popped it into her mouth.

Shocked at this outrage, Fran's own mouth fell open, ready to give a righteous lecture. Then Veronica began to scream. It was the most terrible sound Fran had ever heard a person make, all harsh and sort of cracked, but from the spitting and jumping up and down that went with it, she knew it had to do with the berry.

Mrs Graham rushed out. 'What's wrong? Fran? What have you done to Veronica?'

Hurt, and bewildered by the dreadful noises continuing to issue from Veronica, Fran cried, 'I didn't, I didn't, I told her not to touch, but she wouldn't listen! She's the bad one; she ate one of your special berries!' and turned and ran sobbing down the path.

She forgot to stop, look or listen at the road, and didn't stop at all until she was in her own yard, right up the back under the mulberry tree, where she threw herself on the ground in a tragic heap. As the tears lessened, she tried to think about what had happened, but all she came up with was 'I hate Veronica! I hate Mrs Graham!!' She knew she was going to be in trouble for whatever it was that had upset Veronica, but it wasn't fair, it wasn't her fault.

Hearing her mother calling her, she quickly wiped her face with the hankie pinned to her dress and drooped her way up to the back porch. As she came through the hall, she could hear her mother at the front door, saying 'Oh dear, how dreadful!' Then came Mrs Graham's voice talking about Veronica and the Home and 'def and dum', whatever that was. Fran hid in her room, waiting for her mother's angry voice, for the smack that would surely follow.

Her mother did call her, but for lunch, and in an astonishingly un-angry voice. Fran crept into the kitchen and slid along the bench of the breakfast nook. Her mother put a plate of sandwiches in front of her, muttering under her breath, 'Well what did she expect? Ornamental chilli plants, indeed!'

Fran lifted the corner of one of the sandwiches: Vegemite and cheese and lettuce, but that was shredded, which was a bit special. 'Oh well,' she thought, 'I don't suppose I'd have got banana today anyway, not after what Mrs Graham must have said to Mum.'

She looked up to find her mother just gazing at her, all sort of soft. It was a look Fran had only seen once before on her mother's face, through fluttering lids, when her mother thought she was properly asleep. A dream mother...

'Ah, Franny,' her mother sighed, 'I'll never complain about you talking too much again.'

THE SMALLEST ENTREPRENEUR

DURING the year that Caroline was six, her grandmother often took the opportunity of saying she was so, 'but with the mind of a woman of sixty'. Small for her age, she would frown earnestly as she tried to make sense of the contradictions presented to her by the world. So Caroline proceeded through childhood, like a tiny tug forging determinedly through rather murky waters.

She barely survived the first year of school at the local convent, an ordeal only because of the journey to and from home. In that time and town, strangers offering lollies or rides in cars to children were rare, and, having been told not to accept either, all children walked to school if it was physically possible. To reach hers, Caroline had to walk past the Public School, as she was not allowed to cross the busy Main Road until she was at the official zebra crossing.

The Public School fence was of criss-cross wire set in wooden rails top and bottom, festooned with enemy children lying in wait for Catholic kids, who were glaringly obvious by their far more regimented uniforms.

With clenched teeth and panting heart, Caroline would clutch her school port and walk as close to the road as she dared, trying not to look at her tormenters as they jeered:

'Catholics, Catholics, blah, blah, blah! Boil 'em up, boil 'em up, dipped in tar!'

Coming home was even worse, for then there might be kids outside the fence, waiting for buses, and they might pull her plaits, or snatch her hat off and toss it into a tree, or grab her bag and pass it around

— while she begged and cried — before chucking it into the gutter, or even on to the road.

The torture continued for most of her first year of school, until she acquired a group to walk with, who could yell back equally loudly, unladylike and unoriginal:

'Publics, Publics, blah, blah, blah, etc.'

But the most effective weapon, chanted with righteous noses stuck in the air, was the pompously pacifist:

'Sticks and stones may break my bones but names will never hurt me.

'When I'm dead and in my grave, you'll think of the names you called me!'

Hence Caroline ceased to be a tempting victim and became proudly invincible. She conveyed this confidence to her playmates. On Saturdays she and her weekend friend, a bigger but biddable girl called Margaret, often played in her dad's shed. Here she was usually safe from motherly eyes and ears. As she shared a bedroom with her older sister, Caroline liked the shed's privacy and often played there by herself, making up stories — in which she was always the star.

This afternoon she and Margaret were entertainers, taking turns to 'do acts'. At the time there were lots of silly songs on the radio which were liked by children, although written for adults. Cutesy singers like Doris Day were to blame for many, with lyrics such as, *'On the baby's bottom or the baby's knee, where will the baby's dimple be?'*

Caroline chose to render a similarly appealing song that had so impressed her by its clever twist at the end that she had memorised all the words. 'The Naughty Lady of Shady Lane' had to be sung in a crooning style and included natty deep-voiced asides, like *'Me, oh my, oh what a girl!'* and a long dramatic drawn-out finale *'For she was on-ly...nine... days...o-old!'*

Margaret thought she did it extremely well, praised her effusively, said she ought to be giving singing lessons she was that good! Caroline generously said her friend was good too, but no, Margaret insisted she was not nearly as good as Caroline, Caroline was really good.

It had never occurred before to anyone, including Caroline, that she sang particularly, if at all, well. She nevertheless immediately accepted the judgment and agreed that it probably was a good idea to give singing lessons.

They set about working out how this could be organised; how to find people to teach, how much to charge? Their only experience of selling was of people coming to the doors of their homes to sell raffle tickets or encyclopedias. They knew that even Caroline's mother sometimes bought the raffle tickets, so thought they should model their methods on that, and proceeded to cut up a few pages of Caroline's scrapbook into rough squares for tickets.

'Just going for a walk round the block', she called blithely to her mother as they hurried down the side path, tickets hidden under her cardigan. Not that they were doing anything wrong, but Caroline's mother was inclined to greet most of her ideas with 'Don't be silly!' and this one was too good to be treated so. Her mum'd think it was pretty smart once they had a few people paying for the lessons; she was always wishing for more money.

The two small girls walked importantly past the vacant block next door, deciding against calling at the first house because Caroline knew the lady there already sang very loudly and confidently, at least while washing up.

It took all their combined courage to turn into the next front yard and walk up the cement path and steps to the single barley-sugar-column-supported porch. They looked nervously at the front door, which had a little round window of yellowish crinkled glass.

'You knock,' Caroline said, moving from beside Margaret to slightly behind her.

'But what if there's someone home?' hissed Margaret, 'What will I say?'

'You know, what we said we'd say!' Caroline urged.

'I can't!' wailed Margaret plaintively, softly, but quite definitely.

'Hmph!' Caroline said, with the impatience of her mother, and stepping forward, reached up, lifted and let fall the chrome door knocker.

It dropped back and bounced again onto its chrome plate with an appalling clatter that frightened them both.

They had to stop themselves from following their immediate instinct to run, and, holding fast to each other, forced themselves to wait. It was awfully quiet on the porch and they could hear no sounds from within the house. Or could they?

'Do you think they can see us through that little window?' Margaret whispered.

'N-n-oo...' Caroline said, with absolutely no conviction. Yet as she spoke, she thought she saw a shadowy movement behind the crinkly glass, and, dragging Margaret by her cardigan, turned and bolted down the steps. Neither looked back at the door and neither stopped until they were around the corner and into the next street.

They plopped down on the grassy edge of the footpath; after a minute, each risked a peep at the other's face.

'Nobody home,' Caroline said.

'Nobody home,' Margaret confirmed.

They turned to look at the first house in this street. From the distant safety of the gutter they inspected the door; no spying window. Heartened, they got up, brushing down their minuscule skirts in the appropriate manner, and opened the little wrought iron gate that led to the very neat front yard of buffalo grass lawn.

Before they had reached the front steps a man appeared round the side of the house, pushing a lawn mower down the already tidy grass strip in the middle of the driveway. 'Hello, kids,' he called above the whirring and clacking of his blades. As he reached them he stopped and they shyly responded with hellos. This was, after all, a strange man, whom they probably shouldn't even be talking to, even if he did live just round the corner. But the mower made it all right, somehow.

'What can I do you for?' he said, with a grin that told them this was a sort of joke.

Now that the time had come, Caroline found it difficult to remember what they did want. Margaret poked her with her elbow and hissed, 'The singing!'

'We… we were wondering if you'd like some singing lessons,' she blurted out.

'Why?'

That question threw them momentarily, but Margaret found her normal voice and said rather defiantly, 'She's a real good singer, you know!'

'Hang on a minute,' he said, 'don't tell me she's the one giving the lessons?'

He burst out laughing before either could reply; mightily offended, the girls stalked back down the path and out his silly gate, clanking it shut behind them.

They kept going past the next two houses till they were out of sight of that rude man. Caroline said determinedly as they turned into the third gate, 'I'll say it this time!'

She felt only a faint tremor of anxiety as she knocked. Her small fist made little sound and she was about to do it again when the door was opened and a tall lady stood there. 'Yes?' was all she said.

'We were wondering,' piped up Caroline, 'if you'd like some singing lessons… from us, from me, I mean. I'm a real good singer and… it doesn't cost very much and we've got tickets for it and all…' she wound down.

'I see,' said the lady. 'How much are the lessons?'

'Threepence,' Margaret said eagerly.

'And where do you give these lessons?'

'At my house,' said Caroline, although as she spoke she realised for the first time that it could be a problem hiding the lessons from her mother. She'd have to sneak the people down the side and into her dad's shed.

'So where do you live?' smiled the lady.

'Oh, it's not far; just round the corner really, it wouldn't take you long to get there. I live at 11 Patrick Street.'

'All right, girls, I'll take a lesson, but I think it's getting a bit late for you to be out selling any more today, so I want you to promise me that you'll go straight home if I buy a ticket.'

Both girls were so excited at selling a lesson that they would have been incapable of continuing anyway, so readily agreed to the bargain, swapped a ticket for the lady's threepence and happily headed home.

The new pupil looked at her ticket. Clumsily, with the letters scrambling over each other in the effort to fit the space allotted to them, was pencilled '1 SINGING LESSEN'. An impressive attempt at spelling for their age! Chuckling, she shook her head and went inside to share the joke with her husband. 'Bloody little devils!' he said admiringly, 'They'll go far!'

Caroline and Margaret meanwhile were so overjoyed they could only giggle and shove each other about as they skipped and ran round the corner and up their street. They hid the tickets and the beautiful first silver threepence very carefully in the shed.

It was getting near tea-time, so Margaret went home while Caroline slipped inside to be very good for her mother with a vague sense of making up for having done something behind her back. Tea was delicious — rissoles and gravy, peas, carrots and mashed potatoes — and the pudding was her most favourite at the time, lemon meringue pie. Life was good!

Her mother thought her rather over-excited that night and, fearing she was coming down with something, made her swallow a dose of cod liver oil, just in case. Even that couldn't spoil Caroline's dreams of what she'd buy with all the money she'd get from her singing lessons.

Next morning, after early Mass and the usual Sunday breakfast of exploded saveloys, in which for once Caroline didn't even find any gristly bits, the whole family took to the front yard. Here it was their custom to do various gardening jobs under Mum's supervision while the roast slowly cooked. Then they would be free to read the comics or play till mid-day.

Caroline was on her knees, searching the lawn near the side fence for bindii-eyes to dig out, a job she liked doing because she just hated treading on them in summer. Consequently, she didn't notice someone walk into the driveway and up to her mother, who stood on the porch, arms folded, wondering what business this vaguely familiar woman had with her.

'I thought I'd better call round and see you if you knew about this,' said the woman, holding out a scrappy piece of paper. At the first words, Caroline looked up, horrified. It was the singing lesson lady and she was going to tell her mother about it!

Caroline ducked between the dwarf golden cypresses and the paling fence and made herself as small as she knew how. There she had to stay and hear the story as told to her mother and feel her pride falling into tatters as the two women exclaimed and laughed. Fame and fortune fell with it.

Through her shame Caroline heard her mother calling her in that particular way that meant she was in trouble, 'Car-O-LINE!'

After several such calls, each more peremptory and abrupt than the last, her mother gave the lady a threepence, apologised, thanked her, said goodbye, and began muttering things like, 'Wait till I catch the little beggar!' and 'I hope the whole street doesn't know about this. Oh, how embarrassing!'

Caroline resigned from life, closed her eyes and burrowed deeper into her shelter. She would stay there in the night time dark even, rather than face anybody, ever again.

Sunday dinner smells began to waft to her lair from the kitchen window at the side of the house. The gravelly dirt began to embed itself in her bare knees... and was that black hole a funnelweb spider's?

Tears of sorrow for herself, exiled from the world, hungry and hurting, began to gather. She felt for her hanky; it was not in her pocket. Keeping an eye on the hole, she sniffed, remembered it had been the one with Bambi on it, and burst into real sobs.

Several dark, hairy spider legs appeared at the edge of the hole. Caroline screamed and jumped up, but her legs had gone to sleep and she couldn't walk properly. In terror that she had already been bitten, poisoned, about to die from the legs up, she threw herself out between the dwarf cypresses on to the sunny lawn, calling for her mother and crying bitterly at her fate.

Her father, who'd been watching with stifled amusement from the side window, came to her rescue. The great singer allowed herself to be consoled with cuddles, reassured that this was not yet her swansong, and carried inside to a pre-dinner wash and a post-dinner lecture, reconciled by near tragedy to taking her place in the world once more.

FACING REALITY

THE DRY BUSH crackled in the heat. Long strips of curling bark and spiking fallen branches waited like well-set kindling on a thick layer of gumleaves, pink on brown and slashed with yellow. It was so still that the only movement Ella could see from the back of the ute was their dust trail drifting gently off to the side as her dad drove slowly down the rough track.

When they dropped over the last rocky rise she was as amazed as ever by the sudden secret oasis of green where a horseshoe bend in the creek had created a tiny alluvial flat, thick with softly drooping she oaks and glossy lillipillis. Reaching it, the truck shuddered to a silence that was immediately filled with the busy, echoing rush of the creek.

Ella readied herself to swing over the side of the ute, watching for stinging nettles amongst the tussocks. 'The guardians of the rainforest,' her mother called them, adding grandeur to her daughter's already strong respect for their fine burning bristles. Unfurled bracken shoots were the accepted remedy, their juicy nubs to be applied fiercely to the stung spot, though Ella could never decide if it was the bracken juice or the rubbing that really helped.

Her father said it was neither; it was all psychological, the searching for the shoots creating the distraction from the pain, the shoots themselves being a mere placebo. She had allowed that theory to settle, mostly uncomprehended, somewhere in the back of her brain, having gathered that the whole world could be explained thus, according to her father, but for the moment preferring the one her mother offered, of fairytales and legends, myths, magic and nature itself. Her name even meant 'gift of the elves,' although her father said that was incidental, as she was really called after her great-grandmother.

Towel slung round her neck, elf-like Ella jumped down and edged through the long grass to the passenger door to receive her little brother from her mother's arms. Ben was only three, too small to ride in the back like she did, being seven, or to walk through the tall tussocks, a bleached beige forest amongst which his fair head was easily lost to sight.

She carried him on her hip to the creek edge and set him down safely on the flat rock that was their jumping-across point, holding his hand tightly. Here they must wait for their parents; no chore, as they were always eager to check out the falling height of the creek, with new holes or shelves or stepping stones revealed, and the increasing green weed, floating like combed-out tresses in the current.

'It's dropped at least two inches!' exclaimed her father. 'This is going to be a really bad season.'

'M-mm,' agreed her mother, frowning. 'Anyway, it looks like those water nymphs are really letting their hair down this summer.'

'Maybe they wash it too often,' suggested Ella. 'They must be wasting the water.'

Her mother laughed; her father just shook his head. They each took one of Ben's hands, and let Ella make her leap first. Surefooted in her sandshoes, she scampered over the rocks and through the cluster of young she oaks growing there since the last flood. Rounding the last bend before their special swimming hole, eyes on where she was placing her feet, she yet caught a glimpse ahead of something bright in all the grey-brown of the rocks. She stopped; it was a blue towel.

Nobody else was ever here. She could hear her parents behind her, urging Ben to mind his step, watch that nettle, crunching over the pebbles and thudding on the rocks, but above all she could hear her heart, beating way up in her ears. As the others came close, she put up her hand to halt them and pointed ahead.

In front of their grouped stillness, a dripping figure came into view and picked up the towel; a short, fat man, brown and hairy all over, wearing no swimmers, although he quickly wound the towel around his middle. As he turned, she saw he was bearded, but wildly, not neatly like her father. He flicked up an arm in greeting. Her mother gave her a little shove to keep going, but she wriggled between her parents to come up behind them.

Reaching the man, her father shook hands with him and her mother nodded. He introduced himself as Mike, said he had a cabin over the other side of the mountain. He had a flat, thick sort of voice, and did not open his mouth much when he spoke.

Ella frowned at the intruder from behind her mother's long tie-dyed skirt. She did not like his face at all — his nose was large and fat and somehow pushed up so you saw the holes all the time; there was hair sticking out of them. He had light blue eyes, as pale as the lumps of sanded glass she'd found at the beach, but bright and sharp at the same time.

He's a troll, decided Ella, and I'll bet he has rotten teeth. She knew a few things about trolls, none of them good. Even if he was in disguise, or was only half troll, half person, her mother at least should know better than to trust him. Just then he caught Ella's eye and tried to smile at her. It didn't work — trolls can't smile, they can only laugh — horrible, gloating, evil laughs. And his teeth were a yellowish brown.

She ran nimbly over the big old log suspended across this narrow end of pool to put her towel down on the opposite side. Her parents would surely follow. But no, seemingly unaware of their danger, they were spreading their towels out and sitting down beside the troll, who was still talking.

Ella was a good swimmer, but she was supposed to wait for a grownup before going in the water. Yet she had to do something, and quickly, to catch their attention, shatter the spell he must be weaving. She jumped in with a mighty splash and stayed under for as long as she could.

When she surfaced, they were all standing on the rock ledge looking down at her. Her parents began reprimanding her at once. Taking a deep breath, she kicked off down the long pool away from them, keeping her face in the water. She must get them to come away, even if she got into big trouble, as it certainly sounded she would.

Her parents were dumbfounded; Ella was not usually disobedient, as they repeatedly said to the stranger. He raised his eyebrows sceptically, which made Ella's mother suddenly decide that she disliked him. A lot. Tightlipped, she gave Ben to her husband's charge, unwound her skirt and dived in after her daughter. Ella had reached the pool's end and was inching up the slippery rocks around the 'spa bath' when she heard her mother not far behind, saying, 'Wait for me, Ellie, wait for me' — and she didn't sound angry.

Lowering herself into the smooth round hollow in the rocks, despite today's danger Ella still felt a little of her usual delight in her favourite place on the whole creek. Here the water rushed in with a roar and was forced straight back up again in a perpetual fizz of surprise before it slid like polished silver over the outer edge to become the waterfall and the pool. She could not see her mother from here, but knew she would soon appear. She tried to stay under up to her neck as she used to, but the creek was too low.

Long brown fingers were followed by a body glistening with creek drops and sunshine, as her mother pulled herself up onto the hot rock. She swung her legs over into the spa pool, slid down beside Ella and put an arm around her.

Ella whispered urgently, 'He's a troll, Mummy, you must know he is.'

'Oh, Ella darling, he's not really; he's a schoolteacher, you know.'

'No, no,' pressed Ella, 'he's only pretending! He's bewitching you and Dad, that's why you were talking to him, why you couldn't tell!'

'Now, Ellie, you should know better — trolls can't do that, they're not magic, they're just mean and greedy and ugly.'

Ella thought about that for a minute, while the pool and the creek went on with their familiar hollow gurglings. The rock felt warm and solid against the back of her wet head as she looked up the steep cliffs to the bush edge, where the bladey grass was flowering like duchess plumes. It all looked the same. Her panic began to ease, just slightly. Then she remembered. 'But they eat children, don't they?!'

Her mother hesitated. If trolls weren't true, elves and fairies weren't either, or nymphs or all the other lovely things.

'He's not a troll, Ella, he just looks a bit like one. Anyway, we don't have trolls in Australia; we don't have any creatures that harm people who do the right things, like you do. You think back on all the Aboriginal legends I've read you. We'll start reading them again tonight if you like. Now come on, we'll go back before Daddy thinks we've both drowned.'

That made Ella laugh. Her mother was like a mermaid in the water, and Ella had often heard it said that she took after her mother. Her mother would tell people they were both Aquarians, and whatever that meant, it was a good thing to be, she was sure of that.

'O.K., but I don't like him, whatever he is!'

'Neither do I,' confided her mother, surprising Ella, 'but we won't let him see it. Even nasty people are usually nicer if you're nice to them.'

Not trolls, thought Ella, but knew better now than to say it.

He was gone when they returned. 'Set off back down the creek to where he'd left his motorbike,' said her father.

Hah! Defeated! thought Ella.

'I invited him to call up and visit us sometime,' he added.

Ella's sharp intake of breath caught his attention. 'And as for you, you naughty girl...'

'Oh, did you?!' interrupted her mother.

She shooed Ella off to play with Ben in the shallow pool just upstream. From the low voices and her father's humphs, she knew her mother was trying to explain about the troll. The voices got louder than the creek; now her mother was in trouble. For the stories, and all sorts of things that Ella didn't follow. She heard the 'f…' word a lot; this was big trouble. There was a splash.

Her mother appeared at their pool, her face red, hot-looking. She sat down in the water behind Ben, stretching out her long legs either side of him, her arms around his waist, snuggling her face against his back. He giggled at first, then squirmed free. Her mother bent forward and splashed water over her face, but Ella knew she'd been crying. Ella moved closer, put her arms around her mother's neck, and was hugged back, hard.

It seemed only a minute before she heard a gruff version of her father's voice. 'Come on. We're going.' She lifted her head from her mother's warm damp skin, and looked up at him, squinting against the sun. He'd been for a swim, and he already had all their towels and shoes in his arms. She couldn't see his face properly, but he still sounded angry. He'd talked far too long to that troll; perhaps the troll even gave him something to drink, something that changes people…

Her mother sniffed and sighed. She stood up and went to fetch Ben, who complained loudly. Her father did not speak as he handed Ella her sandshoes; they were still so wet they squished when she stood, but she didn't care. She stomped and splashed through the shallows to the path on the other side and ran ahead of them all to the crossing.

She felt like yelling to burst through the tightness in her chest. Mean, rotten troll! The pool was spoilt, the day was spoilt, everything was spoilt!

Defiantly unsupervised, she jumped across.

That night it was awfully hot in the loft bedroom Ella shared with Ben. The windows were wide open to the night air and the familiar bush noises, but Ella could not fall into proper sleep. Her parents were still talking loudly downstairs.

Dreams and stories and half-hearings mingled as she drifted on the edge of a sticky wakefulness—'Trip trap, trip trap, went the little goat over the bridge. Out leapt the troll, shaking his hairy fist, 'Who's that walking over my bridge?!'…Mo-poke, mo-poke…F…ing hippie bullshit!…'My mother said/I never should/Play with the gypsies/In the wood/If I did/She would say/ Naughty girl/To disobey!'…Mo-poke, mo-poke, mo-poke…got to face reality!'…had enough! had enough! had enough!… Mo-poke.'

Years later, when Ella began reading her favourite stories to her small daughter Chloe, the first troll they met in them brought it all back. She asked her own mother if she remembered the troll/man at the swimming hole.

'Oh, yes,' she said, shaking her head at the same time. 'That was what really brought things to a head with your father and me. I argued for your right to be intuitive about that man, troll or not; he was an unpleasant customer. You and I felt it; we both knew! And we were right. I heard later he got shifted to Correspondence School — too hard on the kids, too many coming home in tears, too many complaints from parents. Your father was so rigid — a schoolteacher was a schoolteacher was a schoolteacher, therefore a good person! He always had to put down any other way of seeing the world but his own.'

'What on earth did you have in common in the first place?' asked Ella, who had maintained an affectionate if guarded relationship with her father throughout the years of separation, divorce, and remarriage of both parents. He was very limited; scared of life, she often thought.

'Oh,' said her mother, 'physical attraction, sex, insecurity, wanting to live in the country — the usual grab bag you get when you fall in love. All normal grounds to get married on then, but I didn't realise you needed more to stay married. That little episode at the creek finally made me see just how different we were. It was time to split.'

'Well, Pete and I are never going to split,' affirmed Ella.

'How do you know?' asked her mother.

'For a start,' said Ella, 'because I married as equally hopeless a hippie throw-back as myself! Chloe's going to have all the fairies she wants!

'Ah, fairies, yes,' said her mother, 'but what about the trolls?'

A LITTLE BIT OF ENGLAND

IT WAS their voices that had first attracted Kathleen to the new neighbours. As they spoke to one another on the bus, their soft voices went up and down in gentle waves instead of the harsh drones and barks of the other passengers. She had realised with a shock that they were speaking proper English, like on the radio.

She'd introduced herself with her best convent manners, desperate for the exotic, someone from another country. Mr and Mrs Foster had come all the way across the sea from England, and yet here she was talking to them on her everyday school bus.

Even though they were old people, with grey hair, and she was only nine, and even though they had no children, Kathleen became a regular weekend visitor. They were growing flowers, a whole glorious paddock of flowers, whilst the farms around them, like Kathleen's, grew everyday beans or peas. Her Dad said they wouldn't make a go of it because they weren't real farmers and only Eyetalians grew flowers anyway.

They treated their serious small visitor as a young lady. Afternoon tea was always served in flowered china cups and saucers on a proper tablecloth; they even used a tea cosy. In summer they would have tea on the closed-in back verandah, in winter by the stove. In their house it was always warm and quiet. They were fond of saying it was their favourite little bit of England.

After tea, they would show her photographs of green and grey places in England and tell her stories about them. They had a book about the Coronation and one about the little Princesses. They had even been to Buckingham Palace.

Mrs Foster had a box of all the cards she'd ever received and she would let Kathleen look through them, explaining who this or that person was. Some of the cards had flowers dried inside them. Violets, cowslips, primroses… flowers that she knew from fairy stories, but these had been real, growing in real meadows, wild in the grass, just like the wet-the-bed daisies did in the paddocks here. English people had picked them there and now she was touching them, on the other side of the world.

Some of the cards held more than flowers; they held dead people's words. Mrs Foster talked about these long ago ladies and gentlemen as if they were just frozen in time. It struck Kathleen as an awesome thing that these people were dead at this very minute. Reading their words aloud now seemed improper, like making them repeat their greetings from the grave.

Mrs Foster had known people who went to the War and died in trenches, people who went to India and died of fevers, people who even stayed at home and died, just 'wasted away'. She had even known ladies who had lost their babies. There were 'thank you for your kind words of sympathy' cards to prove it. Kathleen's mother had a new baby at home, but she couldn't imagine her losing it.

For about a year and a half she'd cherished these visits as her special Sunday treat; her door to another world. Her homeward walks were always rich with replenished fantasies. The paspalum by the roadsides, the falling down fences and overgrown paddocks, the rickety old wooden bridge, the tea-brown creek… all would be transformed to grandeur and beauty fit for the princess she was.

Princesses never trudged, but tripped along, holding the full skirts of their gowns just above the dewy grass with one fair hand…

They'd have trouble here, she often thought, as the exasperatingly sticky paspalum stalks lashed her legs, wishing for the thousandth time that Dad would mow the grass in the middle of their track.

One windy day in autumn she paid a visit when the flower paddock was full of tall, heavy-headed chrysanthemums, sagging a bit as they bunched up to their stakes. Weak in the knees, she thought, like maidens about to faint. She waved to Mr Foster, who was working amongst the rows, tying the flowers up higher with strips of rag. She knocked at the side door, looking forward to the warm kitchen as the wind poked its needling fingers through the weave of her jumper.

Mrs Foster opened the door, smiling, welcoming as ever. Inside, the glass door shut against the wind, the warmth closed around her like a greeting. Mrs Foster led the way into the kitchen. 'My mother's out from England for a few months,' she said over her shoulder.

Kathleen stopped. They hadn't told her anyone was coming, and the mother must have been coming for ages on the ship. She, Kathleen, could have been following the ship in the atlas as it got closer to her own country, her own state, her actual road! Disappointed, a little annoyed, she was nevertheless keen to meet this mother, even fresher out of England than her friends.

'My cousin brought her out, but she's gone on to Brisbane to see her son. Mother, this is our young friend, Kathleen. Kathleen, my mother, Mrs. Bennett.'

As Mrs Foster stepped out of the way, Kathleen saw, extending from the depths of the flowered armchair closest to the stove, a tiny and incredibly bony hand, criss-crossed with purple cords and lumps. She moved forward to take it gingerly and found herself looking down at the smallest grownup she'd ever seen.

Mrs Bennett was shrunken to almost her own size, but wrinkled like the witches in books. She had very thin white hair, her head showing pink between the strands, the ends twisted into a bun at the back. As she smiled, Kathleen realised that this amazingly old lady did look like her Mrs Foster somehow, even though she must be almost dead, she was so very old.

'Hello,' said Kathleen lamely.

'Ah, child, how nice to see you. Come and sit down near me and warm yourself. Isn't it a cold one today? We'll have snow for Christmas at this rate!'

She was still holding Kathleen's hand, patting it with the soft, dry fingers of her other one as she spoke. Kathleen sat down as bid, wondering about the snow.

'Margaret,' the old lady said to Mrs Foster in her thin, shaky, and very English, voice, 'I think we'll have tea now, dear... and some of those lovely date scones of yours. I know how much you like those!' she smiled at Kathleen, who wondered that Mrs Foster had thought that important enough to tell her mother.

Mrs Bennett had the same blue eyes as Mrs Foster, only more faded. Watering a little in their deep bony pockets, they were fixed on Kathleen in a kindly way. 'Now tell me dear, how is your mother? No more trouble with her chest, I trust?'

As Kathleen shook her head in bewilderment, she continued. 'God be praised that you take after your father's side, dear. Our side always had good strong chests; no consumption in our family ...eh, Margaret?' she asked as Mrs Foster reappeared with the tea things.

'No mother, none at all,' she smiled, setting out the cups and saucers on a small table between them.

The old lady peered harder at Kathleen. 'You know, dear, you look very like your father, or rather, like your aunt Charlotte when she was your age.'

'But I haven't got an Aunt Charlotte,' Kathleen managed to say, looking at Mrs Foster for help, who nodded at her, but with a funny little frown and a twist of her eyebrows. What did she mean?

'No, of course you haven't, dear,' said the old lady, 'more's the pity, but surely your father must have told you about his poor sister?'

Kathleen shook her head, a deep frown now furrowing her own small forehead.

'Margaret, pass me those photographs we were looking at earlier: I noticed a lovely one of Charlotte.'

Kathleen put down her cup and got up to follow Mrs Foster enquiringly over to the sideboard, where the latter patted her arm and whispered. 'Don't worry dear, she must think you're one of my nieces. Sometimes she wanders in her mind, gets confused, a bit lost in her past.'

They returned with the album, and the old lady began turning the thick pages, peering at them, sighing a little over some, smiling at others, lost indeed, till she found the one she wanted with a little cry of pleasure and turned it so Kathleen could see it.

'There now! This was taken on your birthday, remember? Your cousins all came to tea and your Aunt Mary played the piano and you all had such a lot of fun... look at the pretty dress I made you. Ah, you looked so sweet in it! Just like the sugarplum fairy. Oh Charlotte, it was only last year... and you've grown so much since then,' she sighed, and sat back in her chair, closing her eyes and looking even smaller and older.

Kathleen looked at the serious little girl in the photograph, at her old-fashioned party dress, white stockings, long ringlets... at her dark eyes looking back. She stood up. 'Um, I have to go now,' she said.

Mrs Bennett opened her eyes and smiled. 'That's a good girl, Charlotte, you run along and do your lessons. And we're having your favourite pudding for lunch today!' She nodded her little head and shook her finger at her, smiling lovingly at the girl. 'That's right, treacle tart!'

Kathleen nodded uncertainly and backed out of the warmth of the stove's circle of chairs towards the door.

'Who's Charlotte?' she whispered to Mrs Foster at the back door.

Mrs Foster sighed. 'She was my oldest sister, her first child; she died when she was only nine. I never knew her, being the youngest.'

'Died! But,' protested Kathleen, 'what could she die of at nine? I'm nine ...'

'Oh dear, don't let it worry you. Children often died in those days. Probably pneumonia ... there wasn't the medicine, you know...'

'Yes,' frowned Kathleen, her voice breaking, 'yes, but … I like treacle tart too! It could have been me!'

She ran down the drive past the unseen rows of fainting maidens, plaits flying, soul fleeing, all the horror and sadness of mortality and old age breaking her heart, followed forever by the eyes of the birthday Charlotte, picked like a flower at nine to lie between the pages of Mrs Foster's album.

THE ROAD TO GREATNESS

SOFT as powder, the ploughed earth was warm under Tessa's bare legs. She wriggled her navy-bloomered bottom like a cat settling amongst cushions until the furrows adapted to her cross-legged position.

She would have preferred a grassy bank dotted with violets and buttercups beside a rippling stream, like in books, but round her way the grass was rank and wild, almost as tall as herself, and the creek was brown and sluggish, its clay banks more popular with black snakes than languid ladies.

Safely hidden from her mother in the dusty tractor paths that kept the hundreds of orange trees in their places, she took the pile of yellow 'wet-the-bed' daisies from her lap and began slitting their stems with her fingernail so she could thread them together. As she did so, she resumed her favourite reverie, of scenarios intended to illuminate the important and difficult decision of which path she should follow to reach the undoubted greatness that awaited her when she grew up: artist, author or ballerina?

She was in the middle of stunning the audience at the Bolshoi with the perfect precision of her pirouettes when her younger sister Liz interrupted, running down the slope skidding to a stop beside her in a small cloud of dust.

'Dad bought a new Sunday paper, it's got different comics and you can win money!'

Her sister plumped down in the next furrow, eagerly spreading out the comic section. 'Sun-Herald Juniors', this page was called, not

'Charlie Chuckles' as in their usual Sunday paper. It had real kids' drawings in it, and beneath them it had their names and addresses and how much they'd won — shillings, 5 or even 10!

She was amazed. Pavlova faded as da Vinci's successor became a better bet. She grabbed the paper, stood up, shook off the more obvious dirt and the forgotten daisy chain and headed up the hill to the house, her sister stumbling behind her.

'Tess, can I do the puzzle? Can I please?'

She frowned down at the child. 'Of course you can, stupid! I haven't got time to do puzzles. I'm going to do drawings!'

But when she sat down and read more carefully, she found the drawings had to be in something called 'Indian Ink'. Her bottle of blue school ink didn't say anything about Indians on it. She would have to talk very hard to convince her mother that this ink was a necessity, just like when she had begged for her Spirax book of beautiful cartridge paper.

Her struggling mother's thoughts turned more to singlets when deciding what was to be bought with the precious child endowment money on those special Tuesdays. With four children and a mostly minus income from the farm, she was a clever manager to whom 'No!' came very easily. She also had no idea of her daughter's destiny and was a great trial to her, always reprimanding her for daydreaming or 'doodling' when she was supposed to be dusting or tidying up her room.

Tuesday came. She ran all the way home from the bus stop, hardly even looking out for snakes, and skidded into the kitchen. 'Don't throw your schoolcase down on the lino like that!' said her mother crossly.

'Sorry,' she said, and then, 'Well?'

'Well what? If you mean that ink, yes, I got it, but you'd better make it last. One and threepence for a little bottle like that! And mind you don't spill it!'

Chooks fed, homework done, tea over, wiping up safely negotiated, kitchen table free; at last she could sit down and begin her real career. She spread newspaper thickly over the laminex, cut a page of her cartridge paper into four, roughly the size of the drawings in the Sun-Herald Juniors, cleaned her school mapping pen and set the tiny bottle of magic ink beside it.

What to draw? In her amateur pencil days, she had usually drawn gum trees or princesses, so she inked her pen and began with one each of those. A stamp cost fourpence, so to make it worthwhile she did two more, variations on the same. Her scratchy pen and the small size of the paper squares made it difficult, but she judged the results at least as good as the ones in the paper. She decided to use her full name, Therese, as it sounded more professional.

Her mother wrote her a note so the nuns would allow her to go down the street at lunchtime and post them next day. As she slipped the envelope through the slot, she was so struck with the enormous significance of her action that she looked around to see if anybody else felt it too — but it seemed not.

Then she waited. For two weeks she waited, hounding her mother each day to be sure she'd really checked the mailbox nailed to the big gumtree at the front gate, worrying that the Editor's letter had blown away or been pinched by a magpie, or that she'd addressed hers incorrectly, that the ink had been the wrong sort after all — and then it came.

Not money, but a certificate, a consolation prize worth having, for it was a points certificate; you could save them up till they reached thirty and cash them in for a pound! Fortune, if not fame, drew closer.

Tessa began flooding the Editor with wads of hopeful tiny drawings, used up her whole sketchbook in miniature vases of flowers, postage stamp size ballerinas and winsome children no bigger than her ink bottle, in different national costumes. As her paper grew scarcer, the drawings grew even smaller.

She would fight her sister for the comic section each Sunday, feverishly scan the Juniors page, look again in disbelief. He still hadn't printed one of hers. Hers were much better; why was she being ignored? Then she got a note from the Assistant Editor, taking pity on her at last and advising the minimum sizes, explaining that the drawings were reduced for publication.

Immediately she offered up her whole last sheet of paper for a Spanish dancer in a polka-dotted dress — a masterpiece, she thought. This new size created a problem because she would need bigger envelopes, so she had to wait till Mum went to town again. And the stamps cost sixpence. With the envelopes, that was over a week's pocket money. It had better be worth it!

She would not send any more until she knew what happened to the dancer. Two, three weeks passed; she drew nothing, sent nothing, in limbo. By the third Sunday, as she opened the comics to that page, the thrill of anticipation had been replaced by one of sick dread. She closed her eyes for a second and made a few rash promises to God, if only …

And there it was, in all its polka-dotted glory:

'Spanish Dancer'

5/- to Therese Nolan (11), Carlton Rd, Erina.

… and yet, until she saw it printed there, she hadn't noticed an awkwardness about the hands, or that stiffness in the folds of the dress, and was the mouth too close to the nose? For a moment she wished they hadn't printed it, she wished she had it back to fix up first, but then Liz looked over her shoulder and shrieked so loudly that the whole family heard and wanted to know what was up.

She was famous now, like it or not. Her parents, forever saying they couldn't draw a straight line to save themselves, and crediting her paternal grandmother as to 'where she got it from', were impressed; not impressed enough, however, to find shillings for drawing paper at the rate she needed it. Singlets must come first.

There was very little opportunity in that house for scrounging, as her mother didn't waste anything, but desperation forged ingenuity. She could usually cut enough unbloodied sections of butcher's paper from round the weekly meat order; she rubbed out old pencil sketches; with silent apologies, she cut the yellowed front and back blank pages out of the only books in the house (an ancient set of the L.M. Montgomery *Anne* books, once belonging to an aunt of her mother's, and Tessa's own bible since she was nine).

She tried begging paper as advance birthday and Christmas presents, but her mother knew her too well and said she wouldn't be able to put up with the look on her face when she had no presents at the real time.

Her second success in print was for a special Father's Day competition; a sentimental version of how she imagined normal families lived. It depicted a slick striped-pyjama'd Dad (certainly not hers) sitting up in bed in a posh bedroom, like in the shop displays, graciously receiving gifts from his two adoring cherubs. None of them looked like they'd been asleep, not a rumpled hairdo amongst them, and she never could draw men very well, but for this she got 15/ — and a lesson in what the public wanted.

The certificates were mounting up. She'd already cashed in one lot for a pound and was well on the way to her second. Getting published was more important, but the criteria for selection was hard to follow. Tessa began specialising in ballerinas en pointe, the Firebird or the Swan usually. She got quite good at legs. Unfortunately the editor didn't notice before she ran out of time and turned 15.

Beanpicking took over as the chief source of pocket money; exam studies took over from daydreaming; worries about the equally troublesome presence of pimples and absence of boys took over from those about careers. She stopped testing out possible captions for her future front page photos: Therese Nolan, the well known author... artist... ballerina....

Untended, the road to greatness disintegrated into a faint footpath, the prints going every which way, often backwards, or right off the track, to be lost in the maze of daily mediocrity.

Tessa got married instead.

A Taste of Olives

THE HILL FARM was a hard place to make a living — stony ground, no water, and the only access a rough steep road.

It had always been the O'Briens'; tall, gaunt people glimpsed occasionally at the produce store, flanked by their two gawkily shy, buck-toothed, beanpole children. They kept to themselves. Real hillbillies, the creekflat kids thought. Real poor too. One day the word got round that the O'Briens had sold up, gone. Where to, nobody knew or cared.

An 'Eyetalian' family, name of Marina or Merino or something like that, had bought it. Any Italians would have been a novelty in that coastal farming district in the late 1950s, but this family wore a particularly exotic mantle.

For a start there was no father, just a woman and her teenage son and daughter. There was also some mystery about why there was no father. It was rumoured he'd been shot in a feud between families at the Sydney Markets, just like in *The Untouchables* show. The family had been paid off, banished to the hill farm. Nobody really believed such a thing possible in Australia, but it made the Merinos, as they were stubbornly called, an irresistible topic of speculation.

The kids didn't go to school and the family rarely left the farm, so nobody saw much of them till the first summer holidays after they came. Bean season in the valley, the regular professional pickers all taken, and the Merinos apparently had a crop too big for them. The farmer at the bottom of their road asked the nearby Mrs Carter and her twelve-year-old daughter, Susan, if they'd help out; he knew they could use the money. Fred Carter had finally given up failing at being a fulltime farmer and had returned to bricklaying and, it was rumoured, to the drink.

So at six the next morning the Carters set off with as heady a mix of excitement and trepidation as any adventurer into foreign lands, armed with their lunch basket and thermos of tea. They didn't normally take tea with them, but Mrs Carter wasn't sure Eyetalians would provide it like the other farmers' wives did — great billies of it, strong, black and heavily sugared, ready to be poured into tin mugs, to wash down the slabs of fruit cake.

Turning off the tar up the Merinos' dirt road took them into unknown territory. It was a stiff climb. They stopped at the top to get their breath back, savouring the unfamiliar aspect of their own faraway little house, nestled amongst the rich green scallops of the rows of orange trees. The track quickly turned a corner and lost them to all that was familiar; the whole bush up here was dry and crackly, unlike their moist ferny patch of forest near the creek. The gums were very tall, but the road was cut so deep and sharp into the hillside that many of their roots hung bare, vainly searching the shaley banks for nourishment.

Coming to an old wooden gate at the end of the road, they lifted its ancient bones far enough aside to squeeze through. Mrs Carter kept nervously smoothing her short hair, her skirt front, her collar and anything else she came across. Susan was worried too; what if they couldn't speak English? What if they couldn't count properly to pay right? What if there was an argument and they waved their hands about and shouted like in the pictures? 'Latin temperament' she knew it was called — what if they had it?

Their shoes puffed pale clouds of dust as they headed up the track to the small house. From there they could see the whole farm on its open shelf cut into the hill, stretching out like a wide apron till it dropped over the edge of a rocky escarpment to their valley below. It was as if the bush had suddenly squatted down, opened its arms to push back its cape of trees, and revealed a bare and gently curving lap.

At the far side of the bean paddock that covered this lap was a shiny red tractor, some full hessian bags already standing on its rear tray. Receiving no response to their timid calls into the house from the bottom step, they walked towards the tractor, on the lookout for their first Eyetalian. As they drew near, a fat boy of about fifteen straightened up from one of the rows.

'Eh! Gooday!' he called, smiling and waving them over with a very foreign flash of gold watch and several gold rings. His black hair, oiled up Elvis-style, kept flopping over his forehead as quickly as he tossed it back. He withdrew a round blue plastic brush, already fitted to his hand, from the straining back pocket of his jeans and ran it through his disobedient locks as he came up to them.

'You Missus Carter, eh?'

'Er, yes,' said my mother, 'Mr Peters said you needed some pickers. This is my daughter Susan.'

He flicked his black eyes over Susan. 'Bean pickin' pretty hard work for a skinny kid like her. She done it before?'

'I've picked beans heaps of times!' Susan flared up indignantly, but was saved from further insult as his sister approached. She was not much taller than Susan but a lot more developed sideways, and wore her long wavy black hair all teased up in front, hairsprayed as if she was going to a dance. Her face, though broad like her brother's, was attractive, and its expression was friendly.

'Eh!' she said, 'We been picking for hours! I'm Christina and thissus my brother Joe.'

'Mrs. Carter,' stated the formal representative of Queen, Country and the English *Woman's Weekly*, 'and Susan.'

'Hiya, Suse,' grinned Christina. 'Put ya stuff over there in the shade and I'll get yers some buckets.'

She swayed over to the shed in her tight black skirt, the effect only slightly spoilt by her rather bandy legs and her boatlike blue thongs. Susan noted with envy the white gathered blouse with its red ribbon drawstring round a very low neckline. Returning with the kero tin buckets in her strong plump arms, Christina bent to put them down. As she did so, her thin gold chain and cross swinging forward, they could see right down her front, past her heavily padded bra to the roll of fat at her waistband. Mrs Carter's raised eyebrows and tight lips said 'Hussy!' but all she actually said was 'U-u-m, where's your mother?', unsure whether they should even stay.

Christina gestured towards the far end of the paddock, where a broad black shape was bent over, picking away from them along the row. At the end the figure straightened up, tin on hip, turned and saw them and threw her free arm up in a sort of salute, yelling a gruff version of the by-now-familiar 'Eh!'

She wore a black scarf on her head, a black blouse, black skirt, black apron and thick black stockings; just like the peasant women in *National Geographic,* thought Susan. Mrs Merino had bent to the next row immediately, so they took their bins to start where Joe indicated with his fat finger.

The morning wore on as all first beanpicking mornings did. Painfully. It was a good heavy crop and they moved slowly, filling their tins often. That was the worst part, straightening up to take the tins along to empty them.

Susan's back muscles were burning but she tried hard to conceal it when she passed Joe, who grinned up knowingly each time. She muttered to her mother that he was absolutely infuriating, he was so patronising. 'Doesn't he realise he's just a fat kid without a father to belt him into place?'

Her mother said they didn't have to be bossed around by a couple of children and that they'd deal directly with Mrs Merino at morning tea. But they didn't stop for morning tea, they worked right on till midday! This was an unheard-of practice in any paddock in Australia, be they beans, peas or potatoes.

At last Mrs Merino rolled up to them, calling, 'Eat, eat! We eat now!'

and was off to the house, beckoning them to follow. They retrieved their basket and followed her on shaky legs, trying to walk erect but not quite succeeding.

By the time they got there, Mrs Merino had brought her family's food out to the verandah and they were hoeing in, sitting along a weathered wooden bench, backs against the wall, legs splayed out. As the new-comers sat primly down on the bench opposite, Mrs Merino's lined brown face broke into a wide grin, revealing many gaps between her stumps of teeth. 'Eh!' she exclaimed again, her hand raised in greeting, clutching a hunk of what looked like hard cake.

These Eyetalians had a strange lunch: bits of a dark cold sausage; little round black things like cherries but with pointy seeds that they unapologetically and proficiently spat out; oval tomatoes that they ate whole like apples; wedges of very dry-looking yellow cheese; and bro-ken-off lumps of the crusty cake stuff that every now and then they dipped into the dish of oil in which the 'cherries' lay glistening. They watched with unconcealed amusement as their pickers unwrapped the greaseproof paper from their neat thin sandwiches of fish paste on soft white sliced bread, and poured out their cups of milky tea.

Mrs Merino tried to offer some of their food. 'Eat!' she kept saying. Mrs Carter politely refused, but bolder Susan thought she'd give some of it a go.

The cake stuff was called 'pa-nay', and Christina reckoned it was bread. As Susan later told her mother, if it was bread, it was awfully stale, and she didn't know how their mother could chew it with so few teeth. 'Where do you get that?' she asked Christina when she'd washed it down. 'Mamma makes it,' said Christina.

Susan shot a glance at her mother. Who ever heard of people making their own bread these days? No wonder she couldn't do it right. Maybe they were too poor to buy proper bread? But no, there was the new tractor and all that gold on fat boy here. Blood money!

She tried a 'cherry' next, but almost instantly spat it out, to her mother's tongue-clicking disgust. 'Well, it's so bitter!' she complained, shuddering at the memory.

'Olives', said Christina, 'from Italia. We love olives!' and she popped another into her mouth, sucking the pip with exaggerated relish. Susan watched, her own mouth involuntarily screwing up.

Christina offered some of the sausage but Susan's erstwhile adventurous spirit quailed at a closer look at its dried blood colour and spots of fat and gristle. 'But it's good, it's salami,' Christina explained, tearing off a chunk with her sharp little teeth. 'Thanks, but I only like devon,' Susan said resolutely.

Mrs Merino and Joe were mopping up the last of the oil from the olives with their bread and taking big gulps from their mugs. Seeing her pickers had finished their tea, Mrs Merino insistently pushed some mugs into their hands, nodding vigorously and saying 'Si, si!' to Mrs Carter's headshakes.

It seemed they had no choice but to accept. 'Oh well, it's thirsty work out there, I suppose we can always do with more tea,' said Mrs Carter.

'No tea…vino!' crowed Mrs Merino, slapping her rough hands on her lap.

'Oh, yes,' said Mrs Carter dubiously as she took a sip, nodding at Susan to be polite and do the same. They were at a total loss; it was dark red like raspberry cordial but it wasn't at all sweet and it made their tongues go furry. Even if it had occurred to Mrs Carter that it mght be alcoholic, it bore no resemblance to either beer or sweet sherry, the sum of her experience, and anyway, 'drinking' in the middle of a working day was inconceivable. Whatever it was, they got through their mugfuls in the interests of good manners and the sacred creed of 'waste not, want not'.

'Bene?' queried Mrs Merino.

'Pardon?' said Mrs Carter.

'She said 'good'… it's good, isn't it?' explained Christina.

'Very nice,' smiled Mrs Carter, rather more readily than before.

The afternoon's picking went more easily. After a while Mrs Carter said to Susan that her back seemed to have got used to it but she had a terrible headache.

'That's funny,' said Susan, 'so do I.' But they lasted out the day, and promised to return on the next. They walked home in tired silence, grateful for the downhill run, mulling over the oddities of their first day amongst foreigners.

Next day Christina picked alongside Susan like an old friend, telling her all about her rich and much older fiancée in Sydney and embarrassing her by asking how many boyfriends she'd had.

Going to an all-girl convent didn't allow Susan such wickedness even if she'd had the access or the wherewithal, but she couldn't admit that to Christina, a woman at fifteen. So, making sure her mother wasn't in earshot, she made some up, promising herself she would confess the lie next week.

Lunchtime was more relaxed too, as Mrs Merino, having guessed they didn't really like the vino, insisted instead on Mrs Carter at least having a little glass of an almost colourless drink she made herself. A sort of tonic, they gathered, called 'grappa', and while she sipped her medicine, the two ladies smiled and nodded at each other, conversing through Christina in a stilted but amiable way.

Susan was surprised that her mother was so at ease with this rough person, as she usually had great pretensions to gentility, but she supposed she felt sorry for her, as the Merinos' house was in an even worse state than theirs. It was so old it had newspapers lining the walls, and its floors were on such an angle that their lounge was propped up on bricks at one end.

On the third day at lunch, Mrs Carter tried to refuse a second glass of tonic, but Mrs Merino grabbed the much slighter woman by the shoulders and stood her up. One broad hand still holding a shoulder, with her other hand she gave each of Mrs Carter's small (32B) breasts several light pats, shaking her head as she did so: 'No milk! No milk!'

She then pushed her gently back down onto the bench, firmly placed the glass of tonic in her hand and motioned her to drink up, affirming 'Bene, bene!' encouragingly.

Susan's mouth fell open at such crude behaviour, and in front of a boy! Her mother went bright pink and then… she giggled. So did Christina and Joe, and Mrs Merino positively roared with laughter. Susan's shock turned to confused embarrassment as her mother simply downed her tonic and joined in.

They went back to the picking, trailing a feeling in the air that Susan couldn't define. Being a wordy little person, she pondered on it until finally, from her store of unused and slightly unclear words, she decided that, being peasants, they must also be the other adjectives that often went with that word. Not only were they 'Latin' but 'earthy' and 'lusty' as well, and whatever that meant, the flavour was strongly here, and she didn't like it.

It was in their food, their drink; in the mother's broad black-aproned hips, her manly hands and gestures, her hearty laugh; in the girl's knowing swagger and heavy eyes when she talked about boys and stuck out her chest and tossed her hair; in the boy's tight jeans and oily awareness of even Susan's faint female qualities… and it was catching. Her mother had caught it; what if she did?

It had already caused her to chalk up one fib for confession. What next? Walking home that evening, still in a righteous huff, Susan silently vowed she wasn't going back to that uncomfortably incomprehensible 'earthiness'. Nor did she, her back having suddenly 'given out' (she confessed that with the boyfriends).

Her mother, however, finished that season and picked for the Merinos for several years. Her breasts didn't get any bigger, but she continued to take the proffered tonic — out of politeness, of course. She spread the word that the Eyetalians were nice people, just a bit more down-to-earth than 'us'. Susan would roll her eyes at this and leave the room. Her mother's uncharacteristic behaviour at the Merinos could be explained by their foreign influence, but not forgiven. Susan felt betrayed.

The Merinos left when Christina turned 18 and married her 40-year-old fiancée, who was setting them all up in a big house near Liverpool, the feud presumably over and the period of exile ended.

'No more beans!' roared Mrs Merino to her flatchested little friend as they toasted each other on her final picking day. 'Flowers — I grow flowers, eh, Missus?!'

When, years later, Susan was finally awakened to what that incomprehensible feeling had been, it struck her like meeting an old friend, barely recognisable because so unfamiliarly resplendent. But, deep down, she knew it:

— it tasted like ripe black olives, golden green olive oil soaking into coarse bread, rough red wine in chipped mugs;

— it smelt like sun-warmed dust, warm sweat and hessian bags;

— it felt like weathered wood and the sun on her face before that was a bad thing.

'Bene, bene!' came the hearty echoes.

'Si,' said the newly-sensual Susan, 'most definitely si!'

FOR BEAUTY

LIKE A MOVIE STAR fallen to earth in their country convent, he offered them his name in his oh-so-romantic accent… 'Carlo Bianchi'… and 200 little pink tongues silently rolled 'Carlo' over and over in their mouths like a Caramello.

The school had been standing at attention for some time. Tarry waves of heat rose from the asphalt but not one girl had wavered or dropped to her black stockinged knees, as often happened. Assembly was always presided over from the verandah by the head nun, Sister Philomena, 'Old Meanie,' broad of shoulder, red of face, black of eye and lightning quick with a cane. Today, whilst all ears took in her ringing Irish voice, all eyes were focused on the man at her side, the visitor who had the older nuns in a dither, the younger ones in a perpetually rising blush, Old Meanie almost caught in a smile, and two hundred adolescent girls in a secret sighing quiver.

No priest, nobody's relative, almost young, and almost handsome, with wavy black hair and flashing smile. Next to Meanie he looked a bit short, but he made up for that in exotica; an artist, an Italian artist, here for a month to paint a mural in their chapel.

'Mr Bianchi' corrected Old Meanie, 'will be using the music room behind the chapel. I expect you to give him the quiet he needs for his work. D-i-s-miss!'

The girls filed into their classrooms in a hum of speculation, adulation and titillation that was as tangible as a swarm of bees in a clover patch, setting even the pre-pubescents athrum with anticipatory tingles, the origin and purpose of which they were entirely ignorant.

Amongst these latter innocents was Catherine McDonald. Catherine came from an outlying farm and had the reputation of being a swot, a goody and a brain. All three were true; Catherine loved learning, especially about Art. Acknowledged as 'good at art' since Infants, she'd been permitted to study it by correspondence for high school. Acknowledged also by the nuns as a 'good girl', Sister Philomena naturally thought of her as the solution to her problem. Mr Bianchi had asked for a helper, a loan of one of the girls at lunchtimes to clean brushes and mix paints.

Philomena was perturbed at the request, as her girls were at very vulnerable ages and must not be exposed to temptation. Of course he was married, and would be above reproach, engaged as he was so constantly in painting sacred subjects, but he was a man, and if his presence had caused even her own firmly suppressed feminine instincts to momentarily flutter within their bonds, what would it do to her girls?

Fourteen-year-old Catherine showed no interest in boys. Nor did she have any; to her they were dumb and dangerous. Thanks to the nuns' evasive sex education, Catherine, like many of her friends, thought kissing could get you pregnant. The safely virginal Catherine was appointed.

She could barely believe such an honour: to watch a real artist at work, to work with him! At eleven she'd spent a day on her own in the New South Wales Art Gallery, overwhelmed by its lofty rooms full of gold frames and brownish oil paintings. When she'd finally re-emerged into the sunlight she was Art-struck the way other girls get horse-struck or boy-struck, but Sister Meanie didn't know this.

Lunchtime finally came. Catherine bolted down her cheese and vegemite sandwiches, combed her hair and smoothed her unruly eyebrows. She wished her tunic was not so old and baggy and shiny. She wished she had fine black lisle stockings instead of wrinkled cotton ones. She wished she did not feel so sick with butterflies…

Crossing the courtyard to the Chapel, she could see through the wide windows that the wall for the mural was already half painted over in white. She knocked at the door of the music room.

'Come in!' she heard, and opened the door to a studio perfume of linseed oil, turps and paint. Mr Bianchi appeared, smiling, before her. He took her hands in his. 'Ah, you must be Catherine! The young artist who is so kind to help me? Yes?'

'Yes, sir,' mumbled Catherine, avoiding his eyes and not knowing how to get her hands back.

He let go to wag his finger at her. 'Ah no, no 'sir'! You must call me Carlo if you are going to work with me. And I shall call you Caterina… is Italian for your name and much easier off the tongue!' as his right hand described a great rolling outward arch.

'Gesticulate' thought Catherine, he's gesticulating. It's because he's a Latin; they always do that in books.

'Come. I show what we must do.'

She followed him over to the long work bench. He began by showing her his drawings for the mural. It was to be a huge oval of Madonna and Child in a delicate garden, with angels peeping down from a blue heaven forming the frame. Awed, Catherine said it would be as beautiful as the Sistine Chapel ceiling.

He laughed, took her elbow and turned her to where he had his paints arrayed; there were tins and tubes and brushes of all sizes and shapes. 'Are you good with colour, Caterina?'

'I… think so,' she said, not sure yet what he would expect her to do, and disconcerted by his warm hand around her arm. Catherine's family were not the touching sort. She could feel the pressure of his fingers through the sleeve of her school blouse. She felt like pulling away but did not want to be thought rude or silly.

'Good!' he said, 'You will make the colours for me. I will mix a little to the colour I want and you then mix a lot for me. Yes?'

She nodded, and he smiled at her again as he released her arm. He worked very quickly, putting a dab of this and that on to the palette until he had made a soft bluish-green. He brought a stool for her to sit on. With a flourish he bade her sit, and tied a large paint-spattered smock round her neck, lifting her hair to do so. She felt his fingers brush her skin, and shivered slightly. Somewhere low down inside her a small ache gently rolled over.

Catherine worked happily until she heard the first bell go for afternoon lessons, when she hurriedly closed up the tins and wiped her hands on the turpsy rag. She took off her smock and called in at the chapel, 'See you tomorrow, Mr Bianchi.'

He turned from undercoating the mural, and waved his brush at her. 'Ciao, Caterina! Grazie, but it is Carlo, remember!'

She smiled and nodded, almost bobbing a curtsy as she backed out the door. She raced to wash her hands before the second bell; mustn't be late, or she might not be allowed to come tomorrow.

All the way home, in the school bus amid the usual cacophony of squeals and giggles, then dawdling in solitude up the long dirt track, she relived his every word and look. He had trusted her to do the work on her own; he did not treat her as a child, but as a fellow artist. Only when faced with her undeniable mother, 'Catherine, you're late! Get changed, feed the dogs, set the table…' did she plummet back to reality.

By next day word of her lunchtime job had spread, and many an envious girl tried to probe her for details, but Catherine held her privilege close and said she was only mixing paints. They rolled their eyes in despair at such an opportunity wasted on this infant who wouldn't know a dreamboat if she fell over him. But this meant he was safely available for them to tempt.

They took extra care with their hair, risked the wrath of Meanie by putting Vaseline on their lips and eyebrows, pulled their belts as tight as possible, and slunk like sirens, instead of running like the scatter-brained fillies they were, when near the chapel.

For Catherine life was only lunchtime; Art encapsulated in time and personified by Carlo. He praised her colour work, and suggested she come earlier, bring her lunch, so they could talk a little before starting work. He asked to see her paintings. She showed them timidly, but he was as encouraging and constructively critical as she could have hoped.

Very soon she was easily calling him Carlo. He told Sister Philomena that Catherine was very helpful, and asked if he might offer her drawing lessons after school in return. Although Catherine was surely doing it for the love of God, Sister Philomena gave permission. When he told her about the lessons Catherine almost hugged him in the excess of her joy, but arrested her upflying hands in time. He did not miss the aborted gesture, patting her shoulder as he passed to show he understood.

He made her draw him in their lessons: details — his hand, his face, his foot, his ear — or quick sketches of figure poses, always urging her to seek the essential lines, to find the 'bones' under the flesh. He talked of how da Vinci had studied anatomy, drawn the muscles and skeletons of dead people, so that when he painted a voluptuously fleshed woman, she appeared real, not just a collection of bumps, because he knew what she was underneath.

Catherine was inspired, worshipping Carlo, whom she felt she knew better than she did anyone else, having so closely traced his features, his body, with her eyes, her drawing fingers. The afternoon sessions were peaceful; no school noises, girls all gone home, nuns safely in the convent. Just the occasional hum of traffic and the scratching and swishing of her charcoal stick as she concentrated on finding Carlo's bones. This total absorption in her work was as near to bliss as she could imagine.

The mural by now was a pale oval glowing in a wall of beautiful blue... 'cielo'. The central figures had their basic colours filled in. The angels were next, but he was having difficulty getting some of their poses right. One afternoon he asked her to pose for him to help with the angels.

'Just the pose, Caterina,' he begged when she baulked at the thought of herself as an angel. 'They will all be pale and plump with blonde or auburn hair. Just give me your bones and I will paint the bodies over them.'

'OK,' she said reluctantly. Carlo showed her how he wanted her to stand, but she was stiff, awkward. He made her spin her arms like windmills and shake her legs like the hokey-pokey till she giggled, then they tried the pose again. She felt warmer, the twist of her body more fluid, her arms more graceful. 'Bene, bene,' murmured Carlo as he drew, his eyes flicking up at her and back down to his paper.

'Now,' he commanded, coming over to demonstrate another. 'You are sitting on the edge of a cloud; stretch out that leg…si, si! And that arm up… oh, but this tunic is ter-r-rible… how can I find your bones in that great bunch of cloth?!'

He stood back and looked at her critically. 'Take off that belt and the fabric will at least flow with your body,' he said. 'It is cutting your shape in half; it does not let your body be beautiful.'

Catherine laughed aloud at the thought of her scrawny body being beautiful, but removed the offending belt. 'Is much better!' smiled Carlo, drawing happily again.

When he had finished, he took her hand to help her up. She stumbled against him, finding her leg quite numb when she put her weight on it. He supported her with his arm around her to a stool. 'Oh, I am so sorry, bambina bella. What have I done to you?'

Catherine found that her arms, however, were far from numb; they were tingling within his firm encirclement. She sat heavily on the stool as he released her.

'Can I see the drawings, please?' she asked, hiding her blushes as she bent to rub her leg.

'Si, if you wish, mia Caterina povera,' unpinning the sheets to bring over to her.

He spread the drawings out on the bench. Catherine could not suppress her cry of shock. He had not drawn just her 'bones,' clad either in angel flesh or school clothes; he had drawn her body, just as it was in her wardrobe mirror. How could he know what she looked like underneath?! He had even drawn her small breasts with their large soft nipples… Catherine could not look at him, could not speak.

'Ah, Caterina, you do not like them! But you make a most beautiful angel.'

'But they're not angels,' she burst out, 'they're me! I thought you would make up the bodies. They'll know it's me!'

'How, cara mia? No one else knows your beauty but I. You did not even know it yourself till this moment. I will make you fat for the mural, do not worry. But I wanted the curve of your back…here…' placing a hand in the small of her back… 'and the path that flows to meet it…' and he traced lightly down the channel of her spine. His fingers set up tiny quivers at each point of contact. 'I want this lovely dip between your shoulders and your neck, I want these hollow shells in front of them, I want these flower buds of your breasts, I want the perfect high domes of your buttocks, the long slender thighs below, the sweetness of your knees, the daintiness of your feet…'

Catherine sat perfectly still, eyes closed, atune to his caressing words and fingertips. Each part he touched seemed to leap towards him in response. That ache at the pit of her tummy lurched alarmingly, her whole body was straining towards him, naked in her beltless tunic.

She felt his hands cupping her hot cheeks, and her eyes flew open. 'You must not worry, Caterina, no one will know it is you. It is a secret beauty between us, yes?'

He was smiling into her eyes as she nodded. 'So come, one last pose for the last angel, eh? An easy one this time.'

He had her kneel on a cushion with her back to him, sit back on her legs and stretch up to rest her folded arms on a chair seat, her chin on her arms. She was glad not to have to face him as she tried to make sense of her confused feelings.

Every now and then he would murmur something in Italian. She was comfortable, drowsy… then he cried 'Finito!' She scrambled up and went to look. He was right. The upward pull of the slender arms, the simple long curving lines of the back, the flaring of the buttocks, the little bare soles exposed beneath them; all were beautiful as he had drawn them.

She smiled up at him. 'Si, bella!' and they both laughed.

The next two weeks flew past as the mural neared completion. The angels were in place, all pale gold and white, decorously draped, plump-ly and anonymously adoring as they peeped through the oval window to earth. It was already softly luminous with colour, like a Fabergé egg in a box of pale blue silk, when he began to apply the gold leaf. From delicate sheets of tissue paper he traced the gold for the fine edgings of the garments, the haloes… the oval began to glow even more, to appear to be about to float away from its restraining wall. It was a masterpiece.

The day before it was to be unveiled and consecrated, she helped him pack up all the paints and brushes. He gave her many partly-used tubes, a few half-sheets of the precious gold leaf, some slightly tatty brushes.

'We will not say goodbye yet, Caterina', he said as she lingered in the doorway, looking at the empty room forlornly. But the next day, their sanctuary gone, she did not see him alone. The mural was admired by all, the artist much congratulated, and after the consecration the school stood in assembly, looking up at his now familiar figure.

He addressed the school — and Catherine/Caterina.

'I would like to thank you all for your hospitality and your consid-eration during my work. I have found much inspiration here. Perhaps when you look at my mural you will remember me and the beauty that God has given us.'

And he bowed and walked away as two hundred pairs of hands clapped desperately, cued by a Sister Philomena not quite ignorant of the frustrated yearnings she was orchestrating.

Catherine found it difficult to believe he would never again be wait-ing for her at lunchtime. But Old Meanie was, tapping a flat parcel. 'It's from Mr Bianchi,' she said, handing it over. 'Well, open it!' she snapped, as Catherine simply clutched it, awaiting dismissal and privacy.

Slowly Catherine unwrapped a book, *Leonardo's Drawings*. The cover bore the head of a demure Madonna, so the vigilant Meanie was satisfied. Yet she frowned at the girl, trying to put her finger on the change in her. 'I was a bit worried about you spending so much time with Mr Bianchi. I must ask you, girl… he didn't try to… er… kiss you, did he?'

'Oh no, Sister!' replied Catherine, obviously shocked.

'Well then, I hope you've learnt something from this experience.'

Oh yes, Sister, smiled Catherine to herself as she hurried out, her book hugged tight against her 'flower buds of breasts.' She had not showed the inscription, which said: 'To Caterina — for beauty — from Carlo Bianchi.'

The now-familiar small ache down there was doing cartwheels.

CRITERION CHRYSALIS

FULL OF innocence and impatience to be otherwise, Victoria and Susan were on their way to mid-morning lectures. It was April 1965, already halfway through the first term of their first year at University, and up till now Nothing had happened.

Suddenly, right in front of them, into the corridor stepped the one elegant male from the beards and baggy trousers set. 'Such a bore, tutorials!' he grimaced, closing a door behind him. 'Ah, Victoria, isn't it? Like to come down to the Criterion with me? I'm meeting a few friends there.'

'Now?' blinked Victoria, off balance for just a second, then, 'Why not?' smiling sweetly at him and ignoring the gasp from Susan. The languid harbinger glanced down at this offsider, misinterpreting her displeasure, and said to Victoria, 'You can bring your friend too...'

It didn't occur to either of them that Susan needed introducing, and from experience, she shouldn't have expected it, but she wanted to be noticed with this group. Its male members exhibited many favourable indications: the trousers were corduroy, the jackets had leather patches on the elbows, those that didn't have beards at least had longish hair, and they smoked pipes or unfiltered Camels. They looked like they read poetry.

So, uncharacteristically emboldened, she spoke up. 'OK. It's too hot to be stuck in a stuffy lecture room anyhow. I'm Susan, by the way.'

Victoria's eyebrows rose in surprise. The tall young man gave a vapid snort of a laugh, pursed his mouth and nodded his head knowingly. 'Adrian,' he replied.

Her existence, her name, acknowledged. That was a start, she supposed. Cursing the mundanity of her given name for the thousandth time, Susan did an immediate mental replay of that scene with various more impressive ones... Evangeline, Charlotte, Sophia... to step up his response: 'He looked at the smaller girl with interest', no, better still, 'He was intrigued by...'

So occupied, she followed them out of the Union building and up the road, Adrian lounging along beside Victoria, briefcase in one hand and a furled umbrella in the other. Not that it looked like rain, but, as he soon revealed, he had been Overseas, being the son of a Professor. Susan decided he had modelled himself on an English fop: well-dressed, nonchalant, clever, lazy. And, she thought, looking at his small pale eyes, up-to-no-good, as her grandmother would say.

On Victoria's other side, Susan felt short, hot, guilty and worried.

For a start, she didn't want to miss her lectures; she enjoyed them.

For another, ladies didn't go into pubs. Did intriguing young women?

For yet another, what to drink? Her mother used to have a gin squash in the car when Dad had a beer on the way home from town on Saturday mornings, but she'd never let Susan taste it. She hadn't really liked beer when she'd tried her Dad's at home, but on her scholarship cheapest was best.

Finally, since she was merely an afterthought on this outing, could she keep up the bravado when faced with a whole group of these disdainful beings?

Totally ignored by her two companions, Susan pretended to be extremely interested in the park across the road and the muddy stormwater canal beyond it as she mulled over this first term. It had all been so awkward and disappointing. For the first few weeks she and Victoria and every other pair of first year girls had self-consciously sauntered across the tarred quadrangles and along the paths between the boring beds of marigolds. They had entered library, lecture room or cafeteria with the same studied glaze, knowing there were watching eyes, but also that they must not show that they knew.

Victoria, and by association, Susan, had attracted the scrutiny and the speculations of several varied quarters. Victoria, the beauty, had expected to be paid due court by either Varsity lads of Ivy League sophistication and wealth or Oxford dons of elegant manners and trousers. So far she had been presented with only slightly smarter replicas of the pimply uncouth youths that had hung around the milkbars in her home town.

Susan, the much lesser light, had been dreaming of ivy-covered walls and ancient halls redolent of scholarship and literature, but had found instead soot-covered brick and fibro, redolent of the steelworks city it served. The students it harboured were mainly studying metallurgy or engineering and loved football and beer, not books.

Victoria had toyed with the inevitable overtures from all camps, naturally only being approached by the leaders. She would flash them her smile, favour them with a glimpse of her fine shoulders by a toss of her long blonde hair, and consider the applicants' potential. She had the confidence that comes from being brought up in the comfort and comparative wealth of the middle classes, being born almost beautiful and pampered as if she was truly so, her assets polished and groomed to full marketability.

She and Susan had been friends all through their convent high school years, despite being from opposite ends of the social strata of their small town. Susan, the brain at school, had no confidence outside it. Not totally unattractive — which she even admitted to herself at times, alone in front of the mirror, carefully practising smiling without showing her poor teeth — but as unnoticed as torchlight in sunshine beside Victoria.

Initially she'd been invited out with Victoria, but Susan had been most unimpressed by that main social scene, where a good time was one where blokes ruled, beer flowed and the girls were privileged if allowed to watch such high points of the evening as schooner swilling competitions. These delights were usually followed by parking at Bar Beach, where the wetly ineffective adolescent kisses and hopeful fumbling did nothing to convince her that the experience was worth repeating. She didn't know whether Victoria fared better.

Not that she was prudish. Despite the warnings of her convent sexual education, so skittish as to invite wild imaginings rather than allay curiosity, she was ready to be deflowered, to bare her freckled bosom for He who would lead her into the groves of love, but it had to be a He who read Donne, who could woo her down the path to perdition with words and poetry, make sex grand and exciting, not awkward and embarrassing and virtually uneventful. Until He appeared, she preferred to stay in the hostel and read.

A few male lesser lights had asked her out on her own, usually for a coffee at the Vienna or to some instructive free do at Uni. They only went as far as sweaty handholding in the bus and a nervous kiss at the door to the hostel. She frightened them off by not being the mild and respectable mouse she looked, by not agreeing with their opinions and by being socially inexperienced enough to say so.

After a poetry reading where she drank several glasses of dreadfully sweet sherry and fell over in the Ladies, she had kissed her escort back, rather fiercely, when he said goodnight at the door. The word got around that she was odd; the timid invitations stopped.

But today might reveal the sort of university life she'd always imagined, even if she was just tagging along. By now they had passed several blocks of grimy brick semis and faded shopfronts, a few car yards and mechanics' workshops, and there it was — The Criterion, clad in shiny brown tiles.

As they neared the public bar entrance, Susan could smell its morning hosed-down coolness, its stale beer and disinfectant, and hear the rough, uneven hum of men's voices, pierced by an occasional burst of laughter. Surely they weren't going in there?

Sweaty, extremely nervous, she glanced at Victoria, who appeared cool and poised as usual, ready to sweep in over the tiled threshold of even this unprepossessing, unknown territory and claim it. But Adrian veered round the side of the pub to a smaller entrance. Susan just had time to notice the sign over the door, saying that minors under 18 were not allowed, before he led them down a dark hall. It hadn't occurred to her before that she was also breaking the law by this reckless undertaking: she had only just turned 17 and she didn't even look that!

Too late to back out. They had already emerged into the brightness of a small beer garden, with several occupied tables over on the shady side. Dozens of strange faces seemed to turn to them as they entered. She knew she was standing there like a schoolgirl, briefcase protectively clutched in front of her too-skinny legs. Dazzled by the sudden light, she could barely see where the other two had gone, but stumbled hopefully forward into the shade. They had stopped at a table which seemed rather full. Please let there be room for me too, prayed Susan, though she doubted God would help her in this multiple wickedness.

Adrian had finished introducing Victoria by the time Susan came up, but he waved a hand vaguely at her — 'Victoria's friend, Susan'. He did not bother saying the others' names again. There was sort of a group mutter in response, and everybody juggled places. When it stopped, Victoria was seated between Adrian and another male. Susan spotted an empty chair at the far corner of the table, but to reach it she had to squeeze awkwardly behind three seated people, holding her briefcase up above their heads, and exposing her damp but hopefully shaven armpits to the assembly.

Bending to stow her bag under the table, she resisted a strong urge to just stay under there. She took a deep breath, surfaced, smoothed her blue checked shift dress (one of three shifts made by her mother especially for her Uni debut) and scraped her metal chair up to the table, ready to smile and face the lot of them. Then she realised she'd need her purse, so scraped back and ducked under again.

Red-faced, she resurfaced, plonked her suddenly childish navy plastic purse on the beery laminex table and squared up once more. Her immediate neighbours nodded at her, then turned their backs to resume their conversations. Across the table, Victoria already had some pale drink in front of her and was holding court, waving her slender hands about and laughing, as if she'd often been in pubs with strangers.

Susan fixedly pretended to be following Victoria's conversation, which she could not actually hear, while she agonised about what to do next, how to get a drink and whether to jump into one of the closed conversations beside her or wait to be spoken to. The sharp leaves of the potted palm behind kept pricking her neck. Her face felt as if it was still red; she only hoped her nose was no more so.

As her embarrassment settled, the faces came into focus. Most of them she'd noticed in aloof twos or threes about the uni. One, however, she recognised with a shock; it was James, her English Lit. tutor, and the unwitting hero of quite a few of her daydreams. Wouldn't he know she ought to be at lectures now? Wouldn't he disapprove? And how come he was here with students?

Just then he looked her way, smiled and said, 'Susan, you don't have a drink. What would you like?'

Rescued, astonished that he even remembered her name, she blurted out, 'Beer, please.'

But he came back with, 'New or old?'

What!?

'Pardon?' she stammered.

'New or old?' he repeated, then understood her expression, 'I expect you prefer new beer, don't you?'

'Oh, yes… new, please.'

He went off to the bar, but it was too late, she caught the amused looks across the table, the rolled eyes, the all-too-obvious signalling… talk about babes in the wood!

One of the blokes gave a short blast of laughter and poked his black-bristled, red-nosed face towards her. 'So what do you normally drink, Suse?'

Unable to think of an answer that would not make things worse, she tried just smiling, but her tormentor had smelt blood. 'It's obviously not beer, so why don't you have your usual — my shout! My pleasure, what's it to be?'

The smile still slashing her face, she was mumbling, 'No, no, really, beer's fine,' when her saviour appeared with her drink and caught the scent of the hunt. 'Susan's clearly a champagne girl, Dave, and you won't get that here. But you hold him to that shout for some other time and place, Susan; I'll be your witness!'

And he actually made the chairs juggle for her, sat beside her, talked to her, smiled at her, drew others into the talk so she felt like she was really there, and so ceased to observe herself pretending to be so. She sipped her beer, ignoring its brown bitterness, accepted another, spilt some, and bent down to fetch her hanky from her bag. Whilst under the table, her eye was caught by Victoria's silver sandals and long tanned legs extending from her short skirt. At the top of each of these legs rested a male hand.

Swiftly sitting up, she looked over at her girlfriend. Victoria appeared unaware of the liberty being taken; perhaps she was drunk? The owners of the hands seemed equally oblivious. All were chatting in a sophisticated sort of a way, passing ironic comments, giving little dismissive sniggers. Victoria was good at that; she had older brothers and sisters who'd been to Uni and they all talked like it.

She was distracted by a sudden noisy surging. People were moving chairs, standing up. Feeling a large warm hand on her bare arm, she shivered, and looked round to find James, her tutor, saying that they were all going for lunch at the Capri, did she want to come? She did, she did, but how to say that she had very little money in that purse and her lunch already packed in her bag?

'You'll enjoy it,' he said. 'Do come; it's my treat!'

She smiled hugely at him, forgetting not to for once, so that her rare dimples showed, and she looked quite pretty. James felt like God for a moment; there was a different girl in there somewhere and he had made her appear.

Susan forgot Victoria and her legs, almost forgot her bag, and as James helped her into his low old open MG, she completely forgot about her own legs, flashing them about carelessly, letting them rise up happily brown and narrow next to the gearstick. They roared off down the road, the hot tarry air feeling almost cool on her flushed face. James patted the bare knee nearest to him.

Susan was ready for anything. She turned her bright eyes upon him. 'Say, James, I'll bet you even know some Donne off by heart, don't you?'

MOTHER LOVE

'ZIP ME UP, would you?' Matt's mother said, presenting her virtually naked back to us all. I assumed she meant me, the only other female there. I'd first met her ten minutes ago, when she'd barely acknowledged me, perhaps because she was in a rush; Matt had said she was going out to lunch.

But who would she have asked to do up that zipper if I hadn't been there? Her son? There was almost no back to this dress, an elegant sheath in a sheeny grey fabric with a faint pattern like bird clawprints in black and a pale, cool sort of pink, like you get in cyclamens.

The zipper started halfway down over her shiny black 'step-ins'. I used to wear ones like these at school to hold my stockings up, but mine were in a very unseductive salmony-pink, 'flesh-coloured', like no human flesh you ever saw. She wasn't wearing stockings, so hers must be acting as a sort of corset, to hold her tummy in. After all, she'd had two kids — and was no spring chicken, as my mother would say.

Her low-set bra was black too, emphasising her pale skin. There was a small bulge between the bra and step-ins. Her flesh looked as if it would feel clammy to the touch; I tried not to as I edged the zipper up. It was a very closely fitting dress. I could hear my mother whispering, 'No wonder she needed the corset!' — or was that my own inherited streak of cattiness?

'Thanks,' she said, throwing me a brief glance over her shoulder. No smile. Not worth the effort? I shrivelled to my most unattractive, irrelevant adolescent self.

She walked off, high-heeled black sandals clicking on the polished floorboards. Her toenails were painted the same shade of pink as her lipstick, an exact match to the pink on her dress. Such conscious attention to detail awed me, despite my defiant pride in my ignorance of feminine artifice. I'd convinced myself that intellectuals didn't need it.

We were all watching as she bent over the sideboard to check her lipstick in the big antique mirror on the wall behind it, the knee-length skirt of her dress rising with her as she stretched. I envied her those legs, with their slender ankles and shapely calves, but not that pale flesh, whose freckles lurked unfulfilled just below the surface.

In the sixties a bronzed body was desirable; being tanned was a good thing, healthy even. It seemed an eccentricity in her not to try to achieve even a faint dusting of gold when everyone else was desperate to become as brown and as fast as possible every summer. Failing and becoming even a little freckled would have been more of a shared human experience, more... common. This seemed an arrogance, an exercising of aristocratic confidence in being different such as I had only ever before encountered in books.

So was the dress. It was very smart, but surely unseemly for a fifty-something-year-old mother. I couldn't imagine my mother in it.

She re-emerged from her bedroom, wearing the sort of hat people wear to the races, according to the society pages of the Sunday papers. A wide-brimmed black straw hat, rather Spanish in style.

My mother only ever wore a hat when out in the paddocks picking beans, and that was just a floppy faded cloth necessity. But I may as well stop comparing them; Matt's mother didn't act like any mother I knew.

Yet I'd seen photos of the snappy besuited and behatted dresser Mum was in her twenties — before all us kids. Dressing up must have been the norm then, as beside her in those street photos even my father wore a hat and suit, probably the same double-breasted navy suit hanging in his wardrobe now, awaiting the next obligatory funeral or wedding.

'See you this evening', Matt's mother called from the hall. 'And don't forget to feed the dog if you go out, Matthew.'

We listened to the front door shut, the heels click down the steps, the car door slam, and the engine start. Her presence had dominated more than a country hick like me; we had all been mere audience. The car revved its way up the steep drive. It was Matt, used to being around her, I suppose, who broke the silence.

'Well, that's the old woman out of the way. Where did you put the flagon?'

A little shocked at such filial disrespect, I hurried to fetch the claret while Matt brought out tumblers.

It was a hot, lazy day, and our preliminary meeting for the Autumn 1966 issue of the Uni literary magazine had so far not been very inspired. The editorial team were successfully lounging on the various pieces of the Parker lounge suite, while I stood propped against the mantelpiece, pen and paper ready to catch any gems that might fall from their lips.

They were all older than me, and far more literary; several of them had had poems published in the last issue. I was lucky to be tolerated here, when all I had produced were dreams and secret scribblings. This was the only group in our small provincial University that I admired, so being permitted to act as their literary lackey was an important chink in the door's opening, hopefully my entrée to acceptance. And just maybe I thought that the ability to spin words into magic would rub off on me if I got close enough.

Red wine, earnest philosophical debates and risqué stories soon restored their spirits. The magazine plans were postponed. On the fringes of their talk as usual, I wandered out to the rear deck; on such a steeply sloping block you were almost at tree top level there.

Matt's house was ultra modern, architect-designed, lots of glass and exposed timbers; it breathed class and taste and culture as well as money.

It had nothing in common with my own home, whose unpainted green-streaked fibro shell contained lino floors, saggy plasterboard walls and a chip heater bathroom of dark dampness — no shower. We still had an outdoor pan toilet that we had to empty and bury ourselves…

I shuddered at the idea of this lot ever seeing my place, while at the same time registering a flash of homesickness.

At least it had been surrounded by trees, not tar and brick and tile like the suburb in which I was flatting. I felt cooler just looking at the deep continuous green of Matt's garden and all the others in this hilly suburb.

'How the other half live, eh?' came Don's voice beside me.

I knew where Don's parents lived. It was on the bus route to Uni, in a suburb of fibro Housing Commission cottages which nobody seemed to have the heart to try to beautify beyond a stiff oleander or two. Don only lived there when he couldn't afford to flat. He in turn knew I was on a scholarship, so the farm I came from could hardly be in the squattocracy league; he could safely assume we were in the same lower half.

'M-mm. Not too hard to take, is it? But where does the family's money come from? Inherited?'

'No, Matt's old man's a geologist with a mining company up north, and that pays well, because he's away for months. I think his family was a bit posh, but not wealthy. Hers are working class made good, quite well off, but they still live where she grew up, in a poky little red brick joint. I've met them — very petty petit bourgeois. No, Matt's old man earns all this; she just spends it.'

'How come they don't live up north, closer to where he works?'

Don laughed. 'Well, he's away from his base in Mount Isa a lot, and anyway, can you really see her in an outback town all covered in red dust, and no arty circles to queen it over?'

'No, I guess not. And you're right, 'queen' is the word, the way she looks down her nose at everyone.'

'Yeah. Well, she does mix it with the best in this hole, because of her drawings. They're clever; have a look at the ones in the hall later. I know she acts as if she thinks she's got more brains than anyone else, and maybe she does. Or maybe it's all bluff, but yes, she can be intimidating. It's the big fish, little pond thing. This town is so small that the academics and the arty types all swim with the big business sharks at parties and gallery openings and concerts. There's so little they can call culture that they can't avoid each other as they might in Sydney.'

'Still, I wouldn't like my husband being away so much. I guess she keeps busy with her art?'

'Yeah, well, that and other things…' Don tailed off, raising his eyebrows cryptically.

Being a literal sort of person, not only have I always been hopeless at figuring out anything cryptic, I hate it. I like things said outright, which, as I had rapidly learnt in my first year at Uni, is considered very banal or naive. So in this second year I intend to keep my mouth shut when I get tempted. I've been practising an enigmatic, cynically imbued lift of one eyebrow as an alternative response. I haven't got it right yet, according to the bathroom mirror; it just looks weird.

Matt joined us, offering the dregs of the flagon.

'How about lunch at Marco's? It's Tuesday — free bread and coffee with the $2 pasta today.'

Pasta sounded great, especially at Marco's where the mugs of 'coffee' could be illicit rough red if you were regulars.

'But what about the magazine…?' I began, before I saw that look on their faces. Talk about eloquent! — a long-suffering, silent sighing wonder as to when this prissy bird would get the priorities right. 'Yeah, right', I nodded. I knew what their unspoken answer was — 'The magazine can get stuffed!'. As I still can't bring myself to speak like that comfortably, maybe I ought to be telling the mirror to get stuffed every morning too.

The others said they'd walk on up to the bus stop. I wondered why they didn't wait for Matt, but the reason was soon plain. This lazy lot had been here before; they knew the house rules.

I went about like a good girl, collecting glasses and taking them through to wash. Matt came back upstairs from putting the dog out in the backyard and feeding it as told, and thanked me for my help. He then quickly went over the floor of the whole living room with the carpet sweeper, and with a damp cloth wiped all surfaces — coffee table, mantelpiece and bookshelf — where we might have stood our glasses. Or leant our greasy proletarian elbows, I thought as I watched in amazement. Even the teak arms of the Parker suite got a wiping. He's well-trained... no, he's afraid of her! I went back to the sink and wiped the glasses dry; I kept on wiping till they sparkled. When he re-appeared to put them away, I ventured, 'Bit fussy, eh? Must keep you on your toes.'

He shrugged. 'It's easier than putting up with her bitching.'

As he was locking up, I looked at the set of ink drawings hanging in the hallway. They were exquisite: half botanical, half fantasy, very detailed, almost miniatures. I had to admire her talent, and said so to Matt. He just grunted. We walked in silence along the well-tended footpaths towards the main road. Matt was usually pretty silent anyhow. I was thinking of our different lots in life, of how we had no say in whose household we landed at birth. I didn't much like my upbringing, but I didn't think Matt had fared any better in the lottery.

Knowing I hadn't been in this suburb before, Matt gestured at a collection of tiled roofs and gable windows above a particularly high wall covered in ivy. 'The big boss of BHP lives there.'

'Wow! Ever been inside?'

'Yeah, his wife's a friend of the old woman's.'

It was real silvertail country. The houses might range from grand mock Tudor to architectural modern, but they all reeked of money. The Beatles had it right: 'Money can't buy me love...'

'Ever think of moving out?' I asked.

'Constantly,' he said bitterly, 'but the oldies are putting me through Uni. I can't afford to.'

We could see the others up at the bus stop waving us to hurry, so we stopped talking and ran for it. As the bus jolted and swayed us through the decreasingly leafy suburbs to the inner city, I thought about the value of his subsidy compared to my scholarship, and the price he must daily pay.

Mine never quite made the fortnight and didn't even stretch to the shoeleather I had to use up when bus fares ran out, but I was independent. I had already paid for it by being such a stay-at-home swot during school, and that had been pure pleasure to me anyway. Poor little rich boy, indeed.

We got out at Hamilton, the city's only migrant suburb.

'Thank Christ for wogs,' said Don, as we started up the main street towards Marco's.

'Amen!' I said, quite smartly for me. And I meant it.

Here Italians had congregated, brightening an otherwise dour and sooty town whose original convict stock had been diluted with the narrowest of suburban respectabilities.

I could pretend I was in another country as I walked past the gaudy blue and pink and yellow semis, with grape vines and figs and tomatoes flourishing in their front yards instead of buffalo grass around savagely spaded beds with borders of pansies or primulas guarding the pruned sticks of rose bushes.

Here you could buy dense crusty white bread that bore as little relationship to the squashy airfilled slices my family ate as the bitter Italian coffee did to the Bushell's Chicory Essence my mother offered to special visitors.

Here the men did not leer; they cooed. Small groups of them would mutter appreciatively as girls walked by. Sometimes they spoke directly, the soft foreign words and the suggestive invitations of their eyes never offending me. Then I would walk with a newfound swaying of hips and tingling of breasts, fantasising about what would happen if I had stopped, smiled, and said 'Si.'

I didn't as yet know, not exactly, what could happen, but I liked the general idea.

Today, because of my male escorts, the men were properly reticent. You had to look over your shoulder to catch their admiration, as I couldn't help doing, just the once. They made me feel like a desirable female, a woman; my student companions did not, except maybe Don. I sometimes caught him glowering intensely at me when he was very drunk, and had decided it was his way of leering, but he looked as if he might devour me if I gave any signals of encouragement. Rabbit scared, I didn't.

There were more restaurants in this suburb than in others, where the Chinese café or the RSL Club had to serve for the rare special occasions when the locals ate out. Here I liked to peek at the diners in the more expensive restaurants we passed and guess what they might be eating: Hungarian goulash, weiner schnitzel, steak Diane, saltimbocca, carpet-bag steak, lobster mornay? Not a $2 spaghetti special, for sure. But not fish and chips either.

On such a hot day many of the doors stood propped open, so I could see inside better than I usually could through the windows. Passing the Venezia, I could see right through to its vine-roofed courtyard. There, in the bright daylight beyond the dim room, as in a framed colour photo I saw Matt's mother, unmistakable in that hat, that dress, sitting so close you'd have to say 'entwined' with a tall, rather fierce-looking man, all wiry hair and beard.

Catching up to Don, I seized his arm. 'Is Matt's father home?' I whispered.

'Not that I heard, why?'

I told him to go back and sneak a look at the Venezia's courtyard, while I waited like an amateur spy, inspecting a shop window a few doors up. It was a pet shop. He returned with a quizzical grin on his face. 'You really are a babe in the woods, aren't you?'

'What d'you mean? Is that Matt's father or not?'

'No, it certainly isn't. That's her lover, you dope. Did you think she was all done up like that for bridge and sandwiches with the girls? Everyone knows about it except Matt's father. Been going on for a few years now. The lover's an architect, quite famous in his field. Apparently his wife knows, but doesn't care. You know, open marriage and all that.'

I felt sick. The backless dress, the black underwear... 'Does Matt know?'

'Oh yeah. He hates her for it. Don't know why. I reckon it just makes her more interesting. Wish my mother would do something as naughty as having an affair; might take the sour look off her face and stop her smoking herself to death. But who'd want her?'

He laughed. I couldn't. I just stared at the fat puppies in the window as they tumbled over each other. Shocked, I knew I'd never be game to admit what I was thinking to these would-be roués, but...

You'd feel different if it was your own mother. Affairs were all right in a book, or for women of the world, but surely that wasn't the sort of love you associate with your mother. And, knowing, how would you look your father in the eye?

'Can't buy me love, oh, o-h-h...'

THREADS OF A TAPESTRY

'VERONA' remained a grand mansion, its pointed towers still preening high above its leadlights and fretted balconies, but it had clearly seen better times than our 1960s. This impoverished aristocrat was showing its age — paintwork had begun to peel, downpipes to detach themselves, slates to slip and let in leaks.

Not that I imagined its current owners would be concerned about restoring it to past glory. For the board of directors of this institution it would be merely a suitably large building to house the successive batches of round-bellied girls and the charitably disapproving nuns who watched over them.

The very age of its gardens was enough to impress me as I sat there waiting in the dark green shadow of the ancient oaks that edged the brilliance of a sunlit lawn. A feeling of being privileged to do so was interwoven with one of gratitude for being there with my own tummy childishly flat. The directors no doubt saw the gardens as a buffer zone, hiding the inmates from the prying public... or the prying personal. Like me.

It had taken me months to find out where Helen's parents had sent her. They'd been afraid the no-good boyo who'd charmed her into this state in our first University year would also con me into telling where she was. As if I didn't hate him too!

Helen had barely been showing when I saw her last, yet here she was, emerging from the polished dimness of the entry hall and strolling towards me with the peculiar waddle of late pregnancy, one hand protecting the advance guard of her stomach.

We kissed awkwardly and sat back on my garden seat.

She looked well, a bit plumper in the face, but as confidently pretty as ever, instantly turning me into a toad, as ever. With the nonchalant gesture I knew so well, she tossed back her long hair, heavy swathes gleaming somewhere between silver and honey-blonde. For some obscure melodramatic reason I'd been afraid they might have made her cut it off: hygiene, retribution, martyrdom, St.Joan, the Scarlet Letter?

'It's OK here,' she said. 'They run a sort of laundry to pay for the place; we have to do a lot of ironing, but you can sit down for that when you're this far gone.' She chatted on about the other girls, the nuns, as if it was just a rather weird convent school, except you didn't have to wear a uniform and the nuns couldn't cane you, presumably because you were already being punished for your sins by this nine months of purgatory… and longer.

I wanted to ask about the pregnancy, the baby: could she feel it like they said? Was she scared? What was going to happen to the baby afterwards? But she kept up such a cool flow of anecdotes that I felt unable to change the tone back to our old intimacy.

We'd been best friends all through our convent school days and, with more difficulty, through that first traumatic year at university. Traumatic for me, anyway. For Helen it had been a coming-out of great success, with admiring suitors from all faculties.

Why she chose that slick little creep as The One confounded everybody. Half Italian, he was goodlooking, but too smooth, too ready with that flashy smile. Her mother was right: a conman. He was not what I'd call intelligent either. Not that I really had anything against metallurgists, but he was hardly on the level of that tall architecture student she'd been seeing, let alone the really distinguished-looking English Honours man.

He'd even talked her into letting him 'do it' in our shared bedsitter, which, although large, was still only one room. I'd heard him cajoling her when they returned late one night, assuring her that 'she' wouldn't hear a thing, she'd never know, she was asleep. Like hell! I'd forgiven her... but not him.

Beside me now Helen's light voice was still tripping on about trivialities. Then I spotted her mother's car coming up the gravel drive from the big gates. Damn! I'd never be able to ask anything in front of her mother. I blamed her for Helen's lack of communication with me since she'd left, and for this strange detachment now, but I felt sure we could have regained our old intimacy in time.

Fuelled perhaps by my resentment at being excluded, I burst through Helen's chatter as I watched her mother get out of the car. 'But what are you going to do with the baby?'

'Oh,' she said, her eyes on her mother's approaching figure too, 'that's all arranged. They've already got a nice couple to take it. I've signed all the papers; they say it's better if you don't see it...'

'Oh Helen!' I put my hand on her arm, tears of sympathy welling unbid.

She stood up, shedding my hand, as she called a musical hello to her mother.

I had always rather admired her mother's strength; a good Catholic mother to her six kids, a patient martyr to their surly but successful father. As I watched she and Helen embrace I realised that the similarity between the two of them was not just physical. I hurriedly wiped my eyes.

'Mum's come to take me out for a picnic,' she explained as she turned back to me.

'Of course you're welcome to join us,' added her mother, 'But I'm afraid I didn't expect you here; I thought you'd have written.'

Doubly shed.

Eight years later, impatiently pregnant with my first child, I was re-arranging, yet again, the impossibly tiny booties, when I suddenly remembered seventeen-year-old Helen, waiting to have her baby to give it away.

We hadn't stayed in touch; her mother would only say she was well when I rang, and somehow Helen was never there when I called. Acknowledging that I was discarded, I still sometimes wondered what she was doing and how she was coping with life. I had missed her.

Now my own heavy roundness weighed me down with understanding, and I crushed the softness of the booties to my face as I cried afresh for her.

Peter and Dianne, old Uni friends, came up from Canberra for a weekend of food and wine and social catching up. I cherished such times as relief from my domestic routine, a brief reconnection to the outside world.

One evening, my baby and toddler asleep, and we adults very relaxed in front of the fire with our after-dinner port, Peter asked if I ever heard from that good-looking blonde bird I used to get around with in first year.

'You mean Helen? No, not for years. Why?'

'Saw her at an Embassy do a few weeks ago. I didn't talk to her… thought I recognised her though. She's still a stunner. Journalist I know said she's apparently having it off with the Ugandan Ambassador: been a bit of a scandal about it because she teaches at the International School.'

'Half her luck', said Dianne. 'I've seen him: he's gorgeous!'

A few busy years later, our family flew to Canberra to spend a week with Peter and Dianne on their weekend bush block. Peter met us in his new Range Rover, which mightily impressed everyone. I drew the front seat.

We were to spend the first night in town, and as he negotiated the long loops of the Canberra road system, he mentioned that he'd run into Helen a few times lately. Seems she'd moved into an upmarket suburb near theirs, where they often did their shopping because the food range was so much better. He'd re-introduced himself outside the cheese shop.

'She has a son now, you know — James, nice looking boy about three, real coffee colour. She's had a rough time, though. They sent the father back home when the news got out...'

'The ambassador?' I asked.

Peter nodded, eyes on the roundabout ahead. 'She lost her job because of it too, but he seems to look after them pretty well. She's an amazing lady; always looking ahead.'

Something in his tone made me look at his face as he spoke: he'd fallen for her all right. So what's new? I thought, rather resentfully, recalling Helen's lifelong trail of lovesick suitors.

Keeping the baby, that's what! I was struck happy, seeing the loss eased, the bootie placed.

Yet I couldn't help wondering how far she was going to extend this life pattern of hers. Then, like a banner unfurling, I saw Helen's cool progress through life, taking and discarding handsome lovers of all creeds and colours for her tapestry, choosing only the best to father her growing brood.

And as if I was still thirteen, I sank again into lumpish mundanity, now labelled Married With Children, grey wool to her scarlet silk.

GROWN UP?

'I've looked at life from both sides now,
From win and lose and still somehow,
It's life's illusions I recall;
I really don't know life at all.'
Joni Mitchell, Both Sides Now, 1967 song

WHAT MORE can I say but 'Amen?' The years twenty to thirty, a mistaken marriage, and yet the miracle of motherhood, are still the part of life 'I really don't know...', and I have the most difficulty revisiting, but I'm working on it.

From thirty to fifty, the years of divorce and single parenthood, I find

I skid around the hard topics; the stories are far less based on autobiographical 'germs', and more light-hearted. There seems to have been more losing than winning, more stumbles, in this era for me.

My art can't imitate life unless I understand it. So you'll find a few fairly light-hearted 'illusions' in the following pages. I don't know why, but I didn't enter many of these stories in competitions. Perhaps I felt them to be too light?

I had thought that when I reached the official age for women to be eligible for the aged pension, the coming of wisdom would accompany it. In a way it did, but only because it coincided with the undertaking and completion of the head-spinning, heart- and gut-wrenching *Rich Land, Wasteland* book. I assume the getting of wisdom will be an ongoing process, and will hopefully deal retrospectively with the gaps in my understanding, so, just in case, I'd also better rack up a bit more experience of the life matters in question, like love.

Before it's too late.

STARMAN

WE ARE HERE to see stars. Even the thin moon is skulking along at tree level so as not to diminish the display. Here on this inland mountain, far from city lights, the more we look, the more we see. I can no longer tell if my eyes are seeing further into space or if the increasing myriads of twinkles are an illusion.

'Myriad'. Now that's a word I'm not often moved to use. It was a favourite when I was a wordstruck child, but only in the purple prose of my school compositions. This is one of those rare real-life times when the language of poets can be used without fear of soppiness. I mouth it softly, lovingly — 'myriad' — to the stardusted velvet above.

One of the group has proved to be an astronomy buff. A little man of wide vocabulary and quirky phrasing, he points upwards, and names — Latin and layman, myth and magic. He has so much knowledge, tossed to us so casually, that I am awed. I'd always meant to learn the night sky, but I have no aptitude for it. I still can't find the Southern Cross reliably; I don't understand how it came to be so iconic. The Saucepan is my only acquaintance.

Someone beats a real saucepan with a spoon, to tell us dinner is ready. We lower our eyes, and our minds. We are but hungry mortals all of a sudden. The campfire draws us back to earth, but the little man is the last to follow the scent of beef stew.

We line up with our tin dishes to receive a ladling of stew and a foil-wrapped potato, roasted in the ashes. I sit cross-legged on a blanket by the fire.

As I unwrap the foil, steam rises, and a smell of charcoal from the burnt skin. I slash the potato with my knife, and the hot mealy heart cries out for butter. But they haven't offered any, and I don't want to appear too cityfied by asking.

The stew is surprisingly good; the beef chunks tender, with whole small onions and squares of bacon in red wine and tomatoes. I smell garlic and rosemary. Bread rolls are being passed round to sop up the juices. Life can only be improved by a mug of red wine, which materialises as if by magic, nudging my left elbow.

It is held by the little starman. 'Thanks,' I mumble through a mouthful of potato, taking the tin mug. He sits down beside me. I feel honoured, chosen, although I assume it's the fire he's after, not me. Others find places on the rugs or sit on rocks.

We eat. I worry about what I can offer in conversation when we have finished. He is no doubt equally well-informed on lots of subjects. I only know about books. I'm not really an outdoors person, I don't know what made me book for this camping tour.

Well, yes I do. Desperation. A need to do something so different from the life I'd shared with Ben that I wouldn't be reminded of him. This is the first night — the stars have worked, until now. I put down my empty plate and risk a look at my dinner companion as I sip the very rough red from my mug. An odd little man. He has a largish head, floppy hair, and a rubbery face, which splits into a huge grin as he catches my eye.

He's not at all my type — not that I'm looking for anyone. Long and lean, that's what I like in a man. Like Ben — the shit!

Yet he reminds me of someone, though I can't think who. He wipes up the last of his meal with bread. Then he reaches for my plate and takes them both over to the wash-up table. He washes them, upturns them to dry, and rejoins me. I am impressed. Housework is not my strong suit, which I suppose I could begin to justify, but he did that so efficiently and simply that a fuss seems out of place. So I merely say 'Thanks' yet again as he sits down.

He raises his mug to clink on mine. 'Clunk', actually, tin on tin.

'Cheers. I'm Niall.'

'Kim. Niall's an unusual name. Where does it come from?'

'Well, my parents were into Celtic myths and legends. Niall means a champion. And don't laugh — they weren't to know I would refuse all my greens and grow up to be a midget!'

But I do laugh, I have to, the way he turned the joke on himself like that. No chip on his shoulder about size.

'So,' he continues, 'what about Kim? Kim as in Kipling?'

'Oh no, my parents didn't read books. It's after Kim Novak, a gorgeous blonde film star of the era. It's so dating! And they ought to have known that I'd have the same drab brown hair and freckles as the rest of the family!'

He has the broadest grin I've ever seen. Even by firelight, I can see he has nice teeth. I don't, so I'm always attracted to people who do.

'Hardly drab,' he says. 'But I don't suppose you've ever seen your own hair by starlight.'

Now I don't normally respond to flattery, but the sheer poetry of that image took my breath away. What a pity he's not long and lean, flashes my supposedly non-partner-seeking mind. Or was it my heart?

I take a large swig of red.

'So… how do you know so much about the stars?'

'Just interest. I like to find out all I can about things that interest me.'

Am I so desperate that I'm imagining innuendoes — intimations of interest in me — in everything he says? Though there is a chemistry building up here. You don't get this close to 40 without at least knowing how to tell that. Maybe camping trips are like ship cruises — temporary and unlikely romances blossom under the stars? It wouldn't hurt to have a fling…

But we're all sharing tents. No sex likely here. Unless you nick off into the bush. No thanks! Bull ants, spiders, scorpions or ticks to bite vulnerable body parts, let alone gravel rash and a bed of stony ground and sharp sticks.

Having sorted that out with myself, I get practical and ask him the question that I scoff at others for asking.

'So what do you do?'

'I'm a writer,' he replies.

I choke on my wine. I have always vowed never to get involved with a writer. They are so selfish, so observant, so prying, so thieving...

'And what do you do, Kim?'

'I'm a writer, too,' I admit.

He laughed, a rich warm sound, a big man's laugh.

The thing is, I always fall for men who don't fit my formula of what's good for me. So even if he's a writer, and short — well, he's smart, and funny, and he has good teeth and — he knows about the stars and... he likes me.

My tentmate appeared to remain asleep as I inched the zipper open, crawled in, inched it closed, crawled over the squeaky plastic floor to my nylon sleeping bag and rustled my way in before zipping that up. Why hasn't someone invented silent zips?

I tried to wriggle myself comfortable as quietly as I could, telling myself that the sleeping bag wasn't making me feel claustrophobic, even though it was. I distracted myself by imagining the starman, out there in his swag, lying on his back looking up at the stars. He'd brought his own gear. I envied him the solitude — and the stars. He'd turned out to be a technical writer, so that objection had been removed. We'd talked a little more before the tour guides decided it was time for campfire singing. One of them had a guitar. Now, not only do I have a nasal, always slightly-off-pitch voice, but I hate organised activities like that.

Remaining the reluctant child I'd been at every birthday party, I stood up and excused myself. By torchlight I found a comfy rock not too far uphill, but out of the firelight, and settled on it to wait out the singers. I wished I'd refilled my mug. It was a bit chilly too. And there were noises in the bush behind me.

Looking up at the majesty of the night sky, I thought of the starman, and suddenly recalled who he'd reminded me of. A musician I'd known long ago, short, comedian-faced, witty, knowledgeable — so like this man. Could they be related?

Up the slope came a torch beam, flickering like a firefly as its light swept from side to side. The torch only illuminated the boots and jean legs of the torch holder, but I guessed it was the starman. Then I giggled — 'the starman is carrying a torch for me!' And that wasn't all he was carrying; he had wine.

As we sat on my cold rock he pointed out more of the intricacies of the twinkling network overhead, until my head was reeling and my neck was aching.

'Stop!' I cried. 'Come back to earth.'

'That's what they all say, eventually,' he said.

Which seemed an odd response, but I wasn't up to critical analysis. Instead I asked him if he had any relations near Coonabarabran, as I'd met someone there who was very like him. He didn't answer straight away, and when he did, again it wasn't quite on the mark.

'There's a great observatory near there. Have you been? I go there now and then. Maybe it was me you saw.'

'No, I never went there, though I heard about it. And this guy — I didn't just see him, I met him, spent time with him, at a music festival. Of course it wasn't you — you'd have remembered me, wouldn't you?'

'Maybe, I don't know — did we sleep together?'

I nearly choked on my mouthful of wine. Then I twigged; he was being funny. I'm so bad at that kind of quick banter that I often don't get it when others do it. I tossed him a light laugh, hoping it sounded sardonic, sophisticated — cool.

Only I wasn't, what with the topic of sex brought into the open like that. Of its own accord, my body was prepping itself, doing those little ripples and throbs, imagining what it'd be like with him, even if my conscious mind was refusing to.

Starman

The group jollity in the camp had now died away into sporadic
'Goodnight' calls, like birds at twilight.

'Better turn in,' I said. ' 'Night'. And stumbled down the hill to chastity in the tent.

And to strange dreams.

About all those clever little rubberfaced men. Not dwarves, but a
separate, select race of men. Like the shape that suddenly jumps out at
you in a dot puzzle that you've been staring at forever, I could now see
them clearly in the midst of crowds, shining out at me wherever they
occurred — maybe one in every thousand people. But what were they
doing amongst us, what were they for? Why didn't anybody else know
about them?

I passed by in the amorphous way of dreams, instantaneous, improbable, turning up in exotic places where I'd never been before —
and catching the eye of what looked like the same little man. Hairstyle
or clothes different, but the face, the whimsical look in the eye, the lift
of the eyebrow, the suppressed grin — cut to a pattern.

Sometimes the little man beckoned, stopped me, spoke. Always a
clever first line, wry and intriguing. Each time that happened I fell for
the language, the intelligence in those eyes — and I went with him. I
knew our couplings were extraordinary, yet no physical details stayed
with me. They were like falling star flashes, special but ephemeral, the
shape lost.

But whether my body lay on desert sands or alpine meadows, reeling
slowly above me was always the vastness of indigo skies spangled with
stars.

I awoke to the banging of the breakfast pan. The tent was empty, the
sun already warming the nylon interior. I ached. The dream was fading
fast; the ache was not. I knew that feeling from a memory of other rare
times, of such long and vigorous and out-of-time lovemaking that it
was a different world to which I awoke and a different body in which
I dwelt.

Some dream!

I dressed, tidied my hair, crawled across the tent floor and unzipped my way out to the fierceness of reality and sunlight. I snuck off to take a pee — it stung — and then to wash my face, wanting a shower and knowing I'd not get one for two days.

Breakfast was baked beans on toast, and I was so hungry I had two servings, not even missing the cracked black pepper and finely chopped chives I would have had to add at home to make them acceptable. Several mugs of tea later, I was able to notice that I hadn't yet seen my starman, which was good, as that dream was lingering — and embarrassing.

I looked around for him again when we were ready to set off on the walk. No show. I asked around.

'Oh yeah, him. Nah, he packed up and took off early, said he'd just remembered something he had to do. Odd little bloke, eh?'

Ah well, probably would have come to nothing.

You'd better find yourself a bloke, I advised myself, if you're going to have wild wet dreams like that every time a fellow mentions sex. Or buy a vibrator. And then I thought — but hang on, I don't need any help if just dreaming about it can be so great.

Only it can't have been just dreaming.

Don't ask me how, but I'm pregnant. Two months gone, my doctor said yesterday. Ben and I broke up nearly four months ago.

The nuns always said that thinking impure thoughts was as bad as committing them — but as effective?

Maybe that's how they do it up there...

I think I'm carrying a little starman.

The Great Escape

SITTING on the verandah, her feet propped on the verandah railing, Christina had been lost in a reminiscent daze as she waited for Bernard to arrive. The higher far mountains were turning from purple to black as the last light left them. It was nearly dark; he should have been here by now. Perhaps he was lost. Hah! wishful thinking. Bernard had always been inconsiderate — but that was thirty years ago; she must stop confusing this middle-aged man with the young lover he'd once been.

They hadn't talked long on the phone; he'd been calling from Brisbane, where he'd run into Ros, a mutual friend with whom Christina had stayed in erratic touch. He'd wanted to call in and see 'dear Christina' on his way back to Sydney, but when she explained how far out of town she was, instead of backing off, as people often did, he'd invited himself for the night.

Did he even know she was on her own now? Hopefully Ros had explained all that; she herself wasn't up to a quick social summary of such upheavals in her life. Christina rolled a cigarette to calm nerves, pass time. She hated waiting. The cigarette felt satisfyingly neat and firm between her fingers.

Since Bernard's call, her student days had been much on her mind. Now she recalled her first attempts at smoking. She and her friend Helen had tried and tried, Kent after Kent, battling the instinctive nausea, persevering for the sake of the sophistication they so desired. Such insecure young girls, so eager to please, to fit in.

These days she insisted that she didn't care how she presented or what she said; people must take her as they found her — although she'd been forced to admit to a faint concern about maintaining such recently-won awareness when faced with Bernard as embodiment of her youth.

Ah, she could hear a car now, he must be at the top gate. She stubbed out her smoke and ducked inside for an involuntary quick look in the mirror, stab of brush on hair, dab of powder on nose. Funny how vanity, presumed dead, insists on resurrecting itself. I just hope he looks his age — or worse. Grabbing the torch, she slipped on her shoes and went to open the yard gate for him, reaching it just as his headlights rounded the last corner of the track.

Braced against the open gate as the lights bounced towards her, blinding her to disadvantage, she smiled into the glare. It was not until he drew up beside her that she could see the driver at all. In the reflected glow of the dashboard lights the grinning face looked rather fierce, almost gruesome, but it was unmistakably Bernard.

Waving him through, she shut the gate, hooked the electric fence on and walked to where he'd pulled up. Greetings were always difficult here, complicated by practical needs like electric fences and gates and turning around and where to park and torchlight. How much easier it would have been in the city, where she'd have simply answered the doorbell and there he would be, in full porchlight — 'Hi Bernard, how lovely to see you!' peck on cheek, quick light hug, disengage — 'Come on through.'

Here she never knew what to do first, and nor did her visitors. They were usually dazed from the long drive in, the anxiety of finding her place, and the incredulity of finally arriving at this tiny island of civilisation in the midst of seemingly never-ending mountain forests. By the time she reached Bernard he'd started to get out of his car, but she called out, 'Better move the car a bit further forward; it'll be covered in possum droppings otherwise!' Checked, he slid back in and moved it to where she directed with her torch.

He got out and unfolded his lanky form, opening his arms to her in the broad theatrical gesture she remembered well, 'Chris!'

'Bernard,' she responded, walking over to the car. With one stride he reached her and violently squashed her to his chest, awkwardly pinning her arms and causing her left hand, holding the torch, to bang hard against the side of the car.

'Ow!' She dropped the torch, which went out. 'Damn!'

He let her go. While feeling about on the ground for the torch, she attempted to greet him with asides in the near dark. 'Hi Bernard… no, don't move!… just hang on a minute… have a good trip? Oh hell, the globe must've blown!' She stood, holding the dead torch, and stretched out her free hand. 'Here, better give me your hand and I'll lead you down. It's a bit rough and there's still a few puddles. Anything you need out of the car?'

'Yeah, hang on, I'll switch on the interior light for a sec.' He did so and grabbed several paper bags and a backpack from the rear seat. She spied on his spotlit bent head as he was scrabbling about amongst the papers on the floor. At least he's gone grey. Still got plenty of hair, though.

He slammed the door shut, slung his bag from his shoulder and arranged his goodies precariously in one curved armful. He took her hand, squeezing it as he said, 'Lead on, Chrissie. God, it's so dark out here!'

'Chrissie'!? She only just managed to keep silent. How could he have forgotten how much she hated that babyish version of her name?

They proceeded carefully, taking small tentative steps, one behind the other, familiar blind leading strange blind, towards the warm glow of the house windows. Of all the arrivals, she thought, this is the worst. 'Mind the steps,' she cautioned. They stumbled along the verandah to the door into the big open room, lit in patches and pools by the high tiny twinkles of low voltage halogen globes.

'Just dump your stuff on the couch,' she gestured, putting the torch on the table. While he did so, she began to unscrew the torch to check the globe. He approached, baulked by this busy mechanical scene. 'God, Christina, can't that wait? Come here and let me say hello properly!'

'Only a loose connection,' she pronounced, screwing it back together. 'You'll thank me later when you want to take a leak outside; might save you stepping on a snake.' She offered her cheek for the looming kiss, but his mouth was clearly aiming elsewhere. Their noses bumped. It was a good excuse to withdraw. 'Um, how about a drink?' she asked, pushing back from his too-firm embrace.

Had he always been so overly demonstrative? She didn't think so. Maybe his wife's influence? Or perhaps he'd done some of those touchy/feely personal communication courses. Whatever the reason, she didn't like it much. Especially since she was stuck with him for the night. Watching him open the wine he'd brought, she suspected that this older Bernard was the sort of person she usually disliked. Too much flourish by half, even wielding a bottle opener.

'Cheers!' they clinked, and drank deeply, he from thirsty habit and she from nervous need. Better watch it, she thought, as she felt the blood rise to her cheeks, the last thing I want is to get drunk.

It was very good wine, rich and purple-tasting, a welcome reminder of what her usual cask tipple was meant to be emulating. She was about to say so when he leant forward earnestly and took her hand. 'So, how did you come to be holed up here all by yourself? Ros told me a bit about what happened, but how come you're still here? Don't you get lonely? Or are you just waiting for it to be sold? What sort of prices do they fetch round here anyway?'

She remembered that he had always talked in great rushes. Youthful enthusiasm then, now simply irritating, like a dentist drilling away at a tooth. What am I supposed to answer? Don't know, ditto, no, ditto, don't know? Or is it an inept cue to spill my guts and fall weeping into his arms?

Reclaiming her hand, she took another sip of wine. 'Look, Bernard,

I'd really rather not talk about all that; just believe me when I say that I like my own small world here and as far as I can envisage I'll be staying. But tell me what's been happening in your life. Did you end up marrying Marjorie?'

He burst out laughing. 'Good God, no!' and, thankfully, began a long and highly detailed description of his two marriages and divorces to women she'd never met, but who were apparently much more desirable than poor Marjorie, and presumably than herself. Could he have forgotten that they'd broken up because of his need, nay, his avowed destiny, to pursue his attraction to Marjorie? How heartbroken she'd been at the time; nineteen, and he, her first lover, after their two years that she'd assumed would stretch on forever, telling her how it was important to move on, follow the flights of the heart, experience life, not to get stuck in the rut of conventional relationships.

It sounded as if he'd followed his own advice. While he was complaining of the outrageously possessive demands of his last girlfriend, she began making up a platter of cheese and biscuits, her cherry tomatoes, home-pickled aubergine strips and fat black Kalamata olives. She put it on the table between them. 'Magnificent!' he carolled.

'No children?' she asked drily, thinking he was rather like a boastful and over-jolly ten-year old himself.

'No. Too busy, you know. Probably just as well, all things considered. I gather you do, though?'

She handed him a photo of her son and daughter and herself, taken at her daughter's wedding the previous year.

'I can't believe you have children this old! I must say your daughter looks every bit as dangerously interesting as her mother was at that age. Not that you still aren't!'

That odd look on his face — surely not a leer?

'You'd dumped me long before her age, Bernard. But tell me, how long have you been in Sydney? Are you at one of the Unis there?'

'Ah no, I moved across to the private sector years ago; PR, you know.

The money's good and I get lots of expenses; it was all getting a bit restrictive on the academic scene. I transferred up from Melbourne about ten years ago, to one of the big firms of solicitors. Got a lovely unit at Kirribilli — you must come and see it next time you're down.'

She made interested, noncommittal noises, covered by the banging of pots and pans and vigorous chopping of vegies as she started dinner. He poured more wine for them both, made a vague offer to help, was rejected as he'd no doubt expected, and began telling her of the great little restaurants he had 'discovered' in Europe. He professed shock that she had never travelled. 'But you were so good at languages, Chris. You must go, though, now that you're free.'

'Can't afford it,' she said, 'Anyway, I've lost the urge — and I'm not free; my daughter's about to have a baby. I want to be around for that, and then I won't want to miss out on its growing up. So I couldn't go for long and I don't want to go at all if it's got to be a whirlwind postcard tour.'

'But that's ridiculous! You mustn't let your children tie you down like that,' he began expostulating, but she interrupted.

'It's not ridiculous to me, and they're not doing it, Bernard, I am. I choose what's important to me nowadays.'

She scraped the vegies off the chopping board into the pan with a determined movement that was underlined by the sizzle as they hit the hot olive oil. Bernard poured himself another glass of wine. As she stirred the vegetables, beautiful garlicky olive oil aroma filling the room, she felt inordinately proud of sticking up for herself, although he seemed such a pompous ass that it was probably a waste to be honest with him. Still, it was good practice.

She added the cooked chick peas, a fresh bay leaf, a jarful of last year's tomatoes and a long splurt of her cask red wine, and put the lid on, moving it aside to simmer for a while. After checking the fire box, she sat down and took up her wine.

'Quite the little country woman, aren't we?' he laughed.

'I grew up with a fuel stove,' she said, thinking that the more he said the less she liked him.

'Oh yes, I'd forgotten. Are your parents still there on the farm? No? Ah, that mother of yours! God, she gave your father a hard time, didn't she?'

'I used to think so when I was young, but as I got older I understood her better, and what she'd had to put up with. Didn't you find that with your parents?'

Even as he answered she realised that he wouldn't have changed his opinions because, not having children himself, he had remained the child, as blinkered in his perceptions and demanding in his wants as ever. Not that having children made everyone grow up, but mostly it did. And taught you about love, she thought.

She looked at his flushed face, rather too fleshy now for such a thin frame, trying to place what else was wrong about it, because although he was so recognisable he was also so different. 'Your glasses!' she exclaimed. 'You don't wear glasses anymore?'

'Contact lenses,' he grinned. 'Glasses were all right for an academic, but they didn't impress the young business women much. Oh, a few lady journos thought I looked like a distinguished writer, but I need to work with them, so they're mostly off limits.'

Endless hunting — how wearying that must be. 'Ah well, at our age most people wear glasses. I do, for reading and working on the computer.'

'Ah, but you're only a kid,' he laughed, 'why, you're years younger than I am!'

'Bernard,' she said, with the ridiculous feeling that this was going to be a revelation, 'I'm 56, so you must be nearly 60.'

He just laughed again; clearly he wasn't ready for revelations yet. She went out onto the verandah to roll a smoke. He followed, talking about the rises or falls of once-mutual friends. Did he never shut up? She directed his attention to the blackness of the night sky, absolutely brimming with the glitter of tiny stars, surely quite different from what he could see in the city? 'Magnificent!' he agreed, and resumed his gossiping.

And so the night dragged on; through dinner (also 'magnificent'), another bottle of excellent red wine (she tasted, he drank), some expensive cheeses he'd brought, and fresh nashis and strawberries from the garden. She refused port and went ahead with the washing up, ignoring his insistence that it was bourgeois to do so, quite spoilt his evening to watch her. 'Well, it spoils my morning to wake up to a pile of dirty dishes,' she'd replied.

That done, she ignored the port bottle he was waving at her and insisted on showing him his room, where the lights were and where the torch was kept. She stoked the firebox, telling him it was fine if he wanted to sit up for a while, but that she was ready for bed. Like Pavlov's dog, he came in on cue.

'So'm I,' he slurred, stumbling round the table towards her.

She moved quickly away from the stove, worried he'd lurch onto it and burn himself.

'Bernard,' she said clearly, 'I suppose I should have told you sooner, but … I don't sleep with men any more.'

With pleasure she watched the struggle for understanding.

'You mean… you…you've given up sex?'

She shook her head, 'Oh no, I sleep with women, well, one at least. You'll probably meet her; she's due here early in the morning. So…,' she spread her hands and shrugged her shoulders, in a fair imitation of helplessness in the face of destiny, 'Goodnight Bernard.'

Through her door she could hear him mutter, 'Bloody Ros could have told me!'

When all was still and quiet she crept out and turned off the lights and banked down the fire.

Just after dawn she awoke to the sound of the reluctant turning over of his car engine. The coward!

She thought of getting up to warn him about the electric fence, but decided he'd probably rather not face her. It was only a short jolt anyway. She giggled heartlessly as she heard the expletive even above the engine. Got him!

As soon as she heard him roar off she got up to shut the gate, left open as she'd expected, and saw him rounding the top corner. The Great Escape!… and that goes for both of us.

Still, she thought, as she snuggled her cold feet back into bed, it would have been nice to be expecting someone.

Live at the Bellevue

THE ONCE FAMOUS Ballroom was almost deserted. Across the expanse of parquetry the laminex-topped tables shone bare, their metal chairs drawn up neatly around them. Only one table spoilt the symmetry.

A woman sat there, alone. Earlier, she had eaten in the dining room, where she had unfortunately chosen the lasagne. Her wiser fellow diners had mostly ordered roast lamb, although she'd heard one risk the fish.

Despite the food, she had enjoyed dining in the quaintly tatty surroundings; the chipped ornate plaster ceiling and dados, the fussy lace curtains at the French doors that led out to the cracked and empty pool, the huge stucco urns of dusty plastic flowers, the carved timber chairs upholstered in velvet whose fluff was now only evident where no bottom had ever sat.

She did not usually have wine, but the atmosphere here was so out of kilter with the motel dining rooms on her normal route that she felt inclined to be reckless. As she sipped, she speculated on the lives of the other diners, all couples. Married, or illicit? Happy, or habitually miserable? They appeared not to notice her scrutiny, but most people only ever gave her a first glance. A lone woman possessing neither youth nor glamour and of nondescript colour and shape held no interest.

It was midweek; she was the last to linger over her coffee, and there was still half the bottle left. The tired waitress suggested she might like to take it with her into the Ballroom, where 'live entertainment' was being offered tonight.

Walking down the strangely sloping hall, once the Grand Gallery, she felt uncharacteristically blasé about carrying a bottle like an old alkie. She went into the Ballroom. It was empty as yet. Choosing a corner table well back from the stage, she happily sank into the obscurity offered by the weak glow from the incongruous fifties wall lights, like orange ice blocks on sticks.

She concentrated on enjoying what remained of the past glory of the room — its vast gilded dome of a ceiling; the local scenes of sandstone gorges and ferny gullies romantically depicted in oils and set in massive gold frames against the panelling; the enormous red velvet curtains, faded folds, fringed feet, that hid the stage. Her imagination filled the Ballroom with the dress suits and silk dresses, perfume and laughter, of toffs up from Sydney for a weekend of mountain air, mineral baths and good times.

Her fancies were interrupted by a spotlight being turned on in a nearby corner of the room. It was too bright for her to see what was happening behind it, but there was a scraping and squawking, the tunings of a PA system.

Wondering when the rest of the audience might arrive, she was trying to read her watch when the light suddenly dimmed. She could now see the seated figure. A soft arpeggio of guitar chords was followed by a sweetly light male voice.

Startled by her unexpected proximity to the 'live entertainment', she considered moving further away, but feared to interrupt him. Wine-drowsed, she chose to believe that he was not aware of her presence, and relaxed to the voice and the music.

He sang love songs, ballads, old favourites; she sipped and floated along. No one else came in. It was as if he was just practising by himself, his eyes closed much of the time. She would have felt silly clapping in an empty room, and even worried a little that he might mind her being there, aware of an element of voyeurism in her solitary watching. He was by no means handsome, but her eyes were drawn to his lips caressing the words, his throat extended to the microphone, his fingers moving, blindly confident, on the guitar strings.

After a while he halted, put down his guitar, stood and stretched. He stepped out from the lighted corner, and she could no longer see his face. 'Would you like to hear anything special?' he asked.

She froze. Invisible, she could not believe he was addressing her. Then a tall silhouette and a faint scent of aftershave materialised at her table. He repeated the question.

'Oh, sorry,' she coughed awkwardly, 'uh, no, no, that was just fine. But please, play whatever you like!'

'Thanks. Um, may I sit down? Seems a bit silly to sit over there when there's only the two us here. Of course it's silly having me at all; they never advertise and there's hardly ever much of an audience, but the old place still tries to keep up appearances. They pay me to do this for three hours Mondays and Wednesday nights; Tuesdays and Thursdays they have bingo, Fridays and Saturdays they have a 50/50 dance band and Sundays they run movies.'

'You don't mind then, not having a proper audience?'

'Oh no, better one person really listening than a roomful of boozers who'd rather have a jukebox. Like you — really listening, I mean.'

'Yes,' she nodded. 'But I didn't think you saw me. I liked the feeling that you were playing for yourself. It sort of took the onus off me; you know, that awful self-consciousness of whether to clap or not? But, yes, I liked your music very much.'

He finished his drink. 'Well, I'd better sing some more for my supper. If you're sure you don't have any requests I'll indulge in a bit of a musical tour then, unless someone else shows up and objects.'

And he did — whimsical songs, sad songs, satirical songs, in a wide range of style and voice, pace and emotion. She was moved, saddened, stimulated and amused in turns. In his breaks he came and sat with her. They talked about the past heydays and present dog days of the old hotel, the mountains, his music. Many of the songs he had been singing were his own compositions, she learnt. She felt so at unaccustomed ease that she ordered another bottle of wine to share, having gathered that he was usually broke.

At eleven he finished his stint, put away the lights and microphone, clicked his guitar case shut and carried it over to her table.

'Well…' he began, his words colliding with her 'Would you like…?', as she indicated the half-full bottle.

They walked along the silent corridors of the long fibro tunnel of bedrooms that had been added in the last big boom of the fifties. It did not occur to her that they made an odd couple — the long thin man carrying a guitar case, the much shorter and wider woman carrying a bottle. It was years since she'd seen herself as part of any couple. He was he and she was she and they were merely continuing their conversation in the only place available at this hour.

Next morning she had a slight headache and a reluctance to get up, but she was due at ten at the next branch on her schedule. The shower was helpfully hot and she managed to dress and pack before a break-fast of tea and cold cardboard toast in the dining room, which looked merely tatty in the lace-filtered daylight.

Mist still shrouded the hotel and the windows were wet and blank with condensation. She walked past the Ballroom without a glance, not wishing to see it also reduced to dust by daylight.

She'd done nothing like this in the three years she'd been travelling round the branches to do the accounts. Neither the occasion nor the man had ever occurred. And wouldn't again, she thought; it was the wine, the music — and he was different.

Checking her room for left-behinds, she found a small blue comb in the bathroom; it had not been there yesterday. She smiled and popped it into her bag.

As she paid her bill at the desk, she noticed the board listing the week's entertainment. She had not asked his last name, nor he hers, not expecting to meet again, but she registered it now, gazing at the faded photograph smiling at her from the board. Robert Miller. She smiled back at him.

The young desk clerk, holding out her receipt, coughed impatiently. She was still smiling as she took it from him. Dotty old bird, he frowned, as he forced his mouth into a suitable response.

Four months later she altered her schedule to come that way again. When she checked in, she glanced at the entertainment board, but he was no longer featuring; the live entertainment had been replaced by a karaoke DJ.

The reluctant clerk had also been replaced, by a pretty girl, who explained that a lot of the construction workers from the resort project nearby were dropping in on week nights now and they liked their entertainment a bit more lively than old Robbo.

She sank down into one of the enormous armchairs and looked out across the valley to the far escarpment, glowing and golden in the late afternoon. Her intention had been to just be there while he sang, to see if he remembered her before she decided what to do next. Now she would have to make a deliberate move to contact him, if she really wanted to.

But he had been nice; she did not think he was accustomed to 'that sort of thing' either. Taking up a local phone book, she found two Millers with the initial 'R'. She copied the numbers down and went to the privacy of her room to make the call, or calls. But what could she say to find out which was the R she wanted?

The first number was engaged, but the second rang on for what seemed like a long time. As she was about to give up, a harrassed female voice said, 'Hello?' She panicked and hung up. She tried the other number again, vowing that if a woman answered this one she would drop the whole idea.

It was answered almost immediately, catching her unprepared, 'Um, I'm not sure if I have the right number, but I'm looking for the Robert who used to be the live entertainment up at the Bellevue?'

From the burst of laughter at the other end she knew it was him. She blundered on. 'Look, you probably don't remember me, but I met you when I stayed at the hotel a few months back.'

'Oh yes, my best audience for months! Of course I remember you, Helen, right?'

What relief, what instant infusion of courage! 'Yes. Look, there's something particular I wanted to see you about, and I wondered if we could meet for a coffee or something, just for half an hour, perhaps in the morning before I head on to Lithgow?'

'Sure. I have a student at ten, so can we make it early, say nine? How about the Primrose Café in the main street? That OK? Great; see you then. Bye!'

She put the phone down and flopped back on the bed. So far, so good.

That night she stuck to the roast and the orange juice and happily got into bed with her new book.

When the alarm went off next morning she was shocked out of a deep sleep. The book had proved hard to put down and she had read for too long. She skipped breakfast in the interests of a longer shower and more careful dressing, but by the time she found the café she felt flushed and nervous, a few minutes late when she had meant to be seated before he arrived.

Pushing open the glass doors, she peered about in the sudden contrasting dimness, hoping he had not beaten her there. But he had. A long figure was unfolding itself — like a waterbird out of its element, she thought — rising from a chair over by the window. She wended her way through the tables, his face becoming more familiar as she got closer. He too was frowning in the effort of recognition.

They smiled and mumbled greetings. He looks as awkward as I feel, she thought. I'll have to get this over quickly or I won't be able to do it at all.

'Will you have coffee? White?' He ordered, then sat back, looking at her, friendly, but quizzical too of course. His eyes smile, she realised.

'How have you been?' he asked. 'You look great; maybe a little fatter in the face since I saw you, but it suits you.'

She leapt desperately into the opening. 'I'm fatter everywhere; I'm pregnant.'

A small 'Oh', then silence.

Hands clasped tightly together on the table edge, she sat back and watched the fleeting emotions chase each other across his face. His eyes were downcast, but she had forgotten what he really looked like, and it seemed important now to memorise his features, to know them later, in the child to come. Like her in muted (or 'mousy' as her mother used to lament) colouring of hair and skin, she registered now that he had a perhaps overly long nose, but a good chin, and a beautifully shaped mouth; she was surprised she'd forgotten that mouth; any boy or girl would be happy to inherit it.

The coffee came. They sugared and stirred with desperate attention for as long as possible.

'Whew!' he whistled at last. 'I take it you're here because I'm the dad, right? Hell, that's pretty amazing news. I mean, that's a hard call for a loner like me…'

She interrupted him. 'Look, it's OK. I don't want you to marry me or anything; I just thought you might like to know, that you might like to stay in touch with… with whatever it is…'

The growing relief on his face burst into a big grin. 'Oh my God! This is amazing! It's just properly hit me: 'it'…'it'…a real live little person is going to happen here! I never thought I'd… but anyway, you bet I want to stay in touch with my kid. My dad lit out when I was four, you know.' He took a deep breath, held it, then let it out with a mighty sigh. 'But are you OK? How will you manage? I don't make much dough, you know, but I…'

Shaking her head, she smiled at his unfeigned delight and concern. 'No need. I'm going to work from home. I own my own place; it's one advantage of being an old maid accountant. I'm just glad you want to be involved at all. It will make a big difference to the baby.'

They sat grinning stupidly at each other at that so-evocative last word. Being more used to the idea, she broke the spell first. 'Sorry to hear you lost the job at the Bellevue. Do you play somewhere else now?'

'Nah, I've stopped bothering with that scene. I've got more guitar students, though, and I'm working flat out on a CD of my own songs to send out. Maybe some big star will want to record one of them and make my fortune. Hah! Jeez, they'd better hurry up, though; this kid thing changes everything. I mean, it's one hell of a long-term gig, isn't it? I'm going to get seriously ambitious now, might even apply for a proper job on the Council road gang!'

She laughed at his expression, then, seeing him check his watch, hurriedly passed him one of her cards. 'My home number's on the back. Do you want me to let you know when it's close?'

'Hey, we'll need to talk before that! I mean, there's all sorts of stuff to discuss, and my mum'll want to meet you. She'll think this is a weird way of getting a grandchild at last, but she's a good old stick; I reckon she'll cope.'

He heaved another great sigh, raising his eyebrows clownishly in the effort of adjusting to this extraordinary turn of events, and stood, muttering apologies about his student and fumbling for a more fitting conclusion to such a meeting. She extended her hand to him. He stooped to take it, then saw she was holding out a small blue comb. 'I think you left this behind,' she said.

Embarrassed, he took it and shoved it into his pocket.

'So, um, did you watch the karaoke at the Bellevue last night?' he asked, his thoughts trailing this more trivial memento back to the venue of their meeting.

Shaking her head, she smiled and stood too. 'No, no, I think I have all the live entertainment I'll be needing for quite some time now.'

Involuntarily, her hand rested lightly on the slight bulge of her besuited tummy. His eyes rested on it as well. He flashed her a crumpled smile, and blinking his suddenly glistening eyes, turned and loped out the door.

Hopeless, she thought as she paid the bill, but definitely nice. She truly didn't want a husband, she was too comfortable in her ways, but for an accidental dad, she couldn't have done better if she'd chosen him.

Or had she?

THE GARAGE

THE WEATHERBOARDS of the old garage were shedding their last faded blue flakes. 'Never got round to painting it,' he thought, stabbed straight after by 'Never will now!'

The shaky doors were propped open, as usual. He drove the Toyota into the darkness, habit blindly guiding its wheels along the oil-spattered strips of cement. The engine died with its familiar diesel screech and shudder.

Before he even had his door open he could hear the girls — 'Daddy! Daddy!' Swinging his long legs down to the ground, he scooped up the two excited children, all flying hair and legs. Their arms twined around his neck, their legs round his waist, as they kissed him, giggling into his beard.

He could smell their warm littlegirlness, the shampoo they always had to be coaxed into using, a slight sourness from Monnie's bib, and a whiff of Vegemite, still evident on the corners of Kate's mouth. Kissing them back, tickling them with his beard till they squealed, he hugged them tight so they couldn't see the damned tears that were coming again. He carried them into the yard like that, dancing about with them as he approached the back door.

'You're early,' came his wife's cool voice.

He stopped, a little dizzy from their whirling. Linda stood in the doorway, one hand shading her eyes from the morning sun. He put the girls down and unsteadily faced her. The same worn jeans on her long legs, an unfamiliar T-shirt hugging her skinny chest. He frowned at it, trying to decipher the writing that dashed across her boobs, still smaller than before Monnie's long breastfeeding. She folded her arms abruptly across the message.

'Uh, yeah,' he said, 'I thought I'd take them to the Reserve.'

'Fine. I'll just give them a wash and get their things.' She shooed the excited girls inside.

Standing awkwardly on the doorstep, he could see the clutter on the breakfast table in the sunroom. Was it really only a month ago that he had sat there, feeding Monnie in her high chair… ? Suddenly too weak to stand, his tall frame crumpled down on to the back step. Head against the architrave, he looked through the sunroom to the kitchen and the dim loungeroom beyond. Between the lounge chairs was the low coffee table he'd made when they were first married. It was still piled with Lin's books, but space enough had been found for a wine bottle, and two glasses. All empty.

The blood rushed to his head. He screwed his eyes shut and clutched his forehead. How had it all changed? They'd been such good mates all through teachers' college, the babies, doing up this house. There would never be any other woman for him… but she, she was… he pressed his head hard on to his bent knees to stop the thoughts, but they kept thrashing about in his mind while their barbed tails flailed his heart.

'I can't stand kissing you anymore,' she'd said. 'You've never even learnt how to kiss properly!' What she'd said that night was so different from his memory of the life they'd shared for ten years, he didn't know what to believe. Linda was usually right, though. But what had she ever seen in him if he was as hopeless as she said? 'I want a life!' she'd hissed, 'Not this boring rut you seem happy with!' Boring? Their girls, boring?

He'd been trying to get things straight in his head ever since he'd moved out…

After she had the kids, Lin had always been busy with her pottery and all. It hadn't seemed unfair that she was tired at night. In bed, when he'd lean closer to kiss her, he could only ever reach her cheek; she'd already be turning away. If he placed a hand on her hip, the tensing of her flesh was enough to convince him to go no further.

It was only sex, after all. They had much more in common than just the physical side of marriage; he'd have to be patient with her, try not to annoy her.

She said she needed some time on her own. A ceramic summer school, only a week, in the school holidays so he could mind the girls. 'Sure, love, sure,' he'd rushed to agree, putting his hand out to pat her arm, hoping for a smile. Wrong move; she'd frowned at his touch and clattered dishes in the sink, tossing at him over her shoulder, 'After all, they're your kids too!'

Indeed they were; he had a great week with the girls. And it was a relief not be worrying about upsetting Lin.

The day before she was due back, Dianne, one of her potting friends, phoned about picking up some special clay Linda had ordered for her. It seemed she hadn't wanted the whole lot and Linda was supposed to weigh it out for her. As Dianne needed it urgently, he told her to come round and they'd work it out.

Lin kept her clay stocks in the garage, so he took Dianne there first. 'Sorry it's such a mess. I've been working on the Toyota when the girls are in bed. We're going up to Linda's parents' farm next week and I don't want any problems with it. Um, your clay's probably over here.'

He slid the heavy, plastic wrapped blocks forward for her to read the labels. 'You weren't interested in the summer school?' he asked.

'Too specialised,' she said, 'and too expensive... and anyway, who'd mind my kids? We don't all have nice husbands like you, Dave!'

Too bloody nice, she thought. Linda needs a good shaking. Leaving him with the kids while she's off with Stewart, their pottery teacher. Everyone at evening class knew about the affair. Linda hadn't been able to resist telling her women friends how terrific it was, what a difference it made with an experienced lover, what a dud Dave was... and the poor bloke himself didn't have a clue what was going on!

Should she tell him now? But what if it fizzled out, as it probably would when Stewart's eye was caught by a new student? If Linda changed her mind about Dave when there was nothing better on offer, then telling him would have hurt him for no good reason.

The right clay found, sliced, weighed and wrapped, he offered her a coffee. They sat out in the garden, the kids happy with drinks and biscuits, playing ladies in the treehouse he'd built them. He was a good dad, she thought; she didn't know another so involved with his kids.

She tried drawing him out a bit, asking about the coming week's holiday. She hadn't realised Linda had grown up in the country; you'd never know with all the bohemian airs she put on. Yet these two had both grown up on cattle properties in northern NSW, and rabbit shooting with her father was to be Dave's main pastime this visit! Bye baby bunting…

Well, that was part of the problem, decided Dianne; Dave had stayed country, and Linda sure hadn't. It still wasn't right, treating him as worthless just because he wasn't exactly a he-man! Probably never had been, despite the shooting; everybody had a rifle in the country.

Not his fault Linda had now reached her sexually crazy time and he couldn't keep up. Blokes could sow their wild oats in their peak late teens but women hitting peak sexuality in their thirties were usually too late, already committed. Dianne had never understood why the timing was so mismatched.

Quiet blokes like Dave always lost out to the macho types who could smell a frustrated housewife a mile away. A woman like Linda wouldn't think twice about walking all over Dave's rights or feelings. She shouldn't be getting away with it. Forget about the sisterhood; what about common humanity and decency?

Dianne revved herself up to drop a hint that he ought to lay down a few laws to Linda and stand up for himself if he wanted to keep her. She put down her cup and turned to him. 'Dave', she began… but a shrill scream from the treehouse had him on his feet and running. Fearing fallen bodies and broken arms, she followed him. But, no, merely a sobbing Monnie who had seen a huge spider and daddy must dead it immediately.

Dianne left with her clay and her misgivings. Probably best to mind her own business, she had concluded. Dave wouldn't have believed her anyway. Only Linda could crush his faith in her, his hopes that the happy days would return.

Yet Linda's way of doing it had been so sudden and so heavy it had all but crushed him too. Everything had been going round and round in his head, cracked like a kaleidoscope. He'd not been able to sleep without pills; the pills left him unable to think when he awoke, and he could not prevent the sudden bouts of weeping, even at school. They had made him take compassionate leave. He hadn't told Lin.

As he heard the girls patter across the sunroom lino, he lifted his head. So heavy.

'Are you all right?' came Linda's impatient voice.

'Um, yeah, just a bit off.' He squinted up at her face, dashed the cursed wetness from his eyes. 'Look, can you take the girls up the street for a little while? Just give me half an hour.' He fished in his pocket. 'Buy them some treats, eh?'

Her instinct was to refuse, but he looked terrible, and she badly wanted the free time today. She sighed deeply and flounced off to get her shoes on. The confused girls nuzzled closer to their hunched-up Dad. Kate patted his shoulder, Monnie sat on his feet, chubby arms around his shins, and began to cry.

'Oh, for God's sake!' said their mother, 'Come on, it's only half an hour. We'll bring Daddy back an ice cream. That'll cheer him up,' she lied, ignoring his beseeching eyes and trembling lips.

When he heard their chatter fade, he got up and slowly walked to the garage.

Licking their ice creams, they turned into the driveway, Kate importantly holding her Dad's cone. Linda halted, frowning, as she noticed that the garage doors were closed. Something colder than ice cream clutched at her heart.

She dragged the girls next door. A hurried whispering had the three of them inside and her neighbour's husband rushing over to Linda's garage.

He put his ear to the door; no engine noise, no noise at all. Linda always got a bit carried away. A bloke like Dave wouldn't gas himself! He dragged the doors apart, peering into the dimness. Dave's Toyota was there all right. Maybe he was having a kip in it if he was feeling crook, but why close the doors after himself like that?

Feeling somehow sneaky, intrusive, he switched on the light. In between the fluorescent flickers he saw the driver's smashed side window. He took a few steps forward, the cold white light stabilised, and he stopped, seeing the blood.

'The wife and I just thought it was a car backfiring,' he told the police.

LEARNING FROM VON

V ON scanned the property as they drove through. It was hard country for fencing; away from the paddocks, where it wasn't rocky and steep, it was boggy, and in between it was overgrown with blackberries and thistles. Most of the holes would have to be dug by hand; no machine could go where goats or frogs or bush fencers like she and Chris could.

'We'll certainly earn our money on this one,' she said to Chris as the homestead gates came into view. He patted her thigh, warm and familiar in old jeans washed pale and soft like chamois, before reluctantly removing his hand to change down gears. Chris and Von were a close couple; they'd been a team, in marriage and in fencing jobs, for more than twenty years.

He nodded ruefully in agreement. 'I reckon you're right, love,' he said, and added with a grin, 'but it won't be the first time, eh?'

As Von hopped out to open the gates, Chris recalled what Bill had said when he'd contacted them about this job. Apparently the new owners had instructed Bill, as the kept-on manager, to have the boundaries fenced exactly on the survey lines. A city group, they knew nothing about the country, any country, let alone this sort. Nobody ever fenced the boundaries round here, just the usable flats and gentle slopes, but Bill said they just wouldn't listen. What they saw on the map was all they wanted to know about. If it belonged to them they wanted it properly possessed. 'Fence on the line, or your job'll be on it.' had been their last words on the subject to Bill.

The stationhands were only used to straightforward paddock fencing

— tractor, posthole digger and the like, so Bill had to call in a private contractor. Chris and Von had worked for him about ten years ago, out the back of Tamworth, real rough country too, so he knew they could handle the job.

He was in the homestead office, doing his hated paperwork, when he heard a vehicle pull up. Coming out on to the verandah, he immediately recognised the same beatup old Toyota truck, khaki canvas awning over the back, trailer behind loaded with gear.

But the couple themselves were not the same. Hard outdoor work takes it out of a man, let alone a woman. Chris was weathered like an ironbark post, but just as straight, probably in better shape than the stationhands, who all seemed to end up bent or broken from their run-ins with horses. Bill put Chris at about 50 or so, which would make Von in her mid-40s. He knew they had no kids, although of course he'd never asked about that.

Von had been quite a looker ten years ago, but no eyes for anyone but Chris, never any trouble with the other blokes on the job. Initially Bill had been taken aback at her being the other half of the 'team', but he'd soon realised that she was as hard a worker as any man. Von was a good sort in more ways than one.

As she stretched the kinks out after the trip, he noted she still had a fine figure. But up close, all the skin you could see — hands and forearms, face and shirtfront V — was ruined; rough, dark mottled reddish brown, the typical overcooked, damaged skin of country people from Celtic backgrounds. The wrong bloodlines for this country for sure. Chris was more fortunate; he had some German in him, and took the sun well, browning without freckles.

Von's auburn hair, with more than a few glints of grey through it now, was tied back in its usual thick plait. Bill had never forgotten seeing it out once, drying, after she'd washed it in the creek. It had been quite spectacular, all loose and fiery down her back and over her shoulders, and lively, like an electrified cape.

The trio had barely exchanged handshakes and reunion how-ya-goings when a battered Hilux pulled in behind them. A lanky young fellow emerged and came over to join them. 'Bill, this is Tommy, our offsider for the job. Tommy, Mr. Hodges, the head bloke here.'

Bill shook his hand. 'Pleased to meet you, Tommy, but call me Bill or you'll make me feel like the old codger I'll be soon enough. Say, I didn't know you'd become a threesome, Chris.'

'Ah well, truth is, Bill, I'm not getting any younger and I'm trying to be a bit smart about it, use my skills more and leave the brawn to young blokes like Tommy here. Yours'll be the first job we've done this way, but Von and me talked it over and this is how it'll be from now on, on big jobs like this anyway.'

Bill nodded. 'Sounds a good idea, so long as there's enough in it for you all. Tommy done a bit of fencing, has he?'

'Yeah, on his folks' place, way out west. Never been off the farm really, till his older brother went and got married. Apparently the new bride's the boss, so things aren't what they used to be at home, are they, mate? Anyway, he's out on his pat malone for the first time in his 28 years, and he's thrown his swag in with us for a season.'

'Good luck to you then, Tom,' grinned Bill, 'but mind these two don't lead you astray. They've been known to play a mean game of rummy; strip you of all your matches if you're not careful!'

Amidst the laughter Bill pointed out the old shearers' huts where they could camp. Hadn't been sheep here for years, all beef now, but the grey slab sheds on their massive ironbark stumps would last forever, and there was water in the tanks, a grove of shady peppercorn trees close by and a little creek just behind. Von sighed with relief. They'd be here about six weeks, so a good camp would be a bonus at the end of a rough day's work.

She headed for the creek to freshen up as soon as they'd unloaded and set up camp. While Tom collected a pile of firewood, Chris hung the Coolgardie safe from a pepper tree and filled its tray with water.

This old-fashioned 'fridge' drew a few jokes and comments these days, but it worked, and it didn't need any power to keep their meat and butter cool. So long as it did Von, it would do him. Like most bushies, they drank their tea black, as milk went off too quickly, but there was always a tube of condensed milk in the 'doings' box for visitors.

With the camp all in order for the cook, Chris took Tom up to the men's quarters to introduce themselves to the regular hands. After working the Valley and the Tablelands for nearly thirty years, Chris usually found he knew at least one bloke on a property this size.

It was dusk when they returned. Von had a fire going and a stew simmering in the cast iron camp oven. With this one pot, plus the billy and a griddle, she could cook just about anything. The boys had brought back half a dozen cold stubbies, a welcoming gift from Bill, but Von ordered them to the creek to wash first. No slacking about such things in her camp.

They didn't usually worry about alcohol during the working week, content to wait to go into town on Saturday nights with the rest of the workers, but seeing it was a gift, and their first night, they were happy to sit round the fire with their beers. Chris toasted the new team, coming up with 'The Fencing Freesome,' after Bill's earlier comment.

Von got quite giggly. Chris told her she sounded like a teenager. Tom thought she looked like one in the firelight. Von patted Chris' knee, 'Never mind, love, I'll be your old woman again tomorrow,' and grinned across at young Tom. It wasn't just the beer: she felt good about this job. With Tom's help it would go quicker and easier. Chris had been getting a bit of arthritis, and they'd been thinking they'd soon have to give up the roving life they loved, but hadn't come up with what to do instead. She sighed contentedly; the stew smelt good, the stars were out, and quiet Tom so far seemed to fit in fine.

One week and many ridges and gullies later, the weary trio still managed to scrub up and smarten up before squeezing into the Toyota for the rattling trip to the little town about 50 kilometres away. Saturday night was Saturday night and even the most tired hand got a spark out of the anticipation of it, especially given that Sunday thankfully remained Sunday, when no tool bigger than a toothbrush need be lifted. And Von liked to dress up now and then — don shoes daintier than her Blundstone boots, a skirt instead of jeans, a little lipstick and perfume — to keep her hand in, she said.

The pub was jumping, with a 50-50 band out the back in the beer garden, and whole families sitting out there for the only entertainment in town on a summer evening. Little kids held hands and jigged about on the edge of the cement 'dance floor,' ran in and out of the throng like rabbits, or sat under tables eating potato chips. Their parents drank beer or rum and coke and variously succumbed to the call of the beat and the more distant one of their youth.

Flopping back down into her chair after a particularly strenuous rock 'n' roll number, Von chaffed Tom for sitting there like a log when all those sweet young things were dying for a dance. He reckoned he couldn't dance, which she reckoned all blokes said, but it turned out that not only had he never been to a dance before, he had never actually tried to dance, not even in private. Von was horrified. Tiredness forgotten, she seized his hands and dragged him up despite his protests. Chris just laughed and went off to replenish the drinks.

Von edged him round the back of the crowd of dancers, where it was a little darker, and for three numbers she cajoled and bullied him into loosening up, listening to the music and moving with it. She was a good teacher; by the time she admitted she was exhausted, he admitted he was just starting to like it. Rejoining Chris and the beers, Von toasted Tommy Twinkletoes, which made him even pinker in the face.

The band took a break while everyone tucked into the sausage sizzle supper put on by the pub. One Saturday night's trade like this kept the publican and his family for a long slow country week. It was well worth the cost of a mountain of sausages, a tray or two of bread rolls and half a gallon of tomato sauce.

Sustained by the supper and more beer, when the music started up again for the last bracket, Von would not allow Tom to remain seated. She and Chris were getting up; so must he. In the habit of obeying Von by now, and also fairly well sustained, Tommy grinned sheepishly but didn't baulk too much when she pushed him in front of a tableful of wistful wallflowers.

He didn't even have to ask. At the sight of a lone male standing with obvious, if silent, intent in front of them, several girls rose at once. This frightened him so much he stuck out his hand to the smallest and therefore least threatening.

She seized it immediately and pulled him onto the floor, delightedly bopping about at the end of his arm like a gay little boat on its tether in a choppy sea. He smiled, she smiled. The music stopped, they clapped. There was barely time to yell their names at each other before the music resumed and they were off jigging around the floor again. 'Sandra,' her name was Sandra, he repeated to himself, afraid he might forget.

They danced the whole bracket nonstop. Thanks, Von, he thought, you were right; this is real easy once y'know how — and it's fun!

He was unprepared for the customary slow number at the end of the night, and tried to explain to Sandra that he couldn't do this sort of thing, but she wasn't taking excuses any more than Von did. His tiny partner clutched him to her and rocked him from side to side so that he got into the rhythm almost immediately. She was extraordinarily strong in the arms. If he could have seen her even smaller mother throwing a calf to the ground, he might have expected the muscles so far hidden under Sandra's youthful flesh.

Shuffling round the floor, half dazed like everyone else, Tom spotted Von and Chris locked close and swaying. Chris was kissing her neck. Tom looked down at Sandra, but she was too far away, it wouldn't work. He knew something was called for after the warm closeness they were sharing, so when the music stopped he quickly bent down and kissed her on the cheek, like he did his cousins or his mother, the only females he'd got that close to. No, never this close…

Sandra giggled; she thought it was cute, him being so shy. It made a nice change, as she would say to her girlfriend on the way home, from having to fight 'em off. 'See ya next Saturday?' she called as she ran off. He managed to nod. Did he have a date? The grin was still on his face as he climbed into the truck.

All three were charged up enough to make the dark miles fly on the drive back to camp, leaving scraps of song and clouds of dust floating behind them for the surprised groups of kangaroos.

The magpies in the peppercorn trees could rouse nobody early the next morning. As the sun climbed and the day heated up, the flies did a better job. By ten a recuperative billy was boiling, and bacon and eggs were on the fry. Sunday stretched gloriously, if a little shakily, ahead. Von suggested a picnic lunch at the swimming hole a few miles away, which the stationhands reckoned had to be seen to be believed.

It did. The river took a sharp bend there, forming a large pool, backed by a wall of rocks shaped like perfect hexagonal plugs, looking as if they'd been hammered end on into the cliff. Apart from the won-der of this cliff, the water was cool, and deep enough for a good swim, a rarity in the creeks round here; its banks were soft and grassy, the nearby willows shady. It was just what they needed, and half a dozen other vaguely wounded Saturdaynighters soon turned up to take the cure as well.

Chris couldn't see the point of getting out of the water in this heat, but Von said she'd had enough, she was wrinkling up like a prune. 'You go on then,' said Chris. 'This way I get to perv on you gadding about in your cossie.'

For his impudence he received a backwards splash from Von's quick foot as she climbed out. She bent for her towel. Chris and the other floating admirers whistled. Wrapping the towel as a sarong, she spun round, blushing, admonishing finger ready, but had to laugh instead of scold when they all submerged to escape.

She flicked back her long wet hair, gathered it together and squeezed most of the water out, then headed for the shade of the big willow. As she walked gingerly across the grass, eyes down on the lookout for bindi-eyes, an irrepressible smile twitched the corners of her lips. Amazing how much good a hearty wolf whistle did for a woman, especially at her age!

Tom was half dozing on the picnic rug. Von's foot poked him in the side.

'Shove over, Rip Van Winkle,' she said, 'I need to collapse.'

She stretched out beside him on her back, looking up through the long waving strands of willow, its million tiny bright green leaves translucent with sunshine.

'Hey, Twinkletoes,' she said, after a lazy while, 'You seeing little Sandra again next week?'

'Looks like it,' Tom murmured sleepily.

'Well, just watch it there, mate. Us private contractors can't afford to get a bad name in a district, you know. We don't want angry fathers complaining about us to the boss, now do we?'

Tom propped himself up on his elbow and squinted down at her. 'Hell, Von, I'm only going to see her at the dance!'

'Yeah, right. A quick whirl round the floor and a quickie out the back, eh? I know you cowboys!'

Tom was too appalled at the accusation to reply. After a minute's stewing, Von sat up and looked at him. He was so pale, she put her hand on his arm in concern. 'You all right, mate?'

He shook her off, obviously upset.

'What, Tom? What's the matter? You reckon you're the one bloke in a million with honest intentions, eh? Look, I'll tell you something not many know, apart from Chris. When I was sixteen, I was swept off my silly feet by a goodlooking cowboy, just passing through and out for a good time. 'Cept I thought I was in love. Anyway, my first time, and of course I got pregnant, didn't I!

'It was a small town; my parents sent me away to get rid of it. They got the best bloke they could afford, but he wasn't good enough. I didn't know till years later that he'd ruined my chances of having any kids.

'When I met Chris I realised what real love was; he'd never have put me at risk like that. Of course I told him about the abortion and all, but if I'd known then about not being able to have kids I could've at least given him the choice, to back out before he got too serious. We tried, hoped, for years...'

Von sighed, blinking away the tears that threatened. 'So you can see why I'm pretty heavily on the girl's side in these Saturday night flings.'

Tom was moved by her story to be equally honest. 'Ah hell, Von, I'm real sorry... about the kids... and the cowboy... that was rotten of him. But it's different with me. You don't understand. I wouldn't... I mean, I've never even kissed a girl on the mouth, let alone...'

Von was appalled; she and Chris had been enjoying sex for years by the time they were Tom's age! The poor bloke! All that wasted time. It wasn't right. She looked afresh at him. Nobody would call him hand-some, but he wasn't badlooking, and he was nice. A girl gave her love more because she liked the boy, or thought she was liked by him, than because of his looks. Poor bugger! Stuck out on the farm, she supposed, school of the air... no opportunity...

Tom lifted his head, embarrassed, but driven to complete his confession, explain his inadequacy. 'I don't really know how to go about that sort of thing with a girl. I'd be afraid to ruin it... you know. And I think I do like Sandra. At least I'd like to be game to kiss her without making a fool of myself. She'd expect a feller my age to have done it all! She'd laugh at me if I mucked up even a kiss. My first kiss... at 28! Hah!'

Von took his hand and held it between her own, patting it gently. 'Don't worry about it Tom, there's a first time for everything, for every-one. It'll come naturally at the time.'

Tom jumped up, pulling away from her, almost in tears. 'Yeah, that's easy for you to say, but you don't know that! You don't know what it's like for a bloke! I'm just a bloody freak!' He turned and strode off at a furious pace.

Chris reached the willow tree just as Tom roared away in the truck, leaving the dust cloud rolling slowly off to the side behind it, an incongruously calm final act for such a wild exit.

'What the bloody hell's going on?' he asked. Von still stood facing away from him. He put a hand on her bare shoulder, gave it the gentlest shake. 'Eh, Von?'

She turned to him with a sigh, frowning, close to tears.

'What's the little bugger done, Von?'

'Nothing, nothing; that's the trouble. Look, love, go and tee up a lift back to camp, will you, maybe for in an hour or so? You and me'd better take a walk; there's something I want to ask you… I think. Something pretty odd. And for once I will take no for an answer from you.'

Chris slipped his hand under the long red tresses, just beginning to crinkle as they dried. Her back was cool, still damp. Drawing her close, he kissed her and nuzzled her neck, whispering into that familiar sweet refuge, 'Love you, Von.'

'Me too, you big dill,' she smiled, kissing him back. 'Now get along.'

He did, wondering what the heck she was up to now. She remained full of surprises for him, but never a nasty one yet. He could always trust Von.

It was a subdued campfire dinner that night. Von did not have her mind on the cooking; the chops grilled dry, the potatoes charred too deeply in the coals, the tinned peas went mushy. If the diners noticed, none cared enough to comment.

Having washed up the dishes in the enamelled tin dish and stacked them on the slab table to dry, Chris tossed the water round the base of the bush lemon tree. 'Your turn tomorrow night, Tom. Reckon we're all still pretty wiped out from last night. I'm turning in. See you in the morning, mate.'

He kissed Von on the cheek, and ran his hand gently over her hair, ' 'Night, love,' before disappearing into the darkness beyond the firelight.

Tom poked the fire needlessly until he could voice the words he had prepared. 'Um, Von, look, I'm sorry for going crook at you and rushing off like that. I know you were only trying to help, motherly like. But you can quit worrying. I've been thinking about it all arvo; it's just too late for me. I'm not going to make a fool of myself. Who needs girls anyway?'

Coming over to sit next to him on the bench, Von put an arm round his shoulder and squeezed. 'You do, mate, you do.' She grabbed his hand and stood up, yanking him to stand too. 'Come on, let's take a walk along the creek. Forget the motherly bit, this is woman to man, all right?'

Next day dawned cloudy, and by the time they reached the fence line a light drizzle had begun. Chris suggested having their cuppa before the sticks all got too wet, and had the billy boiling in minutes with his special technique, which he called 'instant tea'. He would surround the billy on the ground with a crisscross mesh of the thinnest twigs, and gum leaves, making a circular wall right to the top, before lighting it. The heat generated was enormous, the boiling almost instantaneous. Von handed round the hefty breakfast sandwiches of cold roast lamb and choko pickles.

As they sipped the strong tea, eyes flicked and slid over the rims of the mugs, checking out the mood of the day. It was warm, friendly.

'Well,' observed Chris with obvious relief, 'we're a much happier little freesome today, aren't we?'

Through the munching, the agreement was as unanimous as the grins.

The day remained a Drizabone one, and by rights should have generated a fair bit of grumbling by the end of it, over such trifles as slipping on wet rocks when carrying a heavy roll of barbed wire, or a hat that persisted in directing its cold runoff down a neck. Yet it didn't seem to bother any of them beyond a joke or two about swimming two days running and the like. Back at camp, however, they eagerly accepted the offer of hot showers over at the men's quarters. Von went first while the blokes sipped the equally welcome offer of a tot of rum and ostensibly stood guard.

To cook dinner that night they set up the little two-burner gas camping stove in the woolshed, sitting round the harsh white light of the hissing portagas lamp instead of the campfire. 'Like being under a spotlight,' complained Von. A game of cards was suggested but nobody seemed keen. It would be an early one tonight.

'If this rain keeps up we'll be in here quite a bit. I might go up to the house and see if Bill can lend us some candles, eh?' said Chris.

'Lovely idea,' smiled Von. He smiled back, already reaching for his oilskin. 'Right, see you soon then.'

As the door shut behind him, the first awkward silence of the day descended. Tom was fiddling with a matchbox, turning it over and over between his thumbs and index fingers. Von began to drum her fingers loudly on the bench. He looked up in surprise. Having caught his attention, she stopped drumming. 'You better take up whittling or something or you'll drive us all nuts.'

Putting the box out of reach, he laughed with her. They smiled across the table. He stretched out his hand to touch her arm. 'Von…?'

Still smiling, she withdrew her arm and shook her head, but gently, swishing crackles of coppery light round her shoulders from her still-drying hair as she did so.

'No, Tom, that was a one-off favour … and I'm a one-man woman. You know what to do now, so go find a good girl of your own. Just be yourself; you'll be right. Remember, it's called 'making love' because that's what it's supposed to be all about. It's not a competition, or a test.

If you both feel loving, it'll be fine, no matter what actually happens. OK?'

He nodded. In the glare of the gaslight, he could clearly see the lines on her face and the ropey tendons of her neck, but not as clearly as he could see her kind blue eyes and her wide smile.

Von was looking down at her hands, now clasped tensely on the rough table. Please let him understand, she prayed silently, though to whom she could not have said. Aphrodite? Venus?

Tom stood up, stepped back from the glare, turned to go. Von stayed just as she was. She heard his boots on the boards, the squeak of the wooden door latch. A second's silence, then she heard him say, half-strangled with the awkward novelty of it, but loud and clear enough, 'Love you, Von!' before he shut the door behind him.

Von exhaled deeply; she had not even been aware of holding her breath.

It would be OK. And after next Saturday night, it would be even better.

The door opened, and out of the rain and the darkness came Chris, shedding dripping hat and coat as he called, 'Got the candles!'

'Great,' said Von.

Chris glanced anxiously at her as he set two candles in their own wax on the bench. 'Tom gone to bed, has he? Everything still all right there?'

Von nodded to both questions. She patted the bench beside her. He straddled it and threw his arms around her, pulling her close against him, rocking her a little. They were silent for a long time, watching the candle flames flicker in the draughts.

Peace.

Chris finally cleared his throat and spoke. 'I don't know what I did to deserve you, Von. I mean, I've never cared much about money, but I reckon the bible's got it right where it says a good woman's worth her weight in rubies, or something like that. So that makes me a millionaire; only,' he said, squeezing her even closer, 'I don't ever intend to cash in on this little investment!'

Von laughed. 'I think it actually says 'a virtuous woman'!'

'Same thing in my book,' said Chris. 'They don't come any better than you, Von. You 'n' me'll always be a great team; we set our own rules and we stick to 'em. Putting kindness and trust first would do many a po-faced pair a lot more good than their phoney virtues and their private cheating. I reckon you could teach 'em more about real love than they'd ever learn in church.'

Von turned in his arms to face him. She patted his bristly cheek. 'Thanks, Chris for... for everything...' A lump rose in her throat; must be the candlelight making her all sentimental. 'Now how about we blow these out and hit the sack?'

He kissed her before she could stand up and get efficient.

'With pleasure, boss.'

Days of Wine and Warrumbungles

THE FOUR of them had been confined to the hut for two days. Inside it was warm, dim and fuggy. Outside it was cold, white and finely wet; the world ended at the toe of an outstretched foot.

It was a very small tin hut, meant as emergency shelter for bushwalkers caught out on this high and precariously bony ridge. It was not intended for wining and dining, card playing and conversation, sleeping and sex for four.

The two bunks were narrow and served as benches as well as beds, ranged either side of the smallest potbelly stove ever made. On one side of the door stood a small table, and every inch of the dirt floor was taken up by the boxes of food and drink they'd lugged up the mountain from their car.

On the map the track to the hut had been an even line all the way from the valley. In reality it was easily driveable for a fair way, dangerously driveable for a short way, and then barely walkable. Only a mad driver like Dave could have forced the Beetle up that last steep pinch, the car careering and curvetting through the mud like a bee-stung puppy while the other three cheered from below.

Undaunted, they'd all agreed to simply make a few extra trips on foot. But the foot track proved so steep and shaley as to severely strain the calves and ankles when carrying nothing more than a pair of sunglasses, let alone groceries. They'd kept going on the oft-repeated assumption that they must be almost there, trudging the last stretch in silent weariness and increasing dismay, as the hut's size became evident.

'It's only a base; we'll be out walking all day.'

The return walk hadn't been any easier, as the effort of not slipping on the shale made it necessary to torture fresh muscles. By the time they reached the Beetle, they were cursing whoever it was did the shopping, packed the boxes, mentioned the damn Warrumbungles in the first place. Communing with nature was fine, but only with good food and wine at the end of it.

To make one extra trip do, they rationed clothes and books, slung water containers over their backs, sleeping bags off their shoulders, cameras round their necks, jackets round their waists, and heroically left the pillows, the cassette/radio, the scrabble set and the watermelon behind.

It had been almost dark by the time they regained the hut, muscles burning, arms stretched on personal racks. They'd all got very drunk and dined off their assorted deli dainties rather than face woodgathering and the stove. They'd rhapsodised about how the mountain air enhanced the flavours of the Kalamata olives, pickled aubergines, Pecorino, Leyden, pastrami, liverwurst, black bread, pano duro, peach leather and handmade chocolates, washed down by beer, a flagon of cheap but good claret, and, of course, port.

Next morning the first out the door was Dave, the most adventurous of the party, or at least the greatest Hemingway fan. He thought he'd been struck blind as the blanket of damp whiteness assailed him. His yells roused the others, all too stiff to move fast and too hungover to want to. 'It'll lift in a few hours... give us a chance to get organised... loosen up...find some wood... cook a decent breakfast...'

None were game to stray out of sight of the hut. Together, they collected wood close by; alone, they felt the need to constantly call out for reassurance of the existence of the invisible others. Clouds were supposed to be 'up there', but had descended with astonishingly tangible authority here where the elements merged, their hut balanced small and frail in between.

Once the potbelly had been fired up with considerable kero help, and the bacon and eggs were sizzling on top while toast was being expertly burnt by Dave at the open firebox below, they all felt more normal. By the time the coffee pot had done its Vesuvius act, they were being practical, considering pikelets or apple fritters for morning tea. They should enjoy the waiting, said philosophical James; clouds, by their very nature ephemeral, would not stay in one place long.

As they tidied up, there was a certain comfort in each scrunched up empty packet and stacked empty bottle; less to carry back. James' girlfriend, Carla, offered to make a minestrone for lunch; that would use up the tins of kidney beans and tomatoes and some of the vegetables and the rest of the pano duro. A few games of poker after the pikelets were eaten with the last of the peach leather took them happily through to midday.

The minestrone was such a success that they decided to have some of the good red wine with it. Afterwards, Marianne, Hem's most unadventurous and often fractious girlfriend, handed round Camembert and crackers and apples. James' addition of 'just a wee glass of Calvados' gave them the final push to an involuntary quartet of siestas.

They awoke around three to the now familiar silence, and busied themselves repacking the food boxes, planning dinner. As it would doubtless be fine tomorrow, they decided to splurge tonight and make a really rich stew, a sort of Boeuf Bourguignon with root vegies, some sprouts added at the end, and perhaps steamed ginger pudding and cream afterwards? The challenge of one-pot cooking was making them all rather proud of their resilience in the face of adversity.

The dinner took a long time to cook and to consume. Very hearty and flushed by the end of it, they planned a really long walk tomorrow to make up for it. Dave took out the map and plotted a climb up through the moss forests to the very top of the assumed nearby volcanic plug. It appeared that the track diverged to cross a huge scree shortly after passing the hut, where the National Parks Guide described it as dangerous to leave the track.

'Certainly no place to go blundering about in white blindness', admonished Dave.

'That's from snow, stupid', said the overly literal Marianne.

James poured soothing ports all round. Dave stepped outside before retiring, and returned to assure them he could sense a lifting in the atmosphere — he rather thought he was developing an affinity with this place, where heaven and earth meet, you know? feeling at one with the spirits? Marianne told him to shut up about spirits before he gave her the creeps, James accused him of having had too much of the spirits of the grape, and Carla said she wished the atmosphere in here would lift a bit and would whoever did that kindly go outside next time?

It did not seem possible, but the following morning was as absolutely still, wet and white as the one before. Nothing had changed out there. Inside, however, there was a new undercurrent of irritable disbelief. This was going too far; they only had two more days, surely they could expect some decent weather.

Besides, confident of a drier tomorrow, they'd not collected any wood, so they could not even make coffee. The blokes vented their frustration by splitting up sodden branches with the axe. The girls, deprived of this outlet by their partners' macho assumptions, collected twigs and thought of hot showers and cappuccino at their corner café.

It was beginning to feel like playing house in a vacuum; the edge was wearing off even the pleasures of eating. James suggested that, as nature had turned their expedition to her shrine into naught but a gourmet farce, they might as well enter into it with proper gusto. To get them more enthused than their overworked digestions were allow-ing, he opened the rum to spice up the morning coffee. Valiantly, they made a second pot and rallied to discuss how best to cook the chicken.

Aided by a few extra rum rations, Dave, a novice gourmet, suggested cutting it up and simmering it with whole potatoes and onions, a little brandy, and perhaps cream. The others said it was such a good idea he could do it; they were taking up the real challenge of concocting a terrine with the leftover cold meats.

Dave opened the Bourbon to foster inspiration. Culinary activity again filled the hours; potatoes were put on to boil for a salad, cucumbers sliced and salted for a sour cream and mint dressing, and eggs hardboiled to layer in the terrine, which, finally assembled to group satisfaction, was put under weights to set. James decided lunch was developing a Russian flavour, so he opened the vodka. It had not actually been on the shopping list, but he'd bought it on the theory that orange juice without it was bad for the digestion.

Dave's onions sent him weeping outside. Whilst there, with great relief he loudly expelled some of his increasingly uncomfortable accumulated gases. To his astonishment, he heard someone or something respond in kind. He whirled around but could see nothing in the few feet visible. He listened hard, but all he could hear was the soft dripping of the trees. Shivering, he ducked back into the hut and silently poured himself an extra large vodka.

Marianne slipped out soon after to 'make room for lunch', and was consequently in an awkward position when she too thought she heard her bodily functions paraphrased. Her upbringing forced her to attend to matters of cleanliness before survival, while her frantically swivelling eyes revealed nothing beyond the immediate trees. As she adjusted her undies, she suddenly heard footsteps rapping hard and fast close by, and stumbled to the hut, jeans at half-mast.

She lurched in the door, quite incoherent. The others sat her down, patting her shoulders and proffering brandy, till she managed to convey that 'something' was out there. Not wanting to say what noise she'd heard repeated, she just said she had heard 'it' running after her. James pointed to her trailing belt and suggested that it had probably been jangling on the stones. Carla agreed, but gave her another brandy for the shock. Dave said nothing.

To take the poor girl's mind off her fright, they decided to open the two bottles of excellent riesling intended to accompany the chicken. James offered to fetch them from outside where they'd been keeping cold. Despite his sanguine attitude, he could not help looking about rather carefully before venturing far from the door.

Assured, he first stepped behind a tree for some longdrawn and exquisite relief from the effects of their gourmet gorging. It was accompanied by an extraordinary amount of wind, which led him to recall the famous Le Petomane, and, thus occupied, he forgot to be nervous and was rather proud of his own final long, high-pitched note. He had begun walking back when he heard what sounded like a tremolo basso version of the same, twice.

His first thought was that one of his friends had snuck out after him. Annoyed, refusing to look around, he snatched up the wine and re-entered the hut. His friends were still all seated on the bunks, just as he'd left them.

He concentrated on opening the wine. Had it not been so still out there he could have said it was a branch rubbing on another; had he drunk more he could have said it was the DTs; given the circumstances, he decided it was a sort of echo, distorted by the higher mountain of rock that must be very near here. Certain pitches only, he mused, must draw responses; that would be why their voices had not called forth this volcanic echo. How very interesting! he marvelled, and proceeded to pour the wine.

It was a very good riesling and a superb lunch. They boiled the kettle and washed up in the tin dish, then settled into the warm nests of the bunks to sleep the afternoon and the lunch away. On awakening, Carla nipped outside for... well, to make room for dinner.

Dave made coffee and put the chicken on to simmer while Marianne dealt four hands of cards. The coffee boiled. She suggested James should go look for Carla. He replied that it was rude to disturb someone in the midst of their contemplations. She retorted that no one with any sense would be hanging about out there long enough to contemplate anything. He warned it was a well-known fact that a leisurely approach to bodily evacuations was the key to intestinal felicity. She threw the cards at him and told him to go stick his facts up his intestinal orifice.

He grabbed his coat and said that if she felt that strongly about it he'd go find her, but would not be responsible for any constipatory consequences. The tin mug hit the closed door. They heard him calling round the hut, then his voice grew fainter. Dave and Marianne looked at each other. Peeping out the door, Dave called to James not to go too far or he'd get lost. There was no answer, but out of the cottonwool wall in front of them came the muffled sound of heavy running over stone.

They quickly slammed and bolted the door: 'That's it, that's what I heard!' she hissed.

It was time for honesty. He ventured: 'You didn't hear anything else, did you? Um, sort of a farting sound perhaps? I rather fancied I did, but thought I was imagining it… you did?'

Heads cleared, hearts pounded: but what to do about it?

'I'm not going out there again!' she blurted, as if reading his thoughts.

'But they might be injured or something…'

'Yeah, and so might we be if we give it half a chance!'

'Oh, come on, we don't have man-cating animals in the Australian bush: no tigers, wolves…'

'Exactly! So if it's not an animal, what is it?'

He poured them both a vodka, adding orange juice with a vague idea of extra energy being required.

'I've been thinking about that,' he began, but she cut him short.

'Oh Christ, this is not the time for any of your ancient spirit bullshit! Or yetis or yowies or abominable bloody snowmen! I don't want to hear it! I don't want to think about it… I don't believe this is happening to me… it's like a bad late night movie! You brought me here: you make it go away!' she ended in a wail, and threw herself on the bunk, crying hysterically.

He patted her helplessly, then remembered her Valium, never far away, in her bag. He coaxed her to take some with the last of the vodka and orange, murmuring that it'd be all right, he'd keep watch; she should rest, they only had to get through the night; they'd leave in the morning.

When her sobs had subsided into indelicate snores, he covered her with the sleeping bag, stoked the fire and ate an enormous plateful of his chicken stew, washed down by the rest of the brandy. The chicken was terrific; what a pity the others weren't here to appreciate it. After a quick peek outside, through a safely thick blanket of insobriety, he allowed himself to consider just where they might be.

In the midst of some quite ingenious possibilities, he slipped sideways from his seat on the bunk and effortlessly blended his snores with hers. Soon after, the lamp spluttered and went out. Darkness covered them both and filled the little hut with an uneven glow from the cracks in the firebox.

Darkness was descending too on the VW down the mountain, as two figures staggered towards it; the one staggering because of a badly injured ankle, the other because of her weight leaning on him. They collapsed on its familiar bonnet and looked back up at the cloud that sat blankly unrelenting on the mountain above, ending only about 200 metres below the hut.

Fleeing blindly from the invisible pursuer, she had missed the path and fallen heavily down the uneven slope. There she'd huddled in pain and cold and terror, till James' voice, booming her name out of the whiteness on the track above, had ended the nightmare. In the urgency of getting her to a doctor, neither had thought of the two back in the hut — not their probable anxiety nor their possible danger. Now they did, James vowing to call the Ranger about the strange stalker as soon as he'd left her at the hospital.

Next morning, the sun was newly glittering on wet leaves as the last trails of mist floated round the hut and up the gullies in the wake of the rising cloud. The Ranger and the Sergeant approached softly, not wishing to alarm whomever… or whatever… they should find there. The Ranger had a stun gun ready for the worst animal eventuality; the Sergeant had his pistol ready should the animal be one of the human type.

The door was ajar, swinging slightly. They looked significantly at each other, frowned, raised eyebrows, nodded readiness, and advanced. As they came closer, they could see partway into the dim interior. On a bunk lay two inert bodies: asleep? unconscious? dead?

The Sergeant kicked open the door. A pair of yellow eyes flashed towards them in the gloom, and, before they could react, an explosion of long greasy hair and foul smells viciously knocked them both down and bolted over them out the door. Someone screamed.

As the commotion resurrected the bleary victims behind him, the Ranger struggled up onto his bruised elbow to catch a glimpse of an enormous old feral billygoat bounding across the scree, hooves rapping hard and furious on the rocks, a long black sock trailing from his hoary mouth, panic blurting loudly from his rear.

FOR THE LOVE OF FROGS

THE RAW orange scar of the new dam was offensively ugly. Wherever she stood, it leapt out from the subtle shades of the surrounding unskinned bush to catch in the corners of her eyes and accuse her of its injury. Scalped, disembowelled, the shape of the slope forever broken to make this awkwardly perched dish for catching raindrops.

'It's for bushfires,' he boasted to the local blokes. 'We'll be right now even if the pipes from the tanks up top get burnt.'

'It's for bushfires,' she apologised to those rare visitors with an eye for beauty marred and an idea of nature's rights over-ruled. More often she was apologising silently — to the land.

Only part of the scar would ever heal. The exposed bedrock clay was never meant to grow plants; it did not belong to the realm of air and sunlight. While the little dam filled quickly, above the waterline the eroding clay still glared at her. She planted waterlilies, but their beauty called attention to the unnatural setting instead of distracting from it.

'It needs some life,' she said.

'I could put yabbies in,' he offered, momentarily forgetting that she wouldn't let him eat them anyway. For peace, and from laziness, he ate her vegetarian food, but he was a carnivore at heart. When they went to town, he secretly indulged — a hasty meat pie, a sneaky steak sandwich, a charity sausage sandwich at Bunnings.

As he told his mates, she had some weird ideas, but he was on a good wicket here — and he'd always been a sucker for long legs like hers, especially in tight faded jeans, like now.

'Or I could get some tadpoles from the big dam?'

The big dam was a wide and gentle scoop in the land, its edges well-grassed. Deepened years ago from a natural depression, springfed, it had never seemed an interference, had never been ugly.

From its shallows they easily filled a large jar with tadpoles, bulging, brownish grey and semi-transparent. She carried them on their brief bumpy adventure as they saw the world through glass en route, tipped them carefully into their new home, then forgot them.

Until the first thundery summer, when it sounded as if the dam had been taken over by a flock of sheep. Demented sheep.

The big dam being out of sight and sound of the house, they'd never heard its frog chorus. This was it. She laughed incredulously when she identified them in the frog book — the tadpoles had been baby Bleating Tree Frogs.

Gradually she began to hear other frog voices taking bass and tenor roles amongst the sheep chorus. There seemed to be at least four types, she thought. How wonderful! 'Go, frogs!'

But the noise drove him crazy. He'd been in the habit of playing guitar on the verandah in the evenings. Now he complained that he could barely hear the notes over the din from the little dam.

'Play louder,' she suggested. 'Maybe they'll sing along.'

He did not construe this as a sympathetic response. How was his music to develop if:

— she didn't take it seriously, since she was being flippant, thus

— she was undermining his confidence, and

— he couldn't bloody well hear what he was playing!

She liked listening to his guitar-playing, but she loved hearing the frogs' song. It meant the little dam was alive. Throbbing, thrumming with life. It gave the dam a purpose that to her mind helped to make up for the damage done to the land.

This was a particularly electrical summer, with thunder growling across the hills and crashing low over the house, lightning bolts piercing the evening skies or flashing the darkness into fleeting light, and wild rains tattooing on the tin roof like hail or lashing sideways onto the verandah. The Bleating Tree Frogs were in frog heaven.

He gave up outdoor guitar.

Every night they ate dinner on the cool verandah to an accompaniment as insistent as the beating of jungle drums. One such evening he suddenly banged his fist on the table. 'Shut up!' he bellowed to the frogs; to her he exclaimed, 'Look, I can't stand this any longer; I'll have to drain that dam. It'll soon fill up again with all these storms.'

'But you can't. You'd never catch all the frogs. They'll die!'

He shook his head in disbelief at her dopiness. 'So? That's the whole f…..n' point! It's not as if they're in short supply.'

She stared at him. He wasn't joking. The frogs didn't count as living creatures to him; they were simply a nuisance to be rid of. Who was this… this… yobbo sitting there eating her spinach and ricotta lasagne?!

'No,' he said, putting the last forkful into his mouth. 'They have to go.'

Oh no, she wanted to say, you do. It was her place; she had every right to tell him to go — but could she manage on her own? She'd been so lonely after Mara left that she'd leapt into this relationship almost as soon as she was introduced to him.

It was nearly a year since Mara had run off with a Nigerian drummer she met at the markets. Faithless and fickle, yes, but she wouldn't have hurt a fly, let alone hundreds of frogs!

'No', she said, 'We are not draining the dam.'

He blinked. Where had this bossiness come from? He'd soon knock that on the head. 'Well', he said, 'I can't live with those bloody frogs. You'll have to choose between them and me!'

She thought of the harmless brown frogs bleating their little hearts out down there; she looked at him, redfaced and blustering, with mass murder on his mind.

Quickly, while she had the courage, she stood up and said, 'OK, then. You'd better leave. Tomorrow. And I mean it.'

On a drum roll of thunder, she whirled inside, her spirits lifting like a party balloon. Go girl!

The first drops of rain fell as the frogs belted out their approval. Yeah, I know, she silently agreed, I should have done that months ago!

SHELLGRIT

FROM the sea edge of her long rock platform, Rachel turned around to catch the sun's last brushes of old gold on the island's highest trees. This had been a low tide discovery, but that was hours ago; she ought to head back. Sunburnt and salt-encrusted, she tied her towel around her waist.

Searching the darkening cliffs for a landmark to memorise the position of her find, she squinted; there seemed to be something pale... pink?... moving steadily along the top. It looked frothy, insubstantial; then a section of the pink froth detached itself and began making a beckoning gesture.

Rachel snapped to the realisation of how far out she was, with the sea already over her ankles, small waves creaming around her rocks. She concentrated on making her way past the hidden rock pools, alert for their chains of yellow ochre pods.

The incoming tide had spread alarmingly far up the sand by the time she reached there. Scanning the cliff for her apparition, she could only see treetop silhouettes against a bruised sky. The track up was barely visible; on top, it was clearly marked with crushed white shells, luminous in the dusk. There was no sign of her would-be rescuer.

She jogged along the path as quickly as she dared, her sandshoes squelching and scrunching with each stepfall. Fruit bats squealed through the trees above; strange shapes loomed in the shadows. The track veered inland, down through the familiar glade of tall lemon-scented gums that told her the cabins were just over the hill. When the night hum of the generator reached her ears, for once she welcomed it.

As the path became the soft sand of the landward side of the island, she could see the lights of the house on the headland and the five cabins dotted through the trees on the edge of the lagoon. Their cabin's kerosene lamps were lit; Jo would have been back well before dusk from her fishing trip with some of their neighbours. Vegetarian Rachel didn't like watching anyone catch fish, so they had split up for the afternoon.

She hoped Jo had enjoyed herself, as she'd been expressing doubts about this island holiday — the cabins were tatty, fibro, 'jerrybuilt', as her father would say; 'quaint', protested Rachel, for whom the experience of being on a real island was enough. Her awareness had remained acute, of being on a solitary lump of land in the middle of the sea, of its sense of restriction and yet of perfect totality.

They'd been escaping the heat in the airconditioned Rockhampton Post Office, writing a few postcards and debating where to go next. Overhearing them, a middle aged, half-erased gentleman had introduced himself as 'Armstrong' in a voice that was either posh or English. He'd said the islands were far better than the coast here, mentioning a cancellation, a cabin now available on an island an hour's boat ride away; inexpensive, casual, unspoilt. The price being incredibly low, they'd agreed to a week there.

Escorting them to a small fibro house in one of the town's wide streets to buy their tickets, he tossed a few muttered words through the back screen door, beckoned them in, and disappeared.

The 'booking office' was the kitchen. At the table a big woman with starkly hennaed hair sat, overflowing her floral shift, painting her fingernails. She'd thrown them one sharp blue look, and turned half her attention to business, the other half remaining with the five blood-red nails.

She informed them that the boat, the *Shady Lady*, was leaving from Yeppoon in two hours and they should bring all their own food and drink. Rachel handed her the money. One-handed, she wrote out their receipt, and as she handed it to them, Rachel could smell her sweat and stale perfume.

They'd rushed off to buy provisions before driving across to the harbour. Waiting for the boat to appear, they agreed it was smart to be getting out to an island. Reef-protected, the shore here was unattractive, the water flat and lukewarm.

When the *Shady Lady* had nosed up to the jetty, they'd been surprised to see the faded gentleman at the helm. More surprisingly, they learnt that the taciturn giantess was his wife. The island and the boat were owned by them and his twin sister and her husband, who lived over there. The Armstrong children had apparently grown up on the island. Rachel was intrigued, wanting to know more of the story, but their skipper clearly intended to remain a closed book.

The island was casual, all right. Although she was late tonight, Rachel needed a shower to ease her sunburn. Under the single dim light of the 'amenities', she recalled their first tryout of the shower — roofless, with partial tin surrounds for partial modesty, rough cement slab underfoot. Jo's appalled reaction had not been soothed by the large green frogs which lurked there.

Rachel unhooked her top, breasts drooping coolly damp against the hot skin below; the gritty bikini bottom scraped her already tender thighs as she peeled it down. The bucket was already full of brackish water from the well, which always smelt vaguely of something dead. Lowering the canvas bag, she emptied the bucket into it, then hauled the bag back up and secured it. The water dripped lazily through the holes of the no-longer-adjustable rose, but it was refreshing. She left it dripping and the frogs croaking, wrapped her towel around herself and hurried up to the cabin.

'Hi, Jo!' she called.

Jo spun around. 'Oh, Rach, I was getting worried!'

'Yeah, sorry; got a bit worried myself. Stayed too long over the other side. Let's have a beer and I'll tell you about it; I'm parched.'

Pulling on briefs and an oversize T-shirt, she joined Jo out front. Beers in hand, they flopped into canvas chairs facing the water and the twinkling mainland.

'The ocean side is something else, Jo; you wouldn't see a single light from there. I found a great rock platform, really long and thin, and I saw the weirdest thing… only I still don't know what it was… but it waved me in off the rocks 'cause the tide was coming in.'

'What do you mean, 'thing'?'

'Well, I suppose it must have been a person, but it was a strange shape, or in a strange getup. The light was going, I couldn't see properly. Come for a walk with me tomorrow around sunset; we might see it again.'

'Oh Rachel, you and your imagination! Anyway, we're going on that boat trip to the far reef tomorrow, remember?'

'Ah… that's right. Well, maybe we'll be back in time. Anyway, here's to our third tropical day!'

'And night,' added Jo, stretching to clink her beer on Rachel's. The movement lifted one small breast clear of her sarong.

'I'll drink to that,' said Rachel.

Early next morning, they met the brother-in-law, Larry, when he came to fill the kero fridge and lamps. Burnt a dark reddish brown, glistening with sweat, he was clad only in faded navy shorts, above which loomed a massive beer belly and heavy boobs. Sharp light blue eyes gave him a predatory look. Incongruously, his wavy brown hair was oiled back like a matinée romeo's.

In no hurry to leave, lounging against their doorway, he began telling them how each year he 'made a packet' on a prawning boat up the Gulf.

'So who does your job here when you're prawning?' she asked. 'Your wife?'

'Her! Nah, the missus is too delicate to handle garbage 'n' stuff; bit of a' invalid … good for bloody nuthin'. Nah, Chuckie stops over 'ere during the season.'

'Chuckie?'

'Charles,' drawled Larry, 'Lord Muck, me brother-in-law.'

'Ah yes, your wife's family owned this island, I believe?' said Jo.

'Yeah. Useless lot they were. They done nuthin' with the place; said they liked it natural! There weren't no improvements at all, 'part from the house, till I came here in '58… after the oldies'd drowned in that storm.'

He slapped the door jamb. 'Yep, I built all these cabins meself. Dunno what that sappy pair would've done without me sister'n me.'

'Your sister?' echoed Rachel.

'Yeah, Beryl. Dincha meet her when youse paid?'

'Oh … yes, we did,' murmured Rachel, beginning to get a nasty taste in her mouth.

She got up to clear away the breakfast things; Larry took the hint. The girls moved to the back doorway to wave as he climbed into his old jeep.

'Oh my God! Look at his feet!' hissed Jo.

Rachel looked; they were no longer feet, they were broad thick pads of hard calloused dead flesh, greyish-white under the dirt, split with deep and wide ancient cracks all around.

'I feel sick,' she said.

'Ugh! Imagine being in bed with that!' shuddered Jo. 'He's enough to turn any girl lesbian,' she giggled.

But Rachel wasn't listening; she was throwing up in the sink.

She could not go on the boat trip, but insisted Jo went anyway.

'Sunstroke,' pronounced Jo.

'Suppose so,' said Rachel, feeling it more a blow to her heart than her head. The cabins were no longer quaint; they were excrescences.

'Larrybuilt', she thought sourly. How had the twins fallen into the clutches of this awful pair?

Too depressed to cope with her thoughts, she went back to bed. She slept until well after mid-day, waking hot and thirsty amidst damp and twisted sheets. Downing great draughts of water, she splashed more on her face, then wandered round to the southern point of the island in search of a cooling breeze.

She stretched out under a pandanus tree, soothed by the sea's constant rush on the smooth pebbles that floored this small cove. Her mind kept returning to the original Armstrong family of island dwellers, inventing histories for them... recluses, eccentrics, a skeleton in the Armstrong closet? Whatever, they must have had a private income.

This small island on the other side of the world was the perfect hideaway for a couple who needed no other company. They'd have had all they needed: books, music, painting, studying natural history, tropical sunsets, each other... and then the twins. What must it have been like for them, to grow up on an island?

It was difficult to imagine the reserved Charles even taking off his shoes; she could not see him as a boy running half-naked through the shallows. Would they have gone to boarding school? No, School of the Air, probably. But after that, what opportunities for romance? Hard to imagine kindred spirits in Yeppoon.

She could see the rhythm of their cultured island life simply continuing. Except they were no longer children. Rachel frowned; she'd read how close twins could be, and in this isolation extending that closeness must have been practically inevitable. Non-judgemental Rachel sighed with relief; so they may have been happy for a time. But why, oh why, these grotesque later pairings?

Perhaps they married for propriety's sake, or perhaps their parents, thinking them lonely — or knowing they weren't — had wanted to ensure they sought mainland mates. Rachel's fantasy followed the story — the will dictating that the twins must seek partners and marry within two years, as a condition of keeping this island they loved.

But Larry and Beryl?

Rachel could not match up the pairs. It could only have happened as a business arrangement. Neither of the couples appeared to have children, so perhaps the marriages were never consummated… but she baulked at the associated images.

Physical aspects aside, they could not have been so island-sheltered that they didn't realise how destructive it would be to live with some-one you despised, even with separate bedrooms. Rachel thought of her ill-matched parents, boasting now of their fifty years of marriage. No endurance marathon for her, she re-affirmed grimly.

Maybe the prawning season makes up for the rest of the year: Charles over here with Elizabeth, Larry on the loose up north and perhaps even Beryl finding the energy to paint more than her nails red in Rocky — but Rachel did not convince herself.

A dip might clear her head. She let herself drift gently over the slight swells, the rhythm as soothing as the rocking of a cradle. Reluctantly she turned over and began breaststroking back in, idly scanning the cliffs, lower on this side. It wasn't sunset yet; she'd have time to meet Jo at the jetty.

Then she saw it — coming round the bend from where the house must be; a white figure this time. Rachel hurried to shore. Grabbing her towel, she stumbled up the shingle. It was a person, Rachel was sure now, but of what sort she could not make out. But she would; she must catch up. Clawing her way over rocks and tussocks, she climbed to the clifftop, thankful she'd kept her sandshoes on. She reached the glitter of the headland path, head throbbing, legs shaky.

The path ahead was empty. She began to run, but underestimated her weakness, and fell, savagely grazing her knees on the sharp shellgrit. Hobbling to sit on a fallen paperbark trunk, she snuffled back tears of frustration and pain. She allowed herself a half-bitten howl of exasper-ation, eyes tightly closed as if to will it all unhappened.

A slight crunch of shellgrit and a whiff of lavender quickly opened them to a white handkerchief, lace-edged, being dangled in front of her nose by a white-gloved hand.

'Allow me,' said a voice, as thin and English as the finest china tea cup. Rachel's blurry eyes flicked from the hand up a long white sleeve to a high neckline; a sagging and crepey face, heavily and palely powdered, somehow unutterably sad despite the eyes being hidden behind dark sunglasses; pale, almost white hair, stiffly curled, the whole shaded by a large befrilled white parasol, its carved cane handle held tightly in the other glove.

'Thank you,' managed Rachel as she took the handkerchief. The vision nodded slightly and glided on, a hazy white shape on the white path, long skirts ballooning behind it in the breeze.

She tried to tell Jo about it in between gasps as she bathed her poor knees, self-inflicting the necessary agony of teasing out shellgrit fragments. 'It wasn't really an old-fashioned dress, just long. But white gloves!?'

Were it not for the handkerchief soaking in a bowl, Jo would have suggested sunstruck hallucination, an extension of Rachel's imagination. As she hung the thin fabric up to dry, she noted the embroidered initials in one corner: E.A.

'Do you think your ghost could be Mr. A's sister? Larry's wife?'

'Oh no!' cried Rachel, wincing. 'She couldn't possibly be...' but she knew there could be no other explanation on this small island.

As if on cue, they heard Larry's jeep pull up outside.

He appeared in the doorway with a bottle of Dettol. 'Heard one a yers had a bit uv a spill. The missus thought ya might need some a this.'

Taking it, Jo asked him to thank his wife. 'Does she go for a walk every evening? Rach thought she'd seen her up there before.'

'Yeah, well, she can't take any sunlight, see, bein' one a them whiteys ...and a bloody nuisance that is up 'ere, I tell ya!... so she always goes then to get outta the house, get a bitta exercise.'

'Well, tell her we'll return her handkerchief when it's dry: so E.A. stands for…?'

'Ah, that'd be an old one. Elizabeth Armstrong, see? I call 'er Lizzie meself, but 'er family useta go the whole hog. Chuckie still does.'

That night, Rachel drank a great deal of rum for the pain. She awoke in a sweat from a nightmare, where a strange caged white creature, like an albino lemur, its huge sad eyes fixed on hers in mute appeal, paced around and around the inside of its cage, its long tail dragging behind it, while outside, hairy apes slavered and grunted and rattled the bars.

Stumbling to the sink for water, she saw the handkerchief pegged beside the teatowel. Her hand seized it just as Jo called, 'Rach, what are you doing? I'll get you some water; come and lie back down, you idiot!'

'I think we should get you to a doctor, Rach. You must have quite an infection; you're very hot. Larry says we can go back on the mail boat today, OK?'

Rachel nodded, too remote in her fever to argue. It was not until Jo woke her up later that she realised that everything was packed.

'But aren't we coming back? We've still a few days to go…'

'What's the point? You won't be doing anything with those knees; you can hardly stand up! Now come on, Rach, here's the jeep to give us a lift to the jetty.'

'But…' demurred Rachel weakly; there was a bigger 'but', only she couldn't think what it was.

When she glimpsed Charles Armstrong at the wheel of the *Shady Lady* as it passed the mail boat, she remembered briefly. Her hand went to her pocket, scrunching the thin handkerchief. Elizabeth… I'll write… I'll help… somehow…

But, safely back in her southern city, her knees healed, the vividness of her sympathy dimmed, the tropical drama diminished — she didn't get around to it.

Yet she kept the handkerchief, ever intending to. Every so often her eye would come upon it, neatly folded at the back of a drawer, waiting in mute reproach.

Then, through the safety of the solid world that her always practical partners created for her, suddenly there would burst forth the swish of sea on pebbles, the salty circling of unanswered questions… and the gritty guilt of the unanswered appeal.

Oh Rachel, you and your imagination…

GROWING OLD

*'Growing old is like being increasingly penalised
for a crime you haven't committed.'*
Anthony Powell, *Temporary Kings*, 1973

THE DIFFERENT ways and ages at which people become 'old' has always amazed me. And I'm not talking about wrinkles. Some have been stolid senior citizens in training since they were 20; others are still sparkling sprites in their 80s. Some bemoan 'the young of today' and laud the good old days, while others are interested in any new idea, using the context of their years to better examine its worth.

It seems to me that the key difference is that the latter types are keen to live life, up to the very minute they die, while the former spend half their lives winding down; if they aren't actually dying, they aren't really living either. They're merely marking time.

Once upon a lifetime ago I wrote for a retirement village newsletter, and I was struck by the motto, 'Old age is the only guaranteed inheritance'. Like when kids first walk or talk, they'll get there some time. So what's the big deal about how young or old people look at what age? We all end up as just a jangle of bones inside a wrinkly bag of skin. Guaranteed — if we last that long.

But the way we reach the far end of life is a dreadful design, if it is one at all. Few get to go quickly and peacefully in their sleep, as all wish. Many spend years trapped in humiliatingly helpless bodies, or lose their anchors of self, adrift in lost minds and memories. The ones who keep their physical and mental health are the rare ones on whom we all remark — 'Wow! 95 and still sharp as a tack!'

Now, having astonishingly managed to keep stumbling on for almost three-quarters of a century on this earth, while I can point to my concession card — and to the crepey drapery of my neck, a swan analogy turned turkey — as evidence of my right to be accepted as a senior citizen, I'm not sure when I'll be ready to accept being classed as an old lady. I'm just me, still on that journey called life.

GREY MATTERS

S HE HAD almost missed the train. It is already nosing out of Central towards Melbourne as she lurches through the glass doors into the carriage and confronts the narrow aisle. Flustered, she re-aligns herself and her assorted baggage to fit.

Shoulderslung bags bumping each successive seat, her right hand holds her suitcase out in front, bruising her leading shin at each shuffle forward, while her left arm is bent awkwardly behind her back, her wrist at snapping point as the heavy briefcase insistently swings from its short handle.

With a rabbity facial twitch and a vigorous nod she manages, hands-free, to shake her sunglasses down her nose far enough to peer over at the seat numbers as she inches past. Her aisle seat is at the far end of the carriage. Reaching it, she sees that a man reading *The Age* already occupies the window seat.

She begins the lengthy process of disencumberment and disposal.

Briefcase and laptop carrybag stowed in the rack up top; too-heavy-to-lift suitcase shuffled back out to the baggage shelves at the end of the corridor; shoulder bag tucked under seat; briefcase retrieved from rack for forgotten manuscript; briefcase lifted back up to rack; workbook, pencil, pen and rubber, squeezed, with reading glasses, into seat pocket in front; coat removed and squashed beneath her as she finally sits.

She breathes out heavily, glancing at her neighbour for sympathy. Grey hair, blackrimmed glasses, craggy face, about her age, not bad looking, probably tall.

'Bit cramped, isn't it?' she ventures.

'Mmm,' he says, eyebrows raised as he gives a nod of agreement before returning to his *Age*. Rather pointedly, she thinks.

Having released the small table from its clip on the seatback in front of her and arranged her working materials on it, she realises with annoyance that she is far too hot. Even at her slinkiest there is no room for a manoeuvre like cardigan removal without putting his eye out with her elbow.

Embarrassed at so much dithering, but dreading hot flushes more, she retraces the last two stages so she can stand out in the aisle and take off her long black cardigan. She stuffs it beside the armrest. It is too much, it should go on the rack above, but she fears her short jumper might ride up and expose unattractive bits. Flabby bits. As if he'd notice.

She sits back down and unlatches the table again. Stay calm, she tells herself, breathe slowly or you'll get palpitations — 'Be still, my pounding heart' — and it's not from the nearness of you, she telepaths across the invisible wall beside her. But a faint scent of aftershave insists on floating back to question that. Not the spicy flea powder type, associated for her with leering, joke-telling sales reps, but the cologne sort she's always liked. Cool scent on warm skin — the memories set up an almost forgotten rolling tingle somewhere deep beneath her winter woollies.

It's been a few years since she travelled on her own. Then it was the men who used to try and strike up an acquaintance with her, and she who had to cool them off politely so she could read in peace.

He shakes his paper flat. A distinctly irritable sound. Stupid bugger, trying to read a paper that size in this confined space.

Tickets are collected. She starts scanning the manuscript she is to illustrate, taking in nothing at all.

Half an hour passes in this self-conscious separateness of strangers sitting too close together. By then the words of the manuscript are beginning to filter through and images to present themselves as possibilities. She turns back to the beginning with enthusiasm.

The conductor passes down the aisle, repeating as he goes, 'They've put an extra carriage on. Plenty of spare seats there if anyone wants a seat to themselves.'

She does; her neighbour obviously does too. She begins gathering up her things. 'Think I'll take advantage of that offer.'

He nods, feigning nothing.

Could it just be that she's stopped colouring her hair? Her face isn't very wrinkled; does grey hair really put you so out of the running? Maybe she should resume dyeing it. It had begun turning grey at thirty, after the insanity of her marriage breakup, and only at fifty had she decided to reveal whatever her true colour might have become, not wanting to be thought ungracefully attached to youth. She hadn't meant to sever femininity along with it.

She makes two trips for the transfer. 'Have a good journey,' he says as she collects the last of her belongings, polite enough now he is almost rid of her.

Only about half a dozen passengers have moved to the next carriage. All men except herself, and all younger than she, they have congregated loosely towards the front, closest to the adjacent buffet car.

Tossing smiles to each other, comrades in intrepid relocation, they sprawl across the double seats, no longer needing to sit rigidly upright for fear of touching a neighbour. They give exaggerated sighs of relief, begin to trade stories, turn seats around to face each other, make groups. They do not toss smiles back to her — female, old — doubly alien.

At Goulburn a flamboyantly beautiful girl of about nineteen enters the carriage. Seeing the male enclave further along, she halts and chooses the seat across the aisle from the sole female. Who now remembers her own mother telling her 'Make sure you sit near someone safe, like an old lady'. She also remembers when anybody over thirty was old.

The girl takes off her woollen coat, of a shade between shallow sea and spring sky. She flashes a friendly grin at the older woman as she sits down. She bends to undo her shoes, and as she does so, her tinted auburn hair escapes from its loose knot. Waistlength, it glimmers sideways and sweeps the floor beside her showgirl shoes — cherry red patent leather, anklestraps, and high, high heels. She wears navy socks under them; the watcher marvels at the self-confidence such a combination indicates.

Her clothes are eyecatching, carefully orchestrated: cyclamen pink corduroy flares; a tight navy sweater edged with cherry wool embroidery, deep V-neck, sleeves extended to loose points at the wrists, mediaeval style; a long cyclamen chiffon scarf encircles her throat once and floats from her neck in cheerful counterpoint.

Turning her coat inside out, she folds it into a pillow and immediately curls up on the seat like a child. She sleeps. The reds and golds of her hair glow against the pale blue of the coat's satin lining.

The watcher remembers colour. When her hair had still flared darkly round her shoulders like the banner of her Scots inheritance, she'd favoured clear reds and yellows borrowed from flowers to match her summer tan, and the richest ruby and emerald that fabric could mimic to warm her hidden winter body. Were she a young girl in this era of fancy dress anywhere and anytime, she'd live in velvet and silk. She sighs. Long spilt milk, as her mother would say. She wears black or grey these days; kinder to the ageing skin, so they say.

The girl's feet are now exposed to the aisle; there is a hole in one of her socks that touches the watcher's maternal heart. Where sweater and corduroys part company, a crescent of downy skin and an inch of childish undies, white sprigged with blue, touch more than the hearts of men.

The males pass on their way to and from the Men's in the next carriage. Everyone passes on their way to and from the buffet car. The girl and her colours draw all eyes. The younger men give low growls of appreciation, their eyes widen, their lips twitch; the older men, even the very old men, are more restrained, but cannot hide the yearning on their faces. Dazzled, none register the drab shape opposite.

Who cannot help but be voyeur as she studies the sleeper's face — clear cheekbones, strong dark eyebrows, eyelashes so thick and lavishly curling as to be suspect. She does a sketch in her workbook: curve of hips, rippling fall of hair, shoulder hunched against cheek, like a sleeping bird's wing.

A second girl, tall, fair, scrubbed and shining, gets on in Albury and sits in front of the grey watcher, another good girl heeding her mother's advice. Her faded jeans and plain blue sweater outline an exceedingly shapely figure. She dumps her enormous backpack onto the seat.

This girl's hair is thick and straight, silvered sunshine, pulled back into a low ponytail; her forehead domes as high and smooth as a Flemish madonna's; she wears no make-up; her eyes are large and deep blue, her lips as full as the best paperback romances would prescribe. Unlike her more glamorous sister, she seems totally unaware of her charms, her manner lumpish in an old-fashioned schoolgirl way. She settles down to read.

The men now get a double treat. 'What a honey!'…'Yum!' as if they would like to gobble them both up.

The blonde in front does not seem to hear, or if she does, she is ignoring them. The top of her head barely moves from its inclined position. The watcher wonders if those blue eyes flicker up to stun each approaching admirer, or is she truly unaware? Perhaps she is dozing. Whether or no, soon she droops sideways onto her pack. A momentary stirring as she kicks off her boots, then she resettles, tucking her feet up on the seat. She too sleeps.

Appetites rise; the buffet becomes more popular, the aisle a never-ending stream of slightly unbalanced passengers. As the day edges towards more acceptable drinking hours, the buffet becomes primarily the bar. Punctuated by the snapping of ringpulls, the trips to the Men's become more frequent, the comments more audible, less innocent. They don't seem to care that she, the older woman, is awake, that she can hear them. Do they think she's so old as to be deaf as well as sexless? Or is she indeed invisible to them?

The girls wake only to turn briefly, snuggle more comfortably, oblivious to the passing parade of drooling males. Lucky she is there as chaperone — 'the dowager in black bombazine'!

Towards dusk the interior lights come on and the windows reflect views she could not see before. She does a few more quick drawings: arabesques of backs and buttocks, tapered twins of knees, swathes of hair, sleeping-beauty faces. Her own image is visible too now; she has to try hard to ignore herself and look beyond.

She needs fortifying. Returning from the buffet with her cardboard tray, specially built to keep upright her takeaway tea and cellophaned vegetarian pastie 'with sauce', she sees her erstwhile seatmate approaching down the aisle. She waits beside the baggage shelves at the end of the carriage, where there is space for his big frame to pass, and watches him slow down as his eyes devour each girl, right, left.

He cannot help but see her watching as he nears the glass door. Guilt makes him acknowledge her as an agemate. 'Oh, for the capacity of the young to sleep anywhere,' he says, shaking his hoary head.

She nods, but does not smile forgiveness. There had been nothing paternal in his looking. Perving, her son would say.

As she rips open the cellophane, she realises that what angers her most is that he could probably woo these girls into his bed if he wanted. It was unfair that men her age could still be seen as desirable, when their female peers had long been dismissed by them, let alone by handsome 18-year-old youths.

Especially when she knows she had been unable to ignore his

physical presence, his large hand as it held his newspaper, so close — pale olive skin, fine black hairs, well-shaped nails. Nor had she been able to stop her thoughts from leaping on, unbid, unbridled, to caresses.

She sighs for her sensual days. There are other pleasures now, she consoles herself. But not on the railways — the pastie is virtually tasteless. Reaching for the small tub of tomato sauce, she fails to find the corner from which to open it, peers at its oddly shaped top, squeezes a little, and discovers a new form of packaging as tomato sauce squirts all down the front of her black jumper.

As she is dabbing at the mess with a tissue, her chin doubled or even tripled as she tries to see if she has sauce on the ends of her hair too, she glimpses the bold pattern of his sweater as he sways back with his lunch. He would look now, she curses silently, and will not raise her eyes to meet the amusement she knows will be there. Damn him.

She goes to the Ladies to wash off the stains, but makes it worse, since the mirror shows an even more obvious trail of damp tissue fibres embedded in the wool. The train lurches round a corner; she loses her balance and bangs her elbow, hard, against the door. Sitting down on the toilet seat, she cradles her elbow, and bursts into tears — for the pain, the embarrassment, for this frighteningly permanent grey veil now between herself and the world, dividing what is past from what is possible.

She blows her nose, annoyed with her own menopausal tears, and suddenly remembers her laptop out there for the taking. Bringing the wandering mascara back into line, she powders her face and returns.

The fair girl is still lolling against her backpack, but is now eating an apple, reading again. Her observer peeps briefly as she sits back down, but can't see what the book is. She was hoping for a shock; this girl cannot possibly be as wholesome as she looks.

The other girl awakes, sits up, yawns, stretching her arms wide and flashing an enviably taut bare midriff. As she twists up her vivid mass of hair to re-pin it, she catches the older woman's eyes upon her. She smiles. A pardon, a gift; she is used to being watched. 'How much longer, d'you know?' she asks.

'Not long; it's all downhill from here,' says the watcher with a laugh, then turns to the window to blink away a last upsurge of tears — for such girls, such glory, doomed even so to one day cross the line to grey.

COMING OUT

THE CAMP was quiet in the pre-dawn winter dark. Not the quiet of sleep, but of stealth.

A truck is being silently loaded. With what, she can't see, except for the long poles pointing up over the truck cabin, silhouettes even blacker than the sky.

From the relative warmth of her car, she watches the pinpoints of light from torches mounted on headbands, seemingly moving about independently, like fireflies. They spotlight puffs of breath rising in the chilly air. Steam-driven fireflies.

A slim bright crescent moon limns the edge of its sphere that hangs pale as a wish bubble in the still-black sky.

Bodies emerge from tent tunnels, hastily don beanies and coats, head to the portable toilets and then to the dim kitchen tent for a quick cuppa. Afraid of sleeping in, she's been awake for an hour. She'd camped in her car, which, with the back seats down, easily took a mattress for a shortie like herself.

She's already drunk her tea, thermos-stored last night; she's even brushed her teeth, sneakily rinsing and spitting by the side of her car. She doesn't know what the rules of behaviour are for this sort of thing, with no proper bathrooms, yet not private, able to be hidden by bushes and trees, but all together, public, in a paddock…

Because 'this sort of thing' — a protest camp — let alone this 'non-violent direct action', is totally foreign to a conservative person like herself, but as she'd realised at last night's campfire circle and briefing, she isn't alone in that. Until very recently she'd never have been able to imagine coming here, but she knows exactly when that changed…

A hot dry wind had been blowing all day. As it did the day before, which the radio said was the hottest day on record for an October. Under the wildly whipping trees, fallen leaves were crisping and grass bleaching, visibly drying to kindling. The eucalypts in the reserve behind her house had barely regained their mopheads after two years of desperate survival leaf-shooting along the upstretched blackened claws that were all the last bushfire had left.

She had cleared her gutters, worrying about falling off the ladder, saying to herself for the hundredth time that she should be sensible and hire someone to do this, but glad her house was low and her block flat. As she raked the resulting clumps of brown leaves from her lawn, she felt that anything could happen; anything bad, that is.

Which seemed fitting, given the permanent gloom that had descended on her spirits, sinking them deeper with each night's news. Hurricanes, wildfires, repeated floods or seemingly endless drought, polar ice and glaciers melting, coral reefs and river systems dying, low islands being inundated, massive tracts of forest being destroyed and species being lost forever. Even our koalas in danger!

She knows she is depressed; what she can't understand is why her neighbours and family are not.

They will agree that it's unseasonably hot, that the floods are terrible, that the bushfires are getting more severe and frequent, but if she utters the CC words, they roll their eyes, spout denying simplifications, swap reassuring clichés with each other.

The men joke, 'Not turning into a greenie, are you, June?!' then move the conversation safely back to their chosen 'realities' — two cars, mortgages, investments, holidays; a forever upwards scale of consuming to reach life's essentials, like the right sort of coffee maker.

The women purse their lips, shake their heads, but nod knowingly. The Change can affect some women in very funny ways, and since

June's been on her own, they've noticed a few oddities…

Married at nineteen, any wayward attitudes young June might have harboured were nipped in the bud by her older husband Ted, who had turned out to be ultra-conservative, even more so than her own churchgoing, Liberal-voting parents. If asked, she'd have said she was content in their life together, three children binding the attraction of his ongoing good looks, strong arms and steady job.

Since Ted died five years ago, what must be her rogue root stock had put forth new shoots. Free of Ted's preferred TV sports channels and their interminable ads, she has taken to watching the ABC. Glimmers of new areas of knowledge, once-inconceivable attitudes and debates seep into her mind. She has begun to feel increasingly out of kilter with her familiar circles.

Is she just another 'grumpy old woman' undergoing The Change?

Does that explain her distress that our way of life is harming people all over the world, and that we keep exporting the coal that is warming the planet and causing… S-hh-h! … Climate Change! ?

Or as she prefers to call it, Climate Chaos.

S-hh-h!

She is so tired of biting her tongue, when she wants to stand up and shout or shake somebody: 'Wake up!!!' Maybe she'll end up ranting and railing in her leafy suburban streets — Killara's crazy woman. Maybe she should. Repressed emotion makes people get ulcers or cancer or something, her eldest daughter says. Her youngest says hormone therapy might help.

That heatwave ended with a furious storm by evening; like Nature's revenge, she had thought, watching the lightning slash the bruised sky — but she doesn't say that sort of thing aloud. As heavy rain lashed the suburbs, blocking drains and flooding roads, and roof-lifting, tree-crashing-on-power-lines winds howled like throat-singing banshees, she knew that tomorrow's news would have the SES short of volunteers to fix the damage, that the word 'unprecedented' would be employed yet again, that people would complain about the delay in getting electricity back... and yet the link would not be made. More coal mines will be approved.

When all was quiet but for the smattering bursts of raindrops dripping from the trees in small gusts of wind, she turned on the TV for the ABC news. One story was about a 94-year old man — a Kokoda veteran! — from a respectable Sydney suburb, who had been arrested while protesting against a new coal mine up north that will destroy a koala habitat forest — and fuel global warming. It is his third arrest.

She suddenly felt lighter; he certainly isn't letting anyone say 'S-hh-hh!' to him!

Four a.m.

Time to head out.

The truck has already left; now a convoy of as few vehicles as could fit everyone in slowly drives out the gate and up the dirt road, lights low. They tail each other closely, not knowing the route or the destination.

In the back seat of one hard-riding Toyota, she is jammed in beside two thankfully skinny men. About her own age, she guesses, mid-sixties. There were the usual introductory exchanges of names and 'Where're you from?' ... Gosford, Armidale, and herself, Sydney.

Here the second most common question is not 'What do you do?' but 'Done this before?'

'No... yes ... no' .

This is followed by 'what brought you here?'

'It's just plain wrong; the whole process has been as crooked as a dog's hind leg; the offsets are a sick joke. Clearing this forest for a bloody new coal mine has got to be stopped!'

And:

'This place is special; I used to come here with me dad, birdwatching; we'd stay in an old stockman's hut on the Laird's farm. I couldn't NOT come now, for Leard Forest and for the Laird family. I've been down twice already.'

And herself, 'It's the line in the sand for me. I'm so appalled at what they're doing, I had to come. For the koalas... and for my grandkids.'

A sudden braking throws them all forward. The convoy has stopped; windows whirr down to receive the hissed words of the messenger as she jogs along the line.

'There's a roadblock further up ahead; we'll have to detour and walk in. Just follow the leader, stay real close and careful; parking lights only, OK?'

Her heart thuds. Good intentions are translating into action more quickly and of a different sort from the briefing they'd been given last night. A sit-in outside a gate wasn't even trespassing; she'd been ready for that.

But even driving without lights is illegal, isn't it?

Slowly the whole caterpillar loops round at the wide crossroads and creeps back the other way, soon veering off down a smaller road that dips to cross a creek, up the other side, rattles over a grid and bumps along a track across what she thinks are open paddocks. She can see no edging fences either side; are they on private property now? Trespassing?

Over another grid, and trees begin to loom dimly alongside and over the track. They stop. The word comes that all but the drivers are to get out here, and the vehicles are to return to camp, so as not to be a giveaway once dawn breaks. Their driver mumbles a bit about missing out on all the action. Fleetingly she wonders if she should offer to drive back instead, but she's never driven a beast like this — and on dirt roads, in the dark — no.

She slides out of the truck, shrugs on her backpack and stumbles over to where she can hear people talking; why hadn't she thought to bring a torch?

Even in the dark she can tell there are more people here than she'd imagined.

'What's happening?' she whispers to the nearest.

'We've got to walk for about half an hour in to where the guys have put up the tripods, right where the bulldozers are ready to start. New plan is we're stopping them. If we get there quickly enough some of us will lock on. The rest will just sit like we planned, only more in their face, so to speak, in front of the machines.'

'Oh.'

Stopping bulldozers... hard metal, soft bodies... idiot, they won't be moving!

Formed into groups around those who have torches, they move off into the forest. Amid the crunching and crackling, from the muttered expletives she knows she's not the only one tripping over sticks and roots and logs.

She taps the parka-clad man beside her, thinking she recognises him, or his parka, as one of her fellow passengers, the Armidale one. 'Sorry, but would you mind if I held on to you? I'm a bit worried about falling and breaking something and holding everyone up.'

'No problems. I'm probably as much at risk myself!'

'Why aren't we following a track?'

'Because they've likely put up motion sensor cameras on those.'

'Oh.'

Cloak-and-dagger stuff indeed. What would her children say if they could see her now? A giggle escapes at that thought; she tells him why.

'Yeah, mine think I've lost my marbles doing this stuff. But they'll be bloody grateful in years to come that there's still some farmland and bush and clean water left for 'em to live with instead of a wasteland with great bloody holes in the ground draining the aquifers and turning 'em toxic. I could spit chips when I think what this government is letting happen here!'

'Me too. Such a small scrap of forest left for the creatures to live in anyway on these cleared plains; but it was the last straw for me when they agreed to let the company bulldoze it in winter when most things are hibernating or slow at least. I couldn't bear the thought of all the koalas, the bats, the lizards… and even if they escaped as their homes were being bulldozed, where would they go?…'

'S-sh-sh!' is passed down the line. 'Let's keep it quiet, eh?'

Now that sort of 'S-sh-sh!' I can take! she thinks.

The skyline is now showing a paler edge, the darkness surprisingly quickly giving way to a sort of transparent charcoal; no colour here in the forest yet, but shapes of trees and people — and forest floor traps — are visible. She has no idea how long they've been walking; it feels timeless, walking in the dark like that.

Pale apricot is flushing the eastern sky as they halt. Through the trees several huge yellow machines are visible in a wide ochre clearing. Two people have hurried ahead to reconnoitre; no workers there yet, so they wave the rest forward.

Once in the cleared belt, she is shocked at the totality and scale of the bareness, the absence of everything that once lived, flora or fauna, compared to the complex web of life that is the forest lined up in front of her.

'The eve of destruction'… was that a Dylan song? This is the edge, where the opposing values meet, and right now she feels sick at the thought of those machines pushing over this living growth and scraping bare the leaf litter and logs and burrows. She imagines the dazed creatures.

The coal company reckons it would all be fine because they would shake the bigger habitat trees to 'encourage' animals to leave before 'gently' bulldozing the trees and leaving them lie overnight to allow any remaining animals to escape. Looking at the size of the trees in the forest ahead, how gently would they fall to earth when bulldozed? Who did the company think they were they fooling?

More than sick, she is incredulous that some of this has happened already. Just a few days ago this bare earth on which she is standing had been a living forest — full of living things.

And she is angry. 'Righteous anger'... not just for this wanton destruction, but because it is purely for a private company to profit from digging up the very cause of the global warming that looms over her grandchildrens' future. When even the World Bank is warning we must leave 80 per cent of the world's coal in the ground to avert catastrophic warming...!!

However strongly she'd thought she felt before, the reality confronting her steps it up from a symbolic protest; she is ready to do whatever it takes to stop this. She's never been arrested in her life, has had only one speeding ticket (in a borrowed and unfamiliarly pacey car), and can't even cross the road against a 'Don't Walk' light. But this is clearly wrong, and being legal doesn't make it right.

At the waiting edge of the forest — the arboreal death row — she sees that three very tall tripods have been set up by the truck crew, who'd got in before the road block and so had not been forced to carry all the gear so far.

Now two young men and a girl in a koala suit are sitting on their respective platforms, roped to the trees and each other in an intricate and interdependent web. So clever, these young people, and so brave, she marvels. But then, it is their future being wrecked...

Four of her walking companions have locked themselves on to the bulldozers, their arms through metal tubes that would be very difficult to cut away without harming the people, she thinks, wincing at the claustrophobic nature of their choice. Then she sees that one of them is the Armidale man; lying on his back, right under the machine.

Wow. That 'old' bloke. She knows she couldn't do such a thing, would panic at being trapped for perhaps hours.

A team leader, a boy who looks about fifteen, but whom she'd been told was doing a PhD in Classics, calls out. 'Right, just had word that security are on their way. Everyone sit down in front of the machines. They'll call the police, who'll likely come in from the road block, so they'll be here quickly. Don't forget if the cops ask you to move, it's up to each of you whether to obey or not. You may be arrested if you don't. But make sure you have your I.D. on you.'

'I'm asking for a few volunteers as arrestables… hopefully some who don't have dreadlocks and can't be accused of being rent-a-crowd! We need to take photos of the arrests to send the media and Twitter and maybe do some short sound grabs.'

She puts up her hand and takes off her beanie. 'Greyhaired grannies acceptable?' she asks, ruffling her flattened hair as she comes forward into the first slanting rays of sunlight.

'They're the best!' he grins, and a small cheer goes up.

As she passes the dozer, the Armidale man gives her a wink and a sideways nod of approval. Like her dad used to, in her childhood, when she'd done a particularly good job as his helper. It meant 'You little beauty!'

Light of heart, strong of will, she removes the small foam mat from her backpack, unrolls it and places it on the cold earth where she is directed to sit. Too old to risk a chill, she'd decided.

But not too old to stand up for what's right, she commends herself… or rather, sit for what's wrong!

And with a small giggle and a click of her dicky knee, she does.

WHEN SHADOWS FALL

COBWEBS hang lazily from the cracked plaster ceilings. Dust has piled thickly on the frail spheres of the paper lightshades, which sway slightly with each draught, launching small eddies of fluff to rest on the million tiny ledges of the rough stuccoed walls.

The tops of the closely drawn curtains bend under their pleated weights of dust, and, with the easy elegance of long practice, gently shed their overload to the waiting levels below.

These are for books; books in rows on tall shelves and low shelves, in unsteady stacks on floor, coffee table, lounge and piano, in tumbled towers on spare beds and dressing tables. The reserves bide patiently in boxes, cupboards and wardrobes, while those books in current favour are ranged in piles, two deep, at the rear of the dining table.

In the midst of this shadowland of riches, a reading lamp casts a bright circle on the green cloth of that dining table, illuminating also a sprawl of papers and a woman's head bent low over them. Spotlit, backlit, her hair crinkles like tarnished metal, points of light striking bronze and silver amid base gunmetal grey. As she writes, her brown-clad arm moves slowly across the pool of light, the gold clip at the top of the fountain pen twinkling on the upstrokes, the faint scratching of its nib the only sound in the room.

There is a proper desk, but it is occupied by a computer and its entourage. Never used, here under sufferance from somebody's misplaced but insistent organising several years ago, this is the most useless part of the house, for books will not stack on the futuristic contours of these machines. This woman has learnt that simply saying 'yes' removes such people from her life far more quickly than saying what she means.

A loud rapping at the front door shatters the calm. The writer halts, sighs, starts to lay down her pen, but rebukes herself with a sharp little shake of her head, and resumes writing. The over-enthusiastic knocking is repeated. A hunching of her shoulders reiterates her decision to ignore such intrusion.

But the rapping has disturbed the house too. Millions of tiny dust motes shiver and twirl frantically through the air, fragments of plaster tremble undecidedly along the cracks, spiders hurry to their corners, just in case. The spell is broken. The woman frowns as she hears footsteps pass the curtained window in front of her, heading round the back. Then she hears the prolonged squeak of the back gate.

Clearly there will be no escaping this persistence.

Pushing back her chair, she stands stiffly, revealing the red glow of a bar heater in the dark cave under the table, and walks slowly through to the cold kitchen. Her deep, resentful sigh and a tinkle of badly propped china greets the new burst of knocking, somewhat softer on the wood of the back door. Or is it the inherent intimacy of back doors, leading as they do straight into the private lives within, that tones it down?

Since the back door has dropped a little off vertical over the years, she has to lift it clear of the floorboards to open it without dragging. Even the pale wintry light thus revealed has her blinking like a sleepy mole at the dark silhouette on her doorstep. She thinks she recognises the young man from the flats across the road. He's storing things in her garage, having stopped her at the front gate when she was going out one day and asked if he might. He'd noticed she had no car to put in there, he'd said. As she hadn't been in the old garage for years, she had said 'yes' to be rid of him.

She has absolutely no idea what his name is. Her mind flaps around now in a panic to locate it — but did she ever know it?

'Oh, hello...' she begins, but is saved by his simultaneous and far more brisk start.

'Hi, Mrs Embley. Just wanted to ask if you'd mind if I put up a few shelves in the shed?'

Shelves — timber — nails — hammering — noise! 'Uh, no, I don't think that's a good idea: Donald wouldn't like it.'

'Oh, Mr Embley back, is he?'

'Yes, of course. I told you he'd only gone up the street.'

'Yeah, haven't seen him about, but. OK, no worries.' He turns to go.

'Wait!' she calls, louder than she intends. 'It really would be best if you didn't disturb us in the house. Donald needs peace and quiet for his work, you see. Just come and go to the garage as you want, no need to ask. But we'd prefer there to be no extra noise-making, if you understand what I mean?'

'Fair enough,' he nods. 'Catch you later, then.'

What an odd expression, she thinks. But there's a lot she finds odd about the young, like the flapping oversized trousers he is wearing, slung so low on his hips that she fears for their tenure, and the way he bounces along on his equally oversized sneaker soles. He is a tall fellow, and as he refastens the gate with its complicated loops of old belts, she can see his face over the top. She notes his puzzled frown as he glances round her rampantly overgrown yard. The frown is still there when he looks over at her.

He raises his hand in farewell, and disappears. She shivers a little, taking a brief look at the backyard herself before she shuts and bolts the door. Since she has no need to venture beyond the path to the clothesline, she does not usually even register the jungle beyond. Donald used to look after it, but she can't remember how long it is since he went, nor where he said he was going, if he did. Last winter?... or the one before? It was at least one winter anyway, of that she is sure; not that such detail matters — it's been long enough for her to know that he isn't coming back.

Ah dear! I need a cup of tea to settle me down again. Then on to that troublesome chapter five. She has the kettle on before she remembers she has run out of biscuits, at which she curses gently.

Such a waste of time, going shopping. I'll just pop round to the petrol station on the corner again; they keep bread and milk and butter, and a few tins of things, and they certainly have biscuits. It's a pity they don't keep fruit and vegetables, or I'd rarely need to go further.

She sees herself at one end of a piece of elastic, the other end of which is tied to her writing table. The corner of her street is but two doors up, safely reachable and returnable from. The shopping centre, the bank and the post office, are tangibly far, a bus ride away, and she postpones for as long as possible those days when she must break her connection to go there.

Look what happened to Donald.

Switching off the kettle, she goes into the bedroom to fetch her coat. It hangs on one corner of the tall iron bed-end, since the wardrobe, a once-handsome walnut veneered antique, is past accessing. Barely upright, it is a mutual propping of drunkenly askew panels, the base long collapsed under all the books she has stacked in there. The room is dim, the curtains permanently drawn. She has decided that is best, as such things tend to fall down if moved — curtains, hooks, rings, rods, brackets — astonishingly complicated arrangements, impossible for her to replace or fix. By keeping her life simple she manages very well on her own, in her opinion.

Peering at the dressing table where her brush ought to be, she can't see it, but she does see a hat, which she crams over her wiry hair. It turns out to be an old khaki gardening hat, probably Donald's, but the hazed and speckled mirror door of the wardrobe, hanging by one hinge, shows only a dim image, and she leaves the house unconcerned by her reflection.

She returns ten minutes later with her stopgap shopping, having even remembered to clear the mailbox on her way back. She flicks through the pile while the kettle boils, but the letters are mostly for Donald. These publishers can be so pushy. She'll deal with them later.

Now for chapter five! Tea and biscuits at her elbow, the warm glow at her feet, silence and dust and shadows resettling like a protective curtain all around her, she turns to the beginning to reread what she has written, regain the real world.

The title is only a working one, but it has, she feels, a good ring to it: *When Shadows Fall,* by Donald Embley.

CENTRAL VISION

WHEN the train pulled in, her only thought was to find the right carriage. For half an hour she'd stood beside the yellow letter E painted on the edge of the platform, as the station master had told her to. 'Now if you were J, it'd be a different story: we're too small to fit more than F alongside at a time. But with E you know where you are.'

So she had, but she didn't now. Finding no sash lifts on the window beside her seat, she had tried sliding the glass, to no effect. What with the strange humming of this train and all the windows shut, she was feeling quite smothered. Nobody else had opened their windows, either. Probably for the soot; you always expected an eyeful when the train went round corners and you had to be careful not to lean your sleeve on the windowsill, and of course you never wore white on a train journey.

It was cold in here. A bit of autumn sunshiny air would warm it up. The conductor appeared at the end of the carriage. 'Tickets, please.' She would ask him.

As he balanced his way along the aisle she peered at him with interest. Indian? Foreigners were rare where she came from. Reaching her seat, he held out his hand for her ticket, while still talking to someone in front. Even her untrustworthy eyesight told her it was a beautiful hand: fine boned, smooth, a warm dark brown, paler underneath, neat nails. As she passed her ticket to him she was ashamed of her own hand: mottled like a raw sausage, scabbed and scarred from the sun, with knobs of knuckles and distorted stumps of fingers, the nails never quite free of garden dirt.

She asked about the window. He laughed. She'd never seen such white teeth, or such clear whites of eyes. Unexpectedly, the word 'God' popped into her head. This must be how he had designed humans: unblemished, a joy to the eye, and no doubt to the hand as well. We've certainly messed up the plan, she thought, glimpsing the young man in the seat opposite: beer belly already, ears too large, puddingy face, hair a dull brown. Not a gleam or a sparkle about him.

Even this voice was pleasant, riding lightly up and over invisible waves, 'But you do not need to open the windows, madam! The train is air conditioned so it stays an even temperature all the year round. If we were to allow people to open windows it would not work so well.'

'I thought it might have been for the soot... you know, to keep the seats clean...'

With a perplexed little smile he shook his head and moved on.

A bald head popped round the side of the seat in front of her, twisted to look. 'They don't have soot any more, luv. Where you been? The trains are all electric or diesel these days: have been for years!' The eyes rolled, the head withdrew.

She sat back into her corner, drew her cardigan closer. It was still cold, and it smelt, like the inside of an old fridge when you started it up again. And what happened to the stale air they were all breathing out? Surely they weren't 'conditioning' that and giving it back? Why carry on as if it was rationed, when there was a world full of fresh stuff out there?

Trying not to breathe too deeply, she leant her head against the window, watching for the engine. The track curved: sure enough, no smoke, no funnel, just a flat silver nose. Amazing. And she hadn't even noticed! But what would they have done with all those steam engines? Rusting in a paddock somewhere, she supposed, along with the old carriages with their varnished wood, the 'dogbox' compartments where you had to watch out for strange men; the long leather seats, the glass water carafes in their metal holders, the big tin hotwater holders under the seats for your feet...'rusting in a paddock somewhere'... just like her.

It had been over thirty years since she'd left the bush, been on a train, come to any city, let alone the big smoke of Sydney. Closer to forty, really, but it hadn't felt like a long time. The seasons came and went, the work flowed round them, small things happened to denote one year from another. Not all small; it was near ten years since Hec died. Her breath caught, snagging on the familiar pain.

Closing her eyes, wishing him here now, she could almost feel the warmth and bulk of his arm pressing against hers on the armrest; he'd know what to do about windows and such. If they'd had children, one of them would probably be taking her to Sydney to see this specialist. Mavis Callaghan's daughter drove her to Broken Hill that time she had her operation; stayed there with her too.

Her own doctor had booked her in to a sort of guesthouse that belonged to the hospital where she was due tomorrow. She'd have gone to the People's Palace near Central; people used to say it was cheap and clean and handy. Doctor Ryan had said he doubted if it was still there, but if it was, it'd be full of backpackers, whatever they were.

Gazing out at the hazy monotony of the country flashing by, she dozed a little. She'd been up long before dawn that morning to get a lift with Ted Price in his cattle truck; lucky the sales were on that day. It was a four-hour drive, and she'd had a bit of a wait at the station, but she wasn't game to leave her bag there and walk round town... what if the train came early? She'd brought tea and sandwiches with her, so ate her breakfast sitting on a slatted seat in the sun, quite comfortable until the station master had arrived and got her worried about being so far away from E.

Although Doctor Ryan had said it was a long shot, the trip would be worth it if this specialist in Sydney could fix her eyes. She hated not being able to knit or sew or read. She could get about fine, and apparently would always see a bit round the edges, but she was losing the whole centre of her vision. Tiny blood vessels breaking, they said. Made it hard to pass the time indoors, apart from the radio.

Made it a long trip now, although the other passengers seemed to be eating their way to Sydney, judging by the constant stream of them swaying through from the buffet car with cardboard trays of foam boxes and cups, or packets of crisps and cans of drink. They were a mixed bunch. Some of the young ones looked as if they were wearing too large or too small hand-me-downs, or maybe it was fancy dress? Several had short spiky hair of surprising colours, like green, but she didn't trust her eyes on that one; couldn't always be sure whether they were boys or girls either. You didn't see that sort of thing in Boodialla, not that there were many young ones left there at all.

She ate the last of her sandwiches as they wound up and over the mountains and through the string of little ridgetop towns. Her memories, more reliable now than her vision, combined to make this part as exciting as on her very first trip. She even thought she glimpsed the roof of the Hydro-Majestic through the pine trees. She'd never been there, but she'd seen pictures, and she knew Evie Bennett, who'd gone there for her honeymoon. Hadn't done Evie much good; her George had turned out a real bad one...

She awoke from another doze to find they were down in the plains and a boy of about seventeen was sitting next to her, moving his head oddly back and forth on his neck, like a chook. Catching her eye, he briefly raised his eyebrows. She'd have preferred to think of the gesture as a greeting, but it looked more like 'So what are you gawking at?' She could see black cords dangling from plugs in his ears. Hearing aids? A hissing noise seemed to be coming from them. He was ignoring her now as completely as if she wasn't there. You wouldn't get that in Boodialla either. A bit too much sparing of the rod, Hec would have said.

Turning to the window, she saw that the suburbs were thickening, the streetlights just coming on. She was glad Central was the end of the line; no need to panic about getting her bag down with this boy in the way.

No need indeed. He was off down the corridor before the train even stopped. Not that she needed help, but it would have been nice to be asked. She waited till the aisle was clear before reaching up to tug at the handle of her old brown leather overnight bag, letting it drop on to the seat. She put on her coat, lifted the bag onto the floor, then shuffled down the aisle with it in front. It wasn't very heavy, but these narrow aisles made it awkward. She hoped she wouldn't have to carry it too far though.

Emerging into the air at last, she stood for a minute in renewed awe at the many long platforms of Central. The air smelt different from home, but it was hard to say of what. There was a sharpness to it as it hit the back of her nose. Gas?

She walked up to the gate, ticket clutched ready. The inspector seemed very weary, and did not smile at her like the Indian gentleman. Glancing at her return ticket, he simply nodded her through. She hesitated. 'Can you tell me please where I get a train to the North Shore?'

He sighed, and jerked his head round to the right. 'Downstairs.'

Thanking him, she stepped out into the vastness of Central. It was even grander than she remembered, brighter too. She fancied the stained glass windows were more colourful. They must've had a clean-up. The great arched roof rose high above, alive with pigeons.

Voices echoed, kids yelled and laughed, babies cried, loudspeaker announcements ricocheted incomprehensibly; the noise was enormous. There were people everywhere, rushing past, queueing at the food and newspaper stalls or sitting on the big banks of benches. She was sure they were new; long liver-coloured plastic curving things, like slugs. She preferred honest timber; so did Hec.

Ah, he'd have liked to see this again. She'd come down to meet him right here at Central to get married. It was his last leave before he was sent to Egypt. They'd spent their wedding night in the Great Southern Hotel, just down in George Street. Tears came to her eyes. Silly! she chided herself, but she hadn't been here since then, she couldn't help it.

Perhaps she'd better have a cup of tea, get a grip on herself, before she went looking for her train.

Blinking, she moved on, peering about for the tearooms, and unwittingly cutting across the main evening rush to the suburban trains. People baulked, muttered and humphed exasperatedly, several swore under their breaths; then two young girls bumped right into her. She stumbled, turned to apologise, and with a fright met their angry masks of paint and piercings. 'Whyncha look where ya goin', ya stupid old bag?' snarled one, as they whirled around her and on with the crowd.

She had never heard anyone speak so viciously, and to a stranger, over such a small thing. Why were they so angry?

Spotting a space on the nearest bench, she sat down to get out of the way and recover a little. She turned to her neighbour to ask about the tearooms, but the man seemed to be asleep, his head slumped on his chest. He was very untidy; must have had to wait overnight for his train. An open bottle in a brown paper bag was balanced precariously on the seat beside him. She automatically reached to straighten it up before it fell over and spilt. The rustle of the bag woke him; he grabbed it from her, stood up indignantly, swaying over her and releasing waves of foul smells as he hissed, 'Get yer own f...n' grog, bitch!' He lurched off, looking over his shoulder at her and muttering darkly.

Extremely shaken, she looked around for explanations, reassurance, sympathy. No one seemed to have even noticed; they were reading their papers or staring vacantly through her. She turned to her other neighbour, a young woman. 'Excuse me, I really need a cup of tea... could you...' but the girl jumped up immediately, lips pursed, gave a single vehement shake of her head and stalked off. Sighing heavily, she looked about. There was a food stall back over there, but when she stood up with her bag, she felt too weak to force through all those hurrying people again.

She resigned herself to going tealess till she got to her lodgings and simply allowed the rushing tide to take her. They must know where they're going, she thought tiredly. It flowed down an escalator, where she felt a brief remembered panic at its beginning and end, then on into a sort of tunnel.

Finding herself on the slower edge of the current, she stepped aside to catch her breath, and nearly fell over a person lying beside the wall. She bent down, concerned, apologising, but the young man seemed unconscious, although breathing. She put out her hand to stop someone for help, but was expertly avoided by all. Seeing a uniform bustling by, she grabbed at the sleeve; it was a railway person, he'd know what to do.

'This man needs help,' she said.

He laughed. 'Don't we all! Look lady, if I stopped to help every druggie that bombed out down here I'd never get anything done. OK, OK, I'll call Missionbeat to come get him. Don't worry yourself about him. Scum of the earth, all of 'em.'

She frowned at his disappearing back, then down at the young man. It seemed awful to leave him there unprotected. He looked normal enough; hair not shaved nor too long, decent clothes. 'Scum of the earth!' What if this was her son, and everyone ignored him like this? He was someone's son.

She put her bag down beside his head to stop people treading on him as she'd nearly done, and draped her coat over him while she waited till help came.

Jaded end-of-work eyes flicked in brief curiosity to the old woman just standing against the wall, not begging or busking, then down to the body. No one left the rush to approach her; trains were full this time of evening, drinks and dinner and collapse in front of telly awaited. Only an Aboriginal girl stopped and asked her if she could spare any change; to buy medicine for her kid, she said. She gave some. The girl didn't even look at the boy by her feet.

After what seemed a long time, she sat down on the bag, gingerly... it wasn't really meant for that, not like a proper suitcase. Being closer to the boy like this, she patted his shoulder now and then, murmuring comforting words, though he made no sign of hearing. The back of his neck looked thin, and very young.

When the Missionbeat workers arrived, they asked if she knew him, and shook their heads at such foolishness. 'If he hadn't been so out of it he could've knifed you, robbed you, anything! These druggies get pretty desperate. You have to mind your own business in the city, y'know. Now you go straight home, OK?' They unfolded their stretcher and loaded him on. She only just remembered her coat before they headed off down the tunnel.

Folding it over her arm, she picked up her bag and turned back towards the escalators. The crowd had thinned; she could see her way now. The same girl stopped her and asked for change, only this time it was her mother who was sick; she gave her some more anyway.

Up she went, back to the grand area above. She asked an attendant where she could find out about train times and he pointed her across to where the stained glass was lit up most brightly. It was easy crossing the great hall this time. As she passed the benches, she saw that some now had people lying full length on them. The sickly odour of vomit somewhere near underlaid the predominant Central smell of hot chips and disinfectant.

She found out what she wanted, booked her seat, and was directed to the tearooms, which turned out to be just where they used to be. Putting her bag under a table, her coat over a chair, she took a tray and slid it along the chrome rails to the counter. Ordering roast lamb and vegetables and a pot of tea, she noted the steak and kidney pie: Hec would have gone for that.

Tea helped, but she was very tired. The big clock hanging from the glass roof outside said ten past eight. The overnight train to the west left at nine.

She went through the gate to the same platform on which she'd arrived, hours earlier. She checked her seat ticket. Experienced now, she found the yellow H on the platform. 'H' for 'Hec': that was a good sign, a comfort that she was doing the right thing.

Going straight home. Like the man said.

In Boodialla people saw her, and she could see them, well enough. Down here, they were all more blind than she would ever be.

LAST RITES FOR A LOVER

IT IS considered the best nursing home in town. Impeccably decorated, its walls boast original paintings, its staff are smartly uniformed and uniformly personable. They smile out from the reception desks and nursing stations, all of which bear obviously artistic floral arrangements. Even the muzak is upmarket, classically tinged, although Bach might not approve of the interpretation.

Yet still it smacks of hospitals, and worse.

Two visitors are negotiating the labyrinth of its beige corridors for the first time. They are almost tiptoeing in their desire not to disturb the muted ambience into which they have intruded.

'Quite tasteful,' whispers Beth.

'Why bother?' hisses her husband.

For this is the last stop. No exit from here but by box, to pillow and coverlet of stone, or mechanical slide to furnace. 'Ashes to ashes...' ticks the silent metronome behind the muzak. Life here seems only to be marking time between meals and medications, and yet ever so slowly time does pass. An end will come.

Beth and Mike are merely middle-aged; they do not envisage themselves in this place. They are here to visit Dee, once the queen of the town's arty crowd, an admired, although often feared, dramatic and daring merry widow.

Dee is older than all of them; by how much no one has ever known. Her sophisticated maturity had always been part of her power, but 'older' had not meant 'old' then.

They haven't seen her for almost a year, when she'd been a little shaky, but in command. Since then she'd been battling it out at home, refusing all but medical and family visitors. Then the word got around that her Parkinson's had progressed beyond the control of drugs or home care. Word also got around that she had become such a difficult client that the expensive private home care service could no longer find an 'angel' on their books who was willing to tend to her.

The family put her house up for sale.

To wait out your time in this place comes at an even higher cost than angels.

Everyone speculated on what her art collection would fetch at the Sotheby's auction later this year. Friends admitted to chosen others — in strict confidence — to being a teeny bit disappointed that a favourite painting had not been earmarked as a farewell gift for them. Of course not for the financial value, but as a memento...

All said how sad it was, how unfair, how sorry for her they felt — and all had an unkind and immediately suppressed afterthought, a touch of 'My, how the mighty are fallen'. Not that Mike and Beth have come to gloat in any degree; as Beth said, Dee has been their 'dear friend' for years and they ought to visit her.

And here, now, she cannot refuse them entry.

Looking for Dee's room number, they try not to see the pacing or prone shadows doing time in the rooms they pass.

The nurse has told them that Dee is undergoing a drug-free period so they can sort out her conflicting medications. This has led Mike to mistakenly anticipate time with an alert and familar Dee.

But even before they find her door, they hear the metallic clanking. Their prepared smiles fail them as they see she is the captive of the bed, its barred sides raised like a cot. The whole bed rattles continuously with her shaking.

This bothers Mike terribly. Surely they could find a bed that didn't make so much noise; Dee had always been so sensitive to ugly or loud noises. What was the point of all this fancy decor, of what must be the enormous fees, if Dee has to bear this audio abuse as well as the nightmare in which she's trapped?

It seems Dee cannot speak, or even gesture, but her dark eyes immediately fix on them, making two oddly steady points amid the frenetic movements of her body. Mike clutches Beth's arm — they shouldn't be here, Dee would hate them seeing her like this.

But Beth is on autopilot; she moves forward to kiss the pale thudding cheek, avoiding the askew mouth, that had so often wounded her with its patronising smile or small sharp comments that Mike never heard. Her polite peck leaves a glaring smear of orange.

Beth's gaze skids away from this unforgivable grotesquerie — and from those eyes; she focuses on the shuddering drapes of flesh between Dee's chin and chest and addresses her babble to them. 'We won't stay long, Dee. We just called in because we're off to Europe for three months, and we thought...'

She stops, but the 'thought' continues to form silently, take flight, and hover over the rattling bed. They can all see it — how, and why, and probably long before their return, this room will fall sharply into silence.

Dee's eyes snare her visitor's blinking blue confusion. Beth quails; she is suddenly irrationally afraid that Dee might be shamming, might rise up and smite her for her daring. Giving a quick pat to the wasted arm that can no longer withdraw from such liberties, she retreats behind her husband, pushing him forward, like a shield.

Mike finds it harder — that slackly crooked mouth, lips wobbling, saliva threatening to spill from the lower corner. Vivid memories of past passionate kisses collide with his present revulsion. Unable to approach her face, he captures a hand, and presses it gently between his, feeling the frail bones, the tremor constant in the cage, like a panicked bird.

'I'm sorry, Dee, I'm so sorry,' is all he can manage, hoping his eyes, his touch, convey what he cannot say in front of Beth. He can at least remove the indignity of that damned lipstick, and he frees one hand to reach for a tissue.

As he leans closer to wipe her cheek, her eyes sharpen, glint eloquent darts of hatred. Regardless of the wreck of her nervous system, the loss of her physical charms, Dee is still Dee.

How dare he, the long-discarded lover, have power now when she is helpless?

How dare he be able to take new lovers, lovers who could lie still beside him in their sweet exhausted aftermath when she will never know that — or any stillness — again?

Despite her, he manages to make this last touch of her skin a caress. But she holds that intense eye contact, until he fancies his head is beginning to shake from side to side too; she is drawing him into her prison… a ridiculous thought, he knows, but nevertheless he drops the hand, too quickly, and steps back.

He raises his eyebrows at Beth, and they begin to leave, helpless to stop themselves scattering cruelly inappropriate inanities like 'Take care', 'See you when we get back!'. Instinctively they are backing out of the room; the queen might yet press a button, order 'Off with their heads!'

The rattling of the bed follows them as they hurry down the corridor, until the muzak muffles it beyond hearing. But Mike still has it ringing in his head as they sign themselves out; he is not sure that it will ever leave him. Like tinnitus, he worries. And worse, carrying the attendant nightmare image of her…

They escape to the carpark's welcome glare, its metallic dazzle and simmered smells of tar and petrol. Life — ongoing and unmuted. He breathes it in, sighs heavily, swallows. His ears click, the noise stops.

Mike reaches for his keys and the crumpled tissue falls to the ground as he unclenches his hand. He kicks it under the car. Only a small qualm, a wisp of sentiment, follows what once might have become a love token.

Safe in the familiar interior of the car, they wind down the windows and sit in a premature minute's silence.

'I think I need …' Mike begins, and falters, as his lifelong habit of 'affectionate deceit' rises to counteract the unaccustomed urge to honesty brought on by this shock.

Why cause trouble between himself and Beth by telling her about Dee now, after all these years? Let sleeping dogs lie — or bitches! He chokes on an hysterical giggle that becomes a sob.

Beth looks across at him sympathetically and puts a hand on his knee. He frowns at the hand as if it were a stranger's, his gaze moving past the brightly painted orange fingernails — matching that lipstick — to the fingers, already wrinkled, to the folds around the knuckles, to the ropey veins under the over-tanned skin. But the hand's stillness, its ability to just lie there, the fingers shaping themselves to loosely cap his knee, strikes him for the first time as a gift.

Mike pats the hand. 'Poor old girl,' he says. Beth nods, thinking of Dee. But he is looking at his wife, at her carefully made-up face, her freshly waved and tinted hair. Her last chance to score off Dee, he thinks. Only chance.

Dee had been able to put more sex appeal into one glance than Beth had ever possessed, or ever would. Over the two years of their affair, Dee had driven him crazy with desire. Even in her old painting clothes, hair wild and paintstreaked, she had turned him on; it was the look in her eyes, the lift of an eyebrow, the curl of her lips.

They had risked it anywhere, anytime. The memory of their encounters still made his blood race; indeed, he sometimes drew on them to successfully carry out his husbandly duties to Beth.

But Dee had tired of him…

He had been incredulous when she broke it off. It had become too predictable, she said. Dismissed, as passé as last year's hemlines, his pride could no more forgive than his body could forget.

Worse still, in the small social circles of this town, he'd had to keep seeing her, at parties, gallery openings, wine tastings. At least the fact that they were not quite in the same circle spared him the intimacy of dinners, the dangers of sitting too close, touching knees, breathing in her scent.

He couldn't help watching for the signals of a new secret affair, for who would be the lucky man, or had already received her favours, was perhaps the reason for his own loss.

But Dee was clever, controlled; she always called the shots… then.

Shaking his head, he focuses on Beth again.

'Yes? What do you need, dear?' she asks sweetly.

Bringing her hand to his lips, he kisses it, then offers her his neverfail rueful boyish smile.

'I need cheering up after that. Come on, I'll take you to lunch at the new restaurant on the wharf. Seafood, sea breeze — and some decent champagne. We'll have one for poor old Dee.'

Beth splutters, 'Did you see the card on her door? I never knew 'D' stood for Doris!'

Underneath, thinks Mike, they're all bitches. So why do I feel like bawling?

FINAL FLINGS

IT'S 11.00 a.m. at the Berrington RSL. Dot and her friend Alma have come for lunch and a session on the pokies. They do this every Friday, thus avoiding the rush on pension days, which is every second Thursday. Keeping it regular means they won't get confused as to whether it's pension week or not.

As with most of their friends, avoiding confusion is paramount; you don't want 'Them' to suspect Alzheimers/Oldtimers' Disease — shared joke, shared fear.

Dot and Alma have caught a taxi from the Retirement Village. Taxis are more awkward now Alma's on a walking frame, which has to fit in the boot, but the Village bus leaves too early, although it's cheaper and has a special place for walkers and wheelchairs.

This taxi driver is decent enough to lift out the walker for them; some just stay sitting behind the wheel and push the button to open the boot! Dot is fit enough to lift it out if needed; she's older than Alma but she's still got her own hips and knees, though not her teeth.

Now she pushes open the Club's heavy glass door and holds it there for Alma.

'Wouldn't you think they'd have those sliding doors that open by themselves?!' grumbles Alma as she steers herself through. 'What if I was on me own?'

Alma's only been a widow for three years, and still thinks of herself as lacking her other half. Bert always opened doors, paid the bills, put out the garbage and mowed the lawn.

Dot's husband, Fred, died over twenty years ago, so she's used to being on her own. She fills in her week quite nicely, what with tending the potplants out the front of her villa, bowls on Mondays, Tuesdays helping at Vinnies, coffee and windowshopping at the Mall whenever she fancies, the library's books and DVDs and CDs, the occasional day bus trip from the Village, and at least one day out down the Club.

They say 'G'day' to the bloke behind the desk, sign in, and head towards the happy jangle of the poker machines. It's dim in here after outside, but the yellow and purple swirls on the green carpet leap out to guide them. They choose a table halfway between the bar and the pokies.

'I'll get the first round,' says Dot. Actually she gets them all, but they take turns to pay.

Alma manoeuvres herself into the plastic chair, which is too low for her to manage easily. Hip replacements are all very well but they leave you high and dry, so to speak, as far as chairs go. And as for lounges! The squashy type that she used to think of as real comfy are now to be avoided; like quicksand, once she's in she can't get out, as she likes to say.

Dot returns with a port and lemonade for Alma, and a brandy and dry for herself. She'd prefer a middy of New — but not the subsequent frequent trips to the Ladies from so much fluid. She's tried the 'brain over bladder' mantra recommended by a lady who gave a talk at the Village on incontinence problems, but her bladder always seems to get the upper hand.

'Ta, love — cheers!' says Alma.

They sip, look around the room. Alma fluffs out her grey curls and pulls in her chin, but the hanging wattles of skin below it do not follow. Dot understands her friend's need to keep up her feminine image, but wonders when she'll wake up to the fact that none of the old codgers here are paying attention. Nor will they. She and Alma are way over the hill of desirability.

When her Fred went she was only in her early sixties, still able to give and get a glad eye or two. As she had for a time — not that she'd admit it to Alma. She misses the cuddling, the skin-on-skin warmth, but not the rest so much. Yet even so, she and her mate Madge would have had fun here sizing up the aged talent on offer, imagining the possible scenarios — and disasters. But since Madge had a major stroke three years ago, and then a few more, she's not laughing at anything…

Dot sighs, shakes her head. Poor bloody Madge!

Pity Alma's not more down-to-earth like Madge was; she's a bit of a prude, truth be told — too churchy. But Dot has found that her options in friends at this stage of life have narrowed a great deal, are less to do with attitudes or interests in common than how many marbles they have left and how mobile they are.

She and Alma sip in silence. Dot considers starting a conversation, but they've said it all before. And that's not what they're here for. Alma catches her eye. 'Fancy a quick fling before lunch?' she asks, indicating the rows of machines.

'Oh, why not — you only live once, eh? Here, I'll carry your drink for you.'

'They ought to put a drinkholder in these things,' complains Alma as she pulls herself up and over to her walker. 'What if I was on me own?'

Swags and tails of blue tinsel as thick as a man's arm are strung overhead — festive leftovers. They stir slightly in the airconditioning. Beneath them the Penny Arcade beckons. Fluoro beads of light chase each other incessantly around garish cartoon characters as the machines strut their stuff, speaking to the players in cyber trills, with an occasional tinkle of coins.

The big payout noises are much louder, clacking, ratchetting up the hopes of the players — this is the thrill they come for. Lights flash and illuminate the winner; everyone peeks at the mortal so blessed — an ordinary person just like themselves. So it is possible.

And there's Keno and Bingo and the TAB if they get tired of the pokies. In the room beyond are the games for the more active.

Nobody is playing there now — the tables under their traditional brass-hung rows of deep green glass lightshades are calm rectangles of lighter green. That area will burst into clicking action and loud banter and laughter later, when the oldies have gone home for their naps, and the after-work crowd take over.

'Jetsetter!' the flashiest gaming machine proclaims, like a cruel joke to the feeble who sit at its feet. Those in wheelchairs must sit sideways and stretch their arms — pokies are not wheelchair-friendly. Those on interim walkers are lucky.

The games are undemanding. Only one hand, one finger, is needed to play. Lights, sound, but not much action.

A sign warns that 'Your chances of winning the maximum prize are no better than one in a million.' Like the warning on cigarette packets, except that smokers usually enjoy their addiction. No one is doing that here; no one is laughing. They don't have much time left to win the big one.

Dot and Alma do no good. Might as well have lunch. The patterns on the carpet now lead them towards the Bistro. Others are trailing that way too. Walkers like Dot's soon line up at the bain-maries.

'You choose and then you can bags us a table while I order,' Dot says briskly. All the good stuff will be gone if she waits for Alma to dither too long. She suspects that the departed Bert used to choose and order for her, as Alma always has trouble making a decision. She usually 'if's and 'but's about each item on offer, putting-on-weight-wise, then goes back and starts again, appetite-wise.

Dot never met Bert, as Alma only moved into the villa next to hers once he'd gone. To hear Alma talk, he was a saint, but, having caught a few accidentally dropped remarks, Dot has decided that he was probably a bit 'up himself', as her own knockabout Fred would have said.

She pulls her wandering mind back to focus on the food.

This Bistro aims to be classy; there's not a sausage in sight, and snow pea shoots garnish every salad, but it isn't game to do away with the traditional roast meat and vegies.

'I'm having the roast,' Dot says. 'Never bother just for myself at home. What about you, Alma?'

But Alma's recently started getting Meals on Wheels and although they're all right — don't get her wrong, she's not complaining — they're mostly mushy, easy to re-heat in the microwave. Which is just as well, as they deliver too early or too late and she's told them a dozen times that she doesn't want the soup powder but they keep bringing it and even if it does only cost $6 a meal she hates waste and she suspects the mashed potato is that powdered stuff too but she has to eat it because how do you manage the peas otherwise? Anyway, she's now missing her grills and fries and salads, so she chooses the fish and chips and salad quite promptly.

She finds a table and sits looking out to the natural mangroves beyond the un-natural palm trees in front of the veterans' and war widows' villas nearby. They're real handy to the Club, she thinks enviously. Her Bert didn't get sent overseas so she's not eligible. He went deaf from the gun batteries in the army training camps up in north Queensland, where he was a sergeant, but Veterans Affairs said that didn't count.

Her villa is all right, except it's not handy to anywhere else but the hundreds of other villas in the Retirement Village — and the looming next stages, the hostel and the nursing home. Nobody likes to think of themselves as moving up the conveyor belt of old age to those places, although the improved chances of speedier acceptance into them when the need arrives is a prime reason for being in the Village.

It's depressing enough seeing the all-but-last stagers from the hostel wheeled out into the gardens, even though they look sort of normal, chatting to each other and all that. Some even have a smoke, which Alma thinks oughtn't to be allowed, but Dot reckons they probably don't have much else to enjoy, apart from meals and sleep, and since they wouldn't live any longer if they stopped now, why make their last years any more miserable than need be?

A few months after Alma moved in, she thought she might become a volunteer in the nursing home, cheer the really old people up, read the paper to them or something. It hadn't occurred to her that this last stop was so close to the end of the line.

Shrunken and frail, wispy and pale, hardly any with a spark of life in their eyes, they'd been parked around the main room in kind of lie-down wheelchairs — and these were the most mobile, she'd been told. The others were bedbound, and although she'd tried not to look into the four-bed wards as she passed…

She couldn't bear it.

'Like vegetables,' she'd whispered to Dot on their next club day. 'Oh my goodness, I do hope I go before that!'

'You could make sure you do,' Dot had suggested. 'I saw a programme on telly about a group who make plans for dodging that sort of end.' It had made absolute sense to her…

Alma had been horrified. 'Oh, no I couldn't. What would people think! The family! And the church! They won't bury suicides, you know. Oh no, it would be awfully embarrassing!'

'Alma, you'd be dead; you couldn't be embarrassed. But look, forget it. Well then, we'd better do what they say and 'make hay while the sun shines'.

'Don't put off till tomorrow what you can do today,' Alma had re-joined gloomily.

'I always liked "Gather ye rosebuds while ye may," ' the possibly once-naughty Dot had offered.

Alma had blinked and pursed her lips at this, unsure. Still, she hadn't wanted Dot to think she was too hoity-toity, and she liked to have the last word, which wasn't easy around Dot. She'd raised her glass.

'Eat, drink and be merry, for tomorrow we may die!' she'd said bold-ly, half-expecting to be struck down for her wickedness.

'Amen! But actually it's 'Tomorrow we will die.'

Dot had thought better of telling Alma that her old mate Madge was now one of those vegetables; too many strokes. Dot stopped visiting her once Madge's eyes showed there was 'no-one home', as they used to say — and no longer knew her. She was just a body, being spoonfed, her dribbling mouth and her bum wiped by strangers. Dot had wanted to grab a pillow and end this ongoing humiliation for Madge, out of respect for the person she once was.

But then she'd be up for murder! Why couldn't the government see that hers was the decent attitude, not their refusal to legalise such kindness? That TV program had called it 'voluntary euthanasia'. It used to be called 'mercy killing', but she supposed that was a bit blunt for these pussyfooting days.

She'd made a proper Living Will after seeing that show, but her kids could still muck up her planned tidy end; they hadn't liked her talking to them about it at all. Silly buggers; they'll understand when they get old and bits start wearing out and breaking down — and they start losing the selves they knew.

Dot and Alma can't do much about the rosebuds anymore, but at least there's the pleasures of the club while they may.

The dining room is filling up. Some younger ones in their forties or fifties, the old children of the very old, are there with a parent. For the real seniors are mainly singles; not many last the distance in tandem.

The light from the waterside picture windows slants across the room, picking out the men as it polishes bald domes and highlights the odd thick white thatch.

Amongst the women the blue rinses that were so fashionable decades ago are rarely seen. Many still favour perms, although quite a few have succumbed to the fashion of short bangs and tufts of brusque grey.

Alma secretly doesn't approve of this; she thinks it unladylike and unflattering, but she can't say so because Dot has been convinced by her hairdresser to go for the easycare look — 'so long as it's not short enough to be prickly'.

The meals are disposed of, and mostly approved of — Alma bemoaned the lack of beetroot in the salad and left the snow pea shoots untouched — 'Can't fit 'em in me mouth, they're too skinny to hold with your fork and cut 'em, and they're too stiff to fold up properly to catch with your fork that way. Ridiculous!'

As they sit on over a cup of tea, Dot nudges Alma to look at the next table, where an old child with dyed red hair is picking the shoots up in her fingers and nibbling off the leafy bit. Alma is scandalised: 'With her fingers — in public!'

Time to get back to the real business of the day. They intend to try a few different machines, see if their luck changes. It's hard to concentrate in this world of stopstart tunes and ringing bells and stars and neon lights. Some play rousing marches or victory tunes but none finish — like music boxes with a mischievous kid opening and closing the lids, biting off the tunes.

The overall ambience is like a fairground, but they're too old for other than sedentary thrills. Dot and Alma make their choices and settle down to 'do' ten dollars each. 'You never know…'

The lady on the next machine along tells them that her friend Beryl saw someone get a really big one here just yesterday.

Is it possible that Lady Luck could still be hanging about?

'There you go,' nods Alma, 'This week might be our lucky week!'

This week, next week, sometime, never… Dot finds the old rope-skipping tune running through her head, but she doesn't pass it on to Alma, for she suspects Alma actually believes that her dreams might yet come true on one of these flings.

She shakes her head indulgently, and wonders why we do this kind of thing all our lives. Wishing and hoping.

First it's Santa Claus and the tooth fairy, then praying to Someone we aren't even sure is up there — well, that's what some people think, she amends hurriedly, in case He is and He's listening — and from the time we've got a spare penny to bless ourselves with it's the lottery and the lotto or the pokies or the horses or the dogs. Why can't we be happy with what we've got and accept that — afterwards — we might just be pushing up daisies?

Bit late for happily-ever-after and dreams-come-true now, she thinks, looking at Alma, who's anxiously frowning at the dream machine as she plays. She knows that people like Alma will never deal with life's realities. And then they die. Lucky, really.

She sighs.

'Mind me spot, Alma. I'll go get us another drink.'

CLOUDLAND

THERE WAS no end to these mountains. Or so it seemed once you were in them — it was never a question of 'on' them.

Evie had only known the other sort — proud loners that reared up from the middle of a plain, their foothills prostrated low around them; bare-browed mountains where you could climb to the top, spin about, and see everything for miles.

Ben's mountain was but one wave in a great sea of them. From its ridge all you could see, in slashes through the trees, was another mountain. When she'd first come here as a young bride, Ben had taken her to climb a nearby taller ridge so she could get her bearings. He reckoned it would be an easy climb to the top, and they'd get a view, because of its oddly open and grassy north face.

This face had proved so steep that their climbing had been more like vertical crawling, the tussocks providing desperate purchase for hands and feet, but it had been worth it to reach the narrow spine, to stand more in the realm of the three wedge-tailed eagles drifting lazily above them than of the earth.

It was as vast a sea as she had feared; forest-clad mountains crumpled up and down forever, receding from distinctly treed and olive green to pale blue smudges along the horizon.

Ben built their slab house on a little saddle that he'd cleared, halfway between the creek and the ridge. The clearing drew the wallabies, who kept the grass short and green. Evie thought of it as her island in the middle of the forest sea. She could breathe here. It had been a sunny island at first, but the pine trees Ben had planted around the rim of the clearing grew too big in too few years.

Soon only brief slants of morning gold could reach the house, and the slope behind took the sun away early of a winter afternoon. The red boards turned silver, tinged green and lichened grey in the shade of the pines. Her garden plants grew pale and feeble, ceased to flower, and she abandoned them to the possums. Ben dug and netted a vegetable plot beyond the shade and acid of the pines.

She'd become too busy for flowers anyway, with the children and their correspondence lessons. Her two sons liked the pines, using the horizontal branches as ladders, throwing the cones at each other, while the much younger Jennifer sat on the verandah steps and watched longingly.

Sometimes you wouldn't know what the sun was doing for days because they'd be stuck in what Evie called 'Cloudland'. The sky was so close to their mountain that it often merged with the ridges and flowed into the gullies to drip from the trees and shroud her island with a ghostly whiteness. At such times her sunny-day knowledge of what lay beyond its pine-rimmed shores fought to rise above her sense of a cold nothingness, even more alien and unkind than the forest sea.

Yet Ben loved these gently damp days, stomping about outdoors, singing an old nursery song — *'One misty, moisty morning, when cloudy was the weather, There I met an old man clothed all in leather...'* Evie could hear it echoing long after he'd been lost to sight in the cloud.

In Cloudland Evie lost touch with Ben; he couldn't understand why she felt half-smothered, half-blind, praying for the sun which could never come back soon enough. If it lasted a week she feared she might panic. 'Oh please, go back up where you belong!' she would silently beseech the enveloping cloud as yet another day struggled to dawn inside it.

She'd make the long trip to town to escape for a day. As soon as the road began the steep descent down the last hill, she could see the sunlit pasturelands below. A few thousand feet — another country altogether. Once down, she would glance back at the underside of Cloudland, looking as dense and imprenetrable as it felt when trapped inside it. If she had known anyone in town, she might not have gone back, but they were loners, she and Ben. Their family was enough for them.

Well, Evie had plenty of sun now. All day she followed it, moving her chair around the verandahs of the beachside house. She could not get enough of it, concentrating on filling herself with that searing brightness, and with the strong scents of salt and seaweed, so different from those of the mountain — eucalyptus pungent, pine sharp, rainforest damp, woodfire smoky — making sure there was no room for them to seep back in.

On days when the fine sea mist rolled in under the verandahs, its clammy salt breath hazing over the windows, she would shut the curtains tight, hide indoors, and watch television, anything and everything.

She sometimes heard the people around her whispering to each other that she did not remember anything, as if it were a simple, final fact. They did not understand, and she could not tell them, that she might have remembered, had she not fought hard, every minute, to preserve that blank.

The mountain was a large knot in the frayed threads of her life, tied there at first by herself in a bid to survive, and thereafter kept so by all who cared that those few remaining threads should not snap entirely. Her own efforts set her face into a perpetual faint frown and kept her mute. Words could cut a knot.

Ben knew that the events at the mountain were unbelievable, ought not to have happened; it was fair enough that Evie's mind had decided that they hadn't.

But he couldn't stop going back up there. The stories that lay behind Evie's knot of silence were for him retold each week, hammered round his skull and pounded through his veins till he'd often have to pull over, breathless with palpitations. The witnesses still silently accused him — that track, this gully, the old truck, their houses, the whole mountain — even the sky. Evie's Cloudland no longer drew song from him.

His mind wasn't as effective at escape as Evie's, but he'd found if he kept talking of other things, he could manage. As soon as he stopped, the nightmare rerun would start up. Yet still he had to drive along that track… there it was now, the very corner post he'd been putting in that day… he could see it, hear it, like it was yesterday…

At first he'd thought it was the echo of the crowbar head on the clay, pounding in his ears. But he'd looked round, ears and eyes clearing at the same time, and there was Tom, hurtling down the track towards him. He'd dropped the crowbar and stepped out on to the track, frowning at the figure rushing headlong downhill, the trees standing oddly still, the boy going too fast, skinny legs flying out at all angles, a queer harsh sound coming from his open mouth.

'Whoa!' he said, holding out his arms to catch him. 'You'll break a leg like that, you silly beggar! What's after you? The bunyip?'

But Tom wasn't laughing; he was sobbing for breath, just enough words rasping through to form an iron fist in Ben's throat. ' Pete… Pete…the gun… Dad… 'm sorry, 'm sorry…!'

His father was already dragging him towards the truck. 'Where? Where?' The kid could barely speak. 'Rabbitin.' ' Ben knew where then: that cleared slope to the blackberry gully was a favourite afternoon spot for rabbits, where the boys often bagged a few. Cursing the truck into starting, he screamed it up the hill, bumped it off the track and across the tussocky paddock, lurching over half-buried logs and rocks. The gully flew towards them. He could see the dog, he could see Pete's legs… oh Jesus.

He wrenched on the handbrake. He climbed out and stumbled towards the face-down figure, the terrible stillness of it, his own legs dissolving with each step. The dog was barking; it backed off, whimpering, frightened by Ben's strange manner.

Ben fell to his knees, going through the motions, feeling for a pulse, a heartbeat. Not a chance, not with the head like that.

He took off his coat to cover him, but irrrationally felt it was too stiff and heavy, it might hurt, so removed his flannelette shirt and draped it lightly over Pete's head and shoulders. Now there was no blood show-ing, it looked like he was just having a snooze on the grass; insane hope flared for the second or two before the red began to seep through the blue checks.

Somehow he stood, walked back to the truck. He coaxed Tom out of his crying huddle and, sitting on the running board, rocked him like a baby, murmuring, 'There, there, mate, there, there,' staring at the long mountain ridge beyond, at its coldness, that it could have watched this happen, and be the same.

'We have to take him to Mum, mate,' he said eventually. 'Sun's goin' down; she'll be worried.'

This would be even worse — Pete was her first.

They laid out the sacks they kept handy in case they got bogged. Ben slid one under Pete's head, but it was a precious cargo, he needed Tom to help. The boy lifted his brother's legs while Ben cradled the top half and together they laid him on the tray. It was a slow drive. Tom had the worst of it, sitting on the tray, holding onto what had so recently been Pete.

The dog had beaten them home. Evie was waiting at the gate in the row of pine trees, peering through the deepening dusk to where the track came over the ridge. Three-year-old Jennifer was half cradled in her arms and half sitting on the gate, legs dangling over, little heels click-clacking against the wooden slats in time to the last song of in-nocence.

Ben had not thought they'd survive that time. But Tom grew, Jen grew, and somehow they all flinched their way through time and the barrage of memories.

He and Tom developed into a good team. They selectively cleared the ridge tops and the shallow slopes, getting good money for the saw logs of blue gum, blackbutt and stringybark. They weren't greedy, left plenty of shade and seed trees, and stocked up with scrawny Herefords from drier areas to fatten them on the nourishing alpine grasses. They were doing well, taking on more leasehold land for the cattle each year.

Tom had been impatient to be grown enough to really help. Ben knew why, knew whose empty place he wanted to fill, knew the guilt that got him no matter what they said about accidents. He was always telling Tom to slow down, but the boy was his own demon boss. There'd only been two years between Tom and Pete. They'd have been some team…

When Tom was twenty he got serious about a girl from over the next valley. He met her at the local show, stayed on for the dance, and the weekend, and came home a daydreamer. Ben told Tom if he waited six months to get to know this Kathy properly, he could ask her, and in the meantime they'd extend the clearing and build another cottage up the hill a bit. It'd be useful for the hands at mustering even if he didn't go ahead with getting married.

They did a good job on the cottage, made it just like a house in town; milled the timber themselves, even painted the boards. Kathy had been delighted with it. Evie liked her, but had been used to being the only woman on her island for too long. It was eleven-year old Jennifer, the lonely latecomer, who really took to her.

But Kathy didn't stay; not after Tom went.

On the slopes, some of those big trees grow with a twist hidden inside, coiled like a spring, ready to leap the way you didn't intend. This one had sprung uphill instead of down, where its cut should've sent it. Quicker than Ben could take in, it had bounced off a blue gum that sent the trunk spearing down the slope and the massive top sprawling right back on top of its own butt, where Tom was. Usually the safest place, next to the butt like that.

The white mist that soaked the forest was suddenly full of bird cries of alarm, a mass of shivering leaves, crushed eucalyptus tang, ripped red soil, his own voice hoarsely screaming Tom's name as he half ran, half slid through the dampness. Ben could feel the cold air burning his throat as he yelled, slipping over the trunk, parting the springy tangle of branches, climbing through this forest giant-laid-low that was still reverberating with the shock. He was looking for a patch of different colour.

There was no answer, but there was colour; there were the blues and yellows of a check shirt, and there was the red. Tom'd been fair driven into the forest floor by a monster of a branch. Ben scrabbled the dirt away from Tom's face. But Tom no longer had a use for air.

It would've been quick, Ben was thinking he could say to Evie. Ah hell, maybe they shouldn't've been cutting in the mist — Evie'd blame it for sure — but Tom'd been so keen to fill that order for fence posts — a-ah, Tom!

But Evie hadn't become hysterical; she'd simply gone into their bedroom, drawn the curtains and shut the door. She went far away from Cloudland, and this time would not come back, not even for Jen.

In the hospital she seemed calmest when sitting by a window that overlooked the beach and the bright endless ocean. The doctors said she'd blocked all the other out; they thought it best for her not to go back there, so Ben sold part of the mountain and bought a house beside the sea.

He paid Liz, a widow, to live in and look after Evie and Jen and the house. Jen seemed to cope well enough with the new experience of school, and she made a few friends. Perhaps she was a little too quiet, but then she'd copped more of the heavy stuff of life than most. Having a mother cocooned in silence didn't help.

Ben spent Sundays and Mondays at the mountain, having found a caretaker to live up there in exchange for a hand with the fences and the cattle. It was good to have someone to discuss plans with again — like he used to with Evie. The mountain would be Jen's some day, he must keep it in good order for her.

When Jen wanted to do a secretarial course, he paid for it. When she went off to Sydney to work, he helped her find a flat. But when she brought that bloke home and said she wanted to marry him, he had to take her aside and ask whether this Mike could even ride a horse, let alone run a cattle property.

That was when she told him she didn't want it, would never live there. Quiet Jennifer had burst into great sobbing tears, like a dam bursting, it was. Or a knot breaking.

Maybe grandchildren would be the answer. He had to be hanging onto the mountain for someone — all that work — it wasn't as if it was the mountain's fault, though he knew Evie wouldn't have agreed.

Jen and Mike lived in Sydney, didn't visit often. The last time was for Jen's twenty-third birthday, when he'd taken them out for a slap-up lunch. They'd left Evie out of it. And for most of the time out of it she remained, safe on her own island of Now, where the shutters had been closed on their familiar faces, so irretrievably connected to the past. Yet occasionally she peeped out, and Ben felt she saw him, knew him. He still hoped there might be a 'now' for them.

Meanwhile he stuck to his routine, never missing his days at the mountain. People remarked on how well he coped with the tragedies life had dealt him. Then one day his body decided that he'd done it long enough. The doctor said he'd had a stroke, and that a few days of rest would see him right, as there seemed to be no major effects.

But there was one.

Ben had received the gift he'd long been craving — the mountain had ceased to exist.

Given the all-clear to get up, he went out to Evie on the verandah.

Taking a deep breath of sea air, he noticed their double garage as if for the first time. I could fit a boat in there, he thought.

'You know, Evie, we ought to get ourselves a boat. We could take it out on that big lake over the back here, just putt along till we were smack in the middle of all that sunshine and sparkling blue water. Now what's tomorrow? Monday? I could start looking for one tomorrow. Eh, love? What d'you reckon?'

He took her hand and gave it a little shake, like he used to in their younger days when he was keen for her to share his enthusiasm about some plan.

Evie was still looking out to sea, but her frown had relaxed as she sensed something happening, something strange, but not threatening. She looked down at the hand holding hers. It looked so like Ben's hand. She squeezed it gently and risked a look at his face. It was Ben, he had arrived at last. He grinned at her and patted her hand. She almost smiled back.

The low spring sun warmed them as they sat, although there were a few clouds high in the sky. Where they belonged.

Dream run

HER childhood bed had always been a hollow; 'flat on her back' could not apply. The rusted wire mesh had long ago ceased to pretend to be connected to the frame in any cohesive pattern, and the old kapok mattress had followed the gradual decline faithfully.

In winter she curled up in the hollow in a tight flannelette ball, waiting for the warmth of her body to fill the cold cocoon suspended below the insufficient covers — two grey army blankets, with her dressing gown, her overcoat and her school blazer overlapped on top.

In summer she could sit in the hollow cross-legged and do her homework with her book resting on the higher end, almost as good as having a desk. Their house held no such item, and even if the kitchen table wasn't occupied, her mother disliked her 'messing it up' once it had been wiped clean after tea, the symbolic last act of the working day.

They did own a lounge, and even though it was vinyl nobody would dare do other than sit on it, feet firmly on the floor. No lounging allowed. She didn't care; when free to read her treasured library books, she could lie back in her bed's hollow, bent in a neat V, legs stiffly uphill in front of her, head propped comfortably on the slope behind, book balanced at perfect viewing angle in the crook of her lap.

This was an equally useful position for daydreaming, except that the sight of her legs tended to distract her, being so unavoidably visible. Possible destinies for great talent or glorious career paths wavered and were reduced to the immediate — the desperate, hopeless contemplation of her impossible legs.

Adolescence had arrived, other body parts had bulged and filled out to acceptable roundness, but her legs remained obstinately sticklike and calfless. Her daily inspections could detect no sign of any intention to change. She could approve of the shape of the feet at their extremities, especially when she pointed them, so, and turned them to the side to better admire their graceful curve, no lumps or bumps, neat pale toenails.

Her contemplation would move on to the ankles, which she knew from her reading were of great importance. Gentlemen could be driven mad by a glimpse of 'a well-turned' one, though that expression puzzled her — was it the shape, as in woodturning, or the direction, as in ballet? Hers were slim enough, 'trim' enough, but due to the unfortunate lack of curve above them, they would probably go unrecognised as such. Gentlemen might unwittingly keep their sanity, when instead she wanted them shooting themselves in the streets, crying her name, or blocking footpaths and causing traffic jams as she walked by. Or at least looking.

But no amount of flexing, raising one leg after the other in hopeful examination, could create even the impression of calves. Two years of ballet had made no difference. She gave up on her dream of beautiful legs, resigned to a life of leg-based decisions; of taking the indirect approach, facing sideways, crabwalking; of placing one foot well in front of the other like a tightrope walker to confuse the lines and lack of curves; of crossing her legs when sitting. Perhaps long dresses would come back in fashion and she would be able to just flash an ankle to catch her man instead of shameleggedly skulking on seats in her miniskirt.

Under such enforced daily scrutiny, she naturally became very familiar with each small spot and blemish, dip and bump, focused around the long shinbones, gleaming and vulnerable, so close to the surface. That small excavation where she'd got stuck on the barbwire fence; that blue mark where the dreadful Robyn O'Brien had jabbed her with a pen nib in primary school; those craters where she'd gone overboard with the acetic acid in her impatience to be rid of a cluster of small warts she once had; that raised pink scar from a glass shard from the exploding bottles of homemade ginger beer one Christmas…

When she grew up and met the love of her life, he would be fascinated by these imprints of her life, stroking them gently while she told their tales. He would tell her how much he adored the thin brown boniness of her legs, simply because they were hers.

She'd forgotten where she'd read that true love was loving another as oneself, but it became, and remained, the crux of her romantic dreams.

Life happens, regardless of dreams.

Now her bed was flat, and hard, the bedclothes stretched tight and tucked in regimentally, pinning her on her back. Not that she was fighting to do otherwise. Propped against two pillows, her head nodding as it always did, she would lie gazing at the blank wall opposite, or down at the slight shape of her body beneath the pastel pink cotton waffle weave bedspread, at her skeletal arms lying limply above it. They were by far the most colourful things in the room; blue rope-veined, pink scab-spotted amid the clouds of yellow, green and purple bruises from the needles.

When they lifted her in or out of bed or wheelchair, the skin-draped sticks they exposed had as little to do with those firm thin legs of her youth as did the wavering face that confronted her when the well-meaning nurses held a mirror up after doing her hair. 'Now don't we look nice today?'

Like a baby they would wash her in the shower chair, pat her dry, powder her liberally, ease the undies up the sticks, 'Just a little lift now, dear, and we're done.' Every day one of them would give her a gentle massage, to prevent bedsores, to stimulate the unused muscles, faint nerves and sluggish blood vessels. They would rub in cool Vitamin E lotion as they did so, talking all the time, not expecting her to answer.

'You still have lovely skin, dear. I'll bet you broke a few hearts in your day.'

At less than 35kg, she was skinny all over now. No one could tell which bits of her body had ever had any shape of flesh or muscle, ad-mirable or otherwise; there was only the clear shape of bone. Neither did she care any more which way her legs or her self presented; vanity had fallen away with the flesh.

Until yesterday. For the first time, they had put her in the bath sling and left her alone to soak in the warm water for a little while. They meant to be kind, but facing her then, floating straight out in front of her, were the relics of those same legs she used to agonise over. She suddenly remembered the bed, the hollow, and her dreams of the lover who would cherish those legs, forgive them, as she had.

The nurses do, for sympathy, now that she is old, dying.

Her mother must have, for love, when she was new, a baby.

This enforced legfacing also flashed her a retro-image from a book popular when she was a student, *Slaughterhouse Five* by Kurt Vonne-gut. In it a man was captured by extraterrestrials, whose perception of time was concurrent rather than consecutive. Hence they did not see human beings as two-legged creatures, but as 'great millipedes — with babies' legs at one end and old peoples' legs at the other.'

The memory made her laugh, and little did these days. The laugh hurt; so did the sharp revelation that followed it, as she saw herself in much the same way. Always the same hopelessly yearning self inside the same but different body, being carried through life on those same but different legs.

For over sixty years she had been waiting for something that would never happen. No merging of selves or souls had been intense enough, no physical absorption or adoration mutual enough, to be 'true' love. *Le grand passion* had eluded her, and nothing short of the dream had been acceptable. She had said 'no' too often.

Her life — a character lost in the wrong story. These legs would rot like the rest of her and no one would remember the little blue mark, the ginger beer scar — or her.

She closed her eyes tight, pressing the buzzer for the nurse.

'Had enough, have we dear?'

The nurse could not distinguish one trembling nod from another. But the answer was clearly yes.

TRACES OF LIFE

THE BOWL in which she lived was shallow and green, set down and forgotten in an endless forest of bluegums, their mop heads forming its scalloped rim. A bony ridge like a skinny arm offered her bowl to the sky, palm up, tilted for easy drinking.

People said she lived alone here, and that it had been empty before she came. A literal observer would argue that she was alone as she sat at the table, slept in the bed, mused on the verandah. The same blinkered spy would claim the absence of pottery shards or rusting ploughshares as proof that none other had used this skybowl.

For her these things were not so clear. She had slept in a small tent while slowly building her little cabin from the earth and rocks and fallen trees; she could see how her predecessors might have lived so lightly on the land as to leave no traces.

She liked to nourish her intuition and imagination with facts, which were hard to come by for such a remote area, but it seemed possible the gentle Geawegal people may have used this mountain range. Over the years she had found stones that seemed deliberately shaped. She decided they were tools, lost while hunting the red-necked wallabies or camping by the paperbark fringes of the lagoons, the spring-fed 'high altitude perched swamps' unique to these mountains. She would hold the stones, heft their weight, see her coarse and freckled Celtic hands grow dusky fine grained skin, pink palms, pale nails — feel the stored knowledge.

Since this area was for so long untouched by white intruders, she wondered why these earlier bowl-dwellers disappeared. Perhaps they hadn't. Just retreated. There were still hundreds of square miles of wilderness to the north and north-east, terrain too rough even for the greedy cedargetters.

She imagined the People had kept closely to the mountains, only venturing down to the open world of the Kamilarois in times of necessity or desperate whim. Maybe that's how it was: heading over to Bulahdelah and on to the coast for a shellfish treat; a misunderstanding, a trespass; overtaken by the Kamilaroi warriors, a battle; the tribe destroyed in one swift and savage hit, the women and children captured; the mountain bowls left uncared for.

But if not... occasionally the senses played tricks up here.

The air was thinner, the bowl was often filled with cloud like cotton wool, the gumtree trunks shining like wet naked bodies, and between them every now and then a darker stringybark sapling would sway, and she would peer harder. The tall clumps of poa grass would shiver in the wake of something unseen, sticks crack suddenly, then all would be still again: a startled wallaby? Way down in the gully, lights would flicker erratically, like torches held in the hands of dancing bodies: fireflies?

Yet there was a flat grassy spot just about there, perfect for dancing, and she was sure she'd once heard corroboree music from that gully. Had it been just for a mistakable second or two, it could have been wind howling and koalas growling, tree branches clicking and swishing against each other, and the cacophonous chorus of frogs — but not for hours.

See there, now! A dark figure stands erect, proud, gaunt and sinewy, turns smoky eyes towards her — an Eastern Grey kangaroo. 'So who is caring for us now? Who holds my totem, sings my song?' he reproaches with his long look.

There was rarely silence: the trees of the rim of her bowl rustled always, even if ever so slightly, in the updraft from the escarpment below. She-oaks sighed and whispered softly behind the backs of the bigger gums and stringies, restless young girls, impatient with solid men's business. Birds repeatedly called mad questions that yet seemed to need an answer; shy giggles wafted up the slope; courting walla-bies gruffly cleared their throats; night birds boomed of woomera and didge. It was hard to say what human was anymore.

She had owned this bowl for twenty years, but its claim on her was more evident: her skin had begun to gather rough spots like the lichen on its rocks, her hair to turn as grey as the Old Man's Beard that fes-tooned branches in its rain forest gullies, her body to mimic the inex-plicable twists and turns of its angophoras.

People now seemed more loud of voice, brash of manner and empty of meaning than she remembered. The odd newspaper left behind by visitors revealed such idiocies on scales both grand and petty that no matter how quickly she mulched them, the headlines returned to cloud her thoughts for days.

Her city-bred daughter still visited her. She had disapproved of a woman in her fifties moving to such an isolated place, yet as the years passed she could see that her mother was happy. It would not suit her, liking her civilised pleasures and friends and her busy career as an architect too much, but she admired her mother's independence.

Lately, though, she had begun to worry about her. She spoke to her mother's old friends. They too, on their diminishing visits, had noticed changes. After all, they said to each other, she was in her seventies, she should think about moving to town, or at least get a mobile phone. They were finding her difficult to be with; always a bit odd, never quite adept socially, she seemed to have lost the art of conversation altogeth-er. Her range of interests had narrowed so, they agreed, that she had become quite out of touch with the real world.

Real? she would have queried had she heard. Her world here was more real than any she'd ever lived in before.

Yet she had noticed changes too. Over the last summer she had been less inclined to move about. The heat demanded she sit limply in the shade, eyes half-closed, and rest like a wallaby till the coolness of dusk. Then she would work a little in her garden before retiring to the veran-dah to eat and sleep in the fresh mountain dark.

Then the night-dwellers took over; possums patrolled the veran-dah posts, antechinus scurried along the rafters, the tiger quoll sniffed round the bed, a powerful owl peered from the railing, koalas growled in the gums nearby. At dawn, the kookaburra chorus would follow shortly after the first currawong had skittered to a landing on the roof as a pre-wake-up call.

She would lie watching the wallabies in the far clearing sunning their pale underbellies, the crimson rosellas sampling their grass seed crop close by. When the sun's first rays stroked her face, she would get up, more stiffly than she used to, and take her breakfast. Fruit and water did her fine these days; she couldn't be bothered with toast or tea. Sal-ad for lunch and dinner, although she still sometimes boiled the nutty little potatoes that hid under the weeds.

As autumn drew on and the fresher days that usually quickened her energy failed to do so, she spent more time slowly wandering about and finding good sitting spots to enjoy the now welcome warmth of the sun.

One ancient angophora had always attracted her. Fallen before the winds long ago, it had yet clung to the earth with enough roots to live, growing as it lay, horizontally. She'd spent hours cradled in its outstretched curving limbs, reading, thinking, watching the clouds. It would gently sway with the slightest of pressure, but up and down, not side to side, because of its strange growth. It felt like being rocked to sleep and she had often succumbed, calling it her cradle tree.

She liked its botanical name too: *Angophora Floribunda*. As she ap-proached, she took to saying the name aloud, like a greeting to a fan-cifully named Victorian bluestocking, or perhaps a secret password, 'Angophora Floribunda!' Most people would have thought her cra-zy; her daughter only smiled indulgently, as she had often heard her mother murmur words of appreciation or encouragement to so-called inanimate objects.

Near this cradle tree was a round grassy depression in the ground, a smaller bowl within the skybowl. About thirty feet diameter and deep enough to be protected from the wind, it was enticingly warm, a sun-bowl, and peaceful, while the westerlies noisily threatened the trees around it and tore up the slope to the ridge in disappointment when they resisted.

It was only a fifteen-minute walk from the cabin and she began to come there each day once the sun had dried the dew. She decided it must have been a perched swamp once, a water-holding bowl that now was dry but for some ancient and mysterious reason never grew any-thing but soft short green grass. Her daughter could offer no explana-tion. Probably only the People could. She thought they might tell her if she sat quietly, listened intently, for long enough.

By winter she was spending all the sunlight hours there, abandoning her garden and her books, returning reluctantly to the cabin to sleep. She took only water with her for her day's sitting, which might have looked like meditation, but was not. Some of the time she'd watch the creatures; the flocks of tiny thornbills like falling leaves, or the endless pattern of darting skinks playing hide-and-seek in the tussocks that ringed the little sunbowl's edge.

Or she might just close her eyes and listen; she could hear the rus-tling of the angophora's tassels of leaves and the slight rubbing of its convoluted boughs as they crisscrossed each other, and the wallabies' grunts and snorts and coughs as they met and challenged and wooed and mated in their endless social life.

Sometimes she thought she heard other voices, low, soft and secret, but feared to open her eyes, to startle them, make them vanish — or to see what she was not ready for.

She could surely hear the rush and urgent flap of the magpie's swoop, and once looked up to see it hunting off a low-flying wedgetail, which had probably thought she was dead, sitting so still and so exposed. Yet she had never felt more alive.

Except, increasingly, for the daily walk to and from the sunbowl. Her legs did not seem suited to walking anymore, their muscles limp, reluctant. In her sunbowl, sitting with her legs crossed, they formed the perfect base, keeping her balanced, while her upper body felt light, tingling with life. She was glad no one had come to visit for a while; or perhaps they had, but as she was out of sight and hearing of the cabin, she would not have known. Her skin now dry and scaly, mottled brown, her hair a windblown tangle, she had stopped changing her clothes, and barely remembered to eat.

One evening she did not have the energy to return to the cabin, although she knew she should before the cold air seeped into the sunbowl. Then, gradually, she became aware that it was counteracting the night chill with a warmth of its own, radiating back from the rocks below, she supposed, like a natural heat sink.

She shivered with pleasure at this unexpected gift; there was no need to return now. She shivered again with anticipation of the night, knowing she would not sleep, but would see, hear, share, the secrets of the night bowl-dwellers; perhaps, even, of those Others.

She sighed with contentment, her bones warming, relaxing towards the welcoming earth… and was still.

It was a while before anyone knew she was missing; it was another week before they gave up looking. There were many deep gullies round the skybowl's rim, thickly wooded, covered with vines and edged with nettles; she could have fallen down any of them. She could even have walked right on into the wilderness, leaving no traces. After all, she had been getting a bit dotty. They might never discover what had become of her…

By the time her daughter could be reached the search was over.

Supposedly at a conference in Paris, she had actually been on a secret barge holiday down the Loire with her married lover. Guilt quickly followed shock when she was told the news.

Mentally she accepted the lack of conclusions; emotionally she could not. The sole inheritor, she would come for a rare weekend, but never alone, and staying close to the cabin, as if she were a child instead of an almost middle-aged woman.

The sleepless nights there were full of thoughts that would not bear exploring, but no tears had arisen from her grief, choked by the endless uncertainty.

About a year after, having come on her own for once, she felt shame at not caring for the place as her mother had. It was time to force her-self to walk farther afield, perhaps to one of her mother's favourite spots, the cradle tree. Strange to be walking there on her own. She was nervous, almost afraid, though of what she could not say; it was too cold for snakes.

Cresting the last rise before the little gully near which the cradle tree grew, she frowned as she caught the flash of sun on water — where there should be none. She hurried down the slope. The water table must be up higher than usual, she thought. I'm sure there never used to be a soak here; there used to be…

She stopped, checked again the position of the cradle tree, and looked back at the little pool. Her heart began to thump as she realised it was right where the strange grassy hollow had been. In the centre of this new pool was a small green knoll, and from this knoll rose a slim young tree, already about twelve feet tall, limbs gracefully shaping ara-besques and scrolls in imitation of its bigger neighbour.

She fought to comprehend. The last time she had been here, with her mother, they had remarked again on the hollow's mystifying bareness; that could only have been about eighteen months ago. She dropped down by the grassy edge of the glistening pool, staring at the tree. A wind sprang up and the cradle tree began to softly rock and whisper as it always did. The young tree swayed gently in response, its tassels of light green leaves whispering back.

For a long time the daughter sat. She told herself that what she was thinking could not be, yet a less familiar voice from within told her it must be. If only she had been with the searchers, or come here sooner; had she seen this pool then, this tree so suddenly appeared, she would have been sure…

She cleared her throat and addressed the little sapling in the tree-filled silence.

'Angophora Floribunda,' she said, smiling through the tears that welled at last.

ACCREDITATIONS

'Traces of life' — First Prize in The Alan Marshall Short Story Award 2002, Open Section (judge Gillian Mears); published in *artstream*.

'For Beauty' — First Prize & Medal in the Federation of Australian Writers (FAW) NSW Inc. 1999 Short Story of the Year and then First Prize in the 2002 Boroondara Literary Award, Open Short Story, (judge Morris Lurie) then published in the winners' anthology, *It's about time;*

'The Road to Greatness' — First Prize in Society of Women Writers QLD Inc. 2001 Short Story Competition;

'Facing reality' — First Prize in the 2001 George Seddon Competition, Open Short Story (Ballarat Grammar); published online at *artsrush* in 2001;

'Grey matters' — Equal First Prize in the 2002 Hunter Writers' Centre Vacant Lot Award;

'Live at the Bellevue' — First prize in the 2009 FAW Marjorie Barnard Award, and was selected for inclusion in the 2010 Award Winning Australian Writing collection;

'When shadows fall' — one of the ten winners in the 50-Plus News Short Story Competition 2001, published there; broadcast on ABC regional radio 1233 in 2001;

'Central Vision' — 2nd prize in the FAW Manly Peninsula Award 2000 Literary Competition and was Commended in the Roland Robinson 2003 Literary Award and published in the winners' anthology, *A Smudge of Sun;*

'Shellgrit' won Equal 3rd in the 2001 Todhunter Literary Awards (as 'Overruled'); chosen as one of the top 11 entries for the Tasmanian Writers' Prize, published in the Forty South Short Story Anthology 2022.

'A little bit of England' — Commended in the 2001 Henry Lawson Festival Short Story Competition and broadcast on Queensland Storyteller 4RPH in 2001;

'A Taste of Olives' — Commended in the FAW Central Coast 1999 Mona Brand Short Story Competition and awarded one of only two Merits in *The Southern Cross Courier* Literary Competition 2000;

'Dream run' — Highly Commended in the 2001 Bauhinia Literary Awards, Uni. Central Qld., (as 'Learning from legs'); broadcast on Queensland Storyteller 4RPH in 2001;

'Threads of a tapestry' was broadcast on ABC regional radio 1233 in 2001;

'The Great Escape' — Highly Commended in the 2005 Shoalhaven Lyrebird Competition;

'Last rites for a lover' — Highly Commended in the 2015 Tasmanian Society of Women Writers Launceston, Tasmania Literary Award.

'Days of Wine and Warrumbungles' was published in *Skive* online magazine and later in the printed collection, *Next Stop, the best of* Skive *Magazine;*

'Starman' was published in *Island* in the December 2009 issue.

www.ingramcontent.com/pod-product-compliance
Lightning Source LLC
Chambersburg PA
CBHW070241140726
47909CB00018B/1794